White Noise

Sophia Soames

love
Sophie Soames
London 2024

Editing by Debbie McGowan

Proofreading by Sarah Coppin

Formatting K.C Carmine

Being an actor is not the glamorous life Connor Telford once expected. Now he lives in a budget hotel, spending all his time working...or working out. He's on friendlier terms with the catering team on set than he is with his co-stars, and his mum keeps telling him to get a life.

A real life. Con kind of agrees. He plays Detective Cass Powell in the multi-award-winning show *White Noise*, making the audience swoon with his character's skills and charm. Detective Powell has his life all figured out, and when you play someone whose life is picture perfect, it's easy to see that your own life is anything but.

Con doesn't even know how to live anymore. Date? He's not been on one for years. At least, not one that wasn't set up by his agent as a promotional stunt. There's no time to think when your brain is constantly fried. Work. Gym. Sleep. Gym. Work.

Then he meets Matthew Winston.

AUTHOR'S NOTE

This book contains graphic scenes of a sexual nature, including one being acted out that could be perceived as assault.

Trigger warning for one main character coming down with a brief vomiting bug.

This book is set in the United Kingdom, and is edited and proofed using British Spellings.

X

THE HARDEST ROLE OF YOUR LIFE IS BEING YOURSELF.

Con

The gym was crowded, as it always was at this time of night. The office jockeys were riding in with their pale faces and top-of-the-range gear, sweating away on the equipment with stern expressions and loud music pumping through their headphones. Muscleheads showed off their physiques with grunts and bulging veins. Then there was the usual crowd of people who seemed to have nowhere else to go with their screechy voices and stupid conversations that I'd rather not be part of. The gym bunnies. Sculpted girls with ponytails flapping against their backs, everyone flaunting their insane fitness.

Was I being judgemental? I suppose so. I didn't want to stand out or be part of any of this. But despite my obvious dislike of this fine establishment, the fact was the gym was good for me. It calmed my head after a hard day's work and was both productive and healthy for my body. Also, it was in my contract to keep my skin and bones looking exactly like this. Con Telford was expected to maintain his physical appearance. Con Telford needed to look like this...this *fool*.

OK, yes, I was judgmental, mostly because of who I'd become and why I was here, and I was well and truly aware of the absolute fact that I was not special. In any way. I was a kid from the suburbs who'd somehow slipped into acting and had a big break. And now I was filming the sixth season of the show that screamed my name and face from massive adverts on the side of London's buses and billboards along the motorway. That stupid expression on my airbrushed face greeted me wherever I went. My female co-star and I would be gracing the giant billboard in Piccadilly Circus before the next season aired. But for all of that, it was also the show that paid my meagre bills.

Bills. I had to laugh out loud at myself again. I currently resided in a Premier Inn budget hotel on an industrial estate. The glamour was real, I could tell you that. I got picked up by my driver at the arse-crack of dawn each morning, only to spend an hour sitting around by the catering trolley waiting for hair and make-up, then costume. When I'd eventually be called, I'd already have eaten my weight in croissants and usually finished another book on my Kindle. The same routine every day. It would take another hour for the set to get ready and for my co-stars to get their shit together. I ate more croissants than were strictly good for my diet and read a stupid number of books—my mum always joked I could have gained a PhD in some exciting subject if I read textbooks instead of sci-fi novels. She was right, and that kind of made me antsy.

I was a successful actor, which was a total fluke. Success in this line of work was as rare as sparkling unicorns. Trust me. I was lucky, and I knew full well that my career could stall in an instant. I might end up back at Mum's old house next week, who knew? Nothing was stable and certain in the acting world, and I of all people should be looking at getting myself a degree. A fallback option. My co-star Caroline was studying to become a solicitor, dragging her textbooks around on set. There was a whole Twitter community dedicated to finding her textbooks lying around in the previous seasons. It had become a thing. Caroline was a mess at the best of times, but viral Twitter threads were an important part of the show's social media, and her books had become part of the set and were deliberately planted by the props department.

Social media was weird. I tended to leave all that to my agent. Officially, I had perfectly curated social media. Unofficially, I went under the radar as the old me—the one who'd once existed before Con Telford had become a household name. I should probably have got myself a cool, snazzy stage name and have saved my mum from the hordes of fans that had sometimes hung out in her front garden early on in my career. Not that she'd minded, and the fans had usually been nice. Screaming and wanting photos, but yeah. Nice.

The way my thoughts spun while I was doing bench presses and grunting out loud like a wild animal was why the gym was good for me. I could actually hear myself think and not have to worry too much. Nobody knew me in this gym complex. It was too big for me to run into the same people, and I'd managed to keep myself fairly anonymous here with not even a hint of recognition from the reception staff as I flashed my membership card through the automated gates. Nor did I get a friendly goodbye as I tapped myself out. The showers were private and the towels were clean and fluffy, and the best thing was that it was directly opposite the dive of a hotel I currently called home. The area didn't just pride itself on a hotel and some massive industrial buildings. It also hosted a parade of takeaway shops and a snazzy newbuild apartment estate—the kind of estate that hosted mums with prams in the daytime and bored kids up to no good in the evenings—but it suited me. It was anonymous and grey and let me blend into my surroundings without any fuss. I liked that.

I tried to zone out from the music pumping through the air and made my way over to the running machines. This was another good part of the evening because I could work on my lines in peace and quiet. I had them pretty much memorised from the ride back from set earlier, but running and mouthing words was nothing that stood out, and the machine overlooked huge glass windows so I could even practise my facial expressions, all while running like an idiot. It usually made me smile, and nobody took notice anyway. I put my headphones on, silencing my surroundings, established a comfortable pace and rehearsed.

"The autopsy will give us the answers we need."

I paused, waiting for Caroline's line, then turned my head to the right and waved my arms. "I don't have all the answers, Inspector!"

I did. Well, my character always did. He was a cocky little shit. I wasn't. Caroline's lines thundered through my head as she accused Powell of having slept with another witness.

The lines made little sense, but that wasn't my problem. After editing and cutting and pasting the scenes together, things would, as usual, pan out into another award-winning thriller of an episode, where Detective Powell would have been naked at least once, showing off his impressive physique to some five-second extra cast as his bedmate for the night. Or the day. Detective Cass Powell was well-known for not having any preference for what time of day his dick needed servicing. But he would solve the crime and the perpetrators would receive their punishment, and all would be well in the world of the multi-award-winning world of *White Noise*, starring Connor Telford as the incredible Detective Cass Powell.

He didn't seem very incredible to me, and I of all people should know him. The scriptwriters wrote his lines, of course, and the wardrobe team dressed him. I'd had zero control over my hair for the past five years, but those things didn't bother me much. I blew the life into his lungs, over and over again, trying to understand the man who shagged everything that moved, had a daughter he rarely saw and solved crimes for breakfast. Well, I struggled a little bit with the daughter since they had changed the actor who played her every season, and I couldn't even remember who was playing her this time around. Some kid with ambitions surrounded by a showbiz mum and a herd of chaperones to ensure she didn't trip on a lighting wire mid-shoot.

Still, I loved being Cass Powell. I loved who I became on set—someone completely different from the grey-washed Con Telford currently mouthing along to a script while running on a treadmill.

"To the left! Target at six o'clock!" I turned my imaginary gun hard right, trying to keep my pace steady.

My fall from the treadmill was not a gracious one. I'd had enough stunt training to know exactly how to fall in a controlled manner, but I was caught totally off guard by the sweat-drenched skin I'd smacked my arm into. Apparently, the left cheek of the dude who was shouting at me—hurling abuse, no doubt—as he grabbed the front of my T-shirt, roughly hoisted me off the ground and propped me on wobbly Bambi legs while I tried to grasp what was going on. I dragged my headphones from over my ears so I could hear what he was saying.

"You OK?" he asked, clutching the red patch on his face where I had backhand-slapped him with the full force of my wrist. I knew because of the throbbing pain thundering through my bones.

"I'm so, so sorry. I didn't mean to touch you. I was—"

"Yeah, doing your lines. I know. You do it every night. It's kind of freaky to watch."

"Ehhr, do I know you?" I went straight on the defensive, racking my brain. Had I seen this dude before? Stalkers were nothing new, and I'd had my fair share of creeps, but I was pretty sure I'd never laid eyes on him before.

"No. I'm so sorry if I interrupted anything. I won't disturb you again."

"You, didn't disturb anything..." I said, but the guy was already walking away, which was a normal reaction. Not that I made a habit of smacking random people in the face during my workouts. I rubbed my wrist, trying to see where he'd gone.

I should apologise. I should have checked if he was OK. I'd whacked him, and that mark had looked sore.

I didn't like upsetting people. I'd done enough media training to know that things like this could easily end up on the front page of the tabloids with some well-constructed headline screaming *Famous Actor Assaults Gym Goer!* followed by the inevitable lawsuit, and the next thing I knew I'd be down at the Job Centre begging for a minimum-wage job somewhere. The life of an actor was a fragile one.

Yeah, that headline probably wouldn't sell quite as many copies as I imagined; I wasn't *that* famous. I'd never done a Hollywood movie, nor had I ever been sued by anyone, but I was, underneath it all, a decent human being, and I'd hit someone. And he'd just walked away.

Problem was, I couldn't even remember what he'd looked like. Dark hair? Red T-shirt? I'd been a little shocked myself, and now I was struggling to even remember what I'd said…

I'd have to find him and apologise, wouldn't I? It was the decent thing to do.

But as I looked around, he was nowhere to be found.

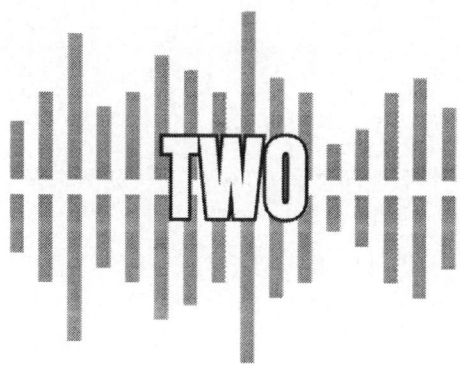

Matt

My face throbbed as I carefully stroked my fingertips over the red mark on my cheek. I couldn't believe what had happened, and it had been completely my fault.

Not that I usually stood around in the gym and watched people run. I wasn't a creep. But there were only so many times you could watch someone almost kill themselves on a treadmill, and I hadn't been thinking. I somehow slipped into teacher mode and wanted to tell the guy who was about to fall flat on his face that his shoelaces were undone, make sure he didn't hurt himself. He fell anyway, and now I'd have to stand in front of my classes for the next week with this bruise on my face and a high probability of a matching black eye. There was already a tinge of green forming under my eye.

The whole incident had taken me back to my own schooldays, triggering a wild range of junk in my head that I didn't really want to remember. I'd once hit this kid square in the face over him calling me some derogatory name or other. He'd hit back. My one and only teenaged detention, and I'd been forced to spend it in a room with that very guy. We'd never spoken again.

These days, I sat through intervention meetings with my own students and dished out the same punishments. Nothing had changed, apart from that as a teacher, I tried. I spoke to these kids like grown-ups, but I remembered how that had felt. I tried to see them. I tried to be a better teacher than the ones I'd had growing up, but at the end of the day, I was human. Something I was once again reminded of as I grimaced into the mirror.

Story of my life.

I snapped a quick selfie—not out of vanity, but out of self-pity—wondering if I could call in sick for the coming week, send the picture to the head and ask for some compassionate time off. My headteacher was an understanding soul, and nobody knew better than me how it would look going into work in the morning with a black eye and a mangled face. Everyone would be asking questions, raising concerns over an imaginary abusive partner or something. I shuddered. I'd just have to tell the truth.

Not that anyone would believe the truth. *Oh, my face? Got into a fight with that Cass Powell off TV, mate. Was nothing. You should see the state of him!*

I cringed a little at the thought. Children could be cruel at the best of times, and being a teacher, a certified proper adult with a degree, didn't mean shit when you were dealing with kids. You stood at the front of that classroom, and you were judged on every inch of your worn-out body. I'd learnt all those things the hard way as a kid myself.

Now I thought carefully about what I wore. My shirts were smart and tailored to fit, my tie always on point and subtle. On my ID, I had a neutral expression on my stern face, and I went to the gym like a good human being, not just to make sure that those shirts looked good over my skin, but also because it was no mean feat being a teacher. I may not have been lifting weights, but life in an inner-city school meant that I was on my feet all day long. I'd given up on counting my steps because I'd hit the target every day without fail, and you needed strength to deal with the fights, the gangs, the threats. The kids who dealt with life very differently from how I'd grown up.

I'd taken this job, my first teaching job, with gratitude, thinking I would move on within the year to a better school in a nicer area with gentler students and better attitudes. Yet years later, there I was, head of Year 8, still trying to instil a love of maths and history into kids whose life experiences I could barely comprehend. I had compassion, of course I did, but it was a hard pill to swallow when you tried to help these students only to be stabbed in the back as soon as you let your guard down.

It wasn't all hopeless. I'd gain a few kudos points on my form kids' scoresheets, walking into class looking like I'd just won a round against Tyson Fury, and it wasn't as if I'd been

"Hey..."

There he was. I even knew his name. His real name. Inspector Cass Powell.

"You, all right, mate? I'm so, so sorry."

His name was not Cass Powell. I knew that. But my mind was suddenly blank. He was taller up close. Broader. Freshly showered and wearing a wrinkled tracksuit.

"I'm..." I stuttered out. I was better than this, but he had this strange air about him. "I'm OK, thank you. No harm done."

I took a step back. He moved with me and reached out to grab my arm.

"I didn't mean to hit you like that. I was in my own world, and I didn't see you."

"It's all right. Honestly."

OK, words apparently didn't work with this guy because now he'd pulled my hood down, the touch of his fingertips light on my skin as he inspected my cheek.

"You should have that checked out. It looks sore."

Concern? Who is this guy? Yeah, yeah, yeah. Calm down, head. This was not a romance movie, and I was no famous actor. This was me, an ordinary high school teacher who'd had an accidental altercation with Connor Telford's hand. His very fine hand that was attached to the rest of him, and he was staring at me while I was no doubt standing here drooling like a moron. Because Connor Telford was...I wasn't going to mention the wet dreams. But he was. One. Big. Sheet destroying. Wet. Dream.

"It's fine. You can barely see it," I countered, pulling my hoodie back up over my head.

"Mate, can I do anything? I feel really bad."

He felt bad? I was getting a hard-on just hearing him talk. His hand was still firmly attached to my arm. I should have him arrested for assault. Well, not really. Well, yes. Assault on my brain. Attraction was one thing, and attractive he was, but personal space was also a thing, and apparently, Connor Telford had no sense of it.

Connor Telford. Funny how I could remember now! Actor Connor Telford had won, like, *all the Baftas*. I may...or may not...have watched every episode of *White Noise*. He was downright filthy in that series, always getting his kit off, and his arse was legendary. Every episode had at least one scene of full nudity involving Cass Powell showering or getting down and dirty, usually with a woman, sometimes with a man. Sometimes with both.

He was a gay icon. A bi icon. A hot-as-hell-dude icon whose heated gaze stared at me in Tesco as I browsed the magazines. *Men's Health, GQ, Attitude*—he'd fronted them all, and now he was fronting me as I put my hand on his chest and gently pushed him away.

"I'm absolutely fine, but thank you for your concern. It was nice meeting you."

Meeting him? What the almighty Christ was I on about?

"Can I at least...I don't know. Get you a taxi home? Buy you a drink?"

"I'm *fine*," I insisted, though I sounded anything but fine. My voice was back to that juvenile squeak it did when I was nervous. He made me nervous.

Scrap that. I made myself nervous.

"Look, I'm fine. I just need to go get some noodles and then I have thirty odd essays on the French Revolution to go through, which I'm already dreading, and then I need to pass out before I have to get up and lead assembly tomorrow."

I was oversharing. Again. Being myself. Yes. This was me. Always me. A slight mess on the outside, an even bigger mess on the inside.

"The French Revolution? You just whooshed me right back to secondary school. I take it you're a teacher?"

Why were we even having this conversation? All right, yes, I'd started it, but only because he'd been in my face.

"History and maths. Lucky me, eh?"

"If I could do it all again, I would have paid better attention in history. Back then, it was all boring, and now I love it. I even watch documentaries on the History Channel."

He was grinning. My stomach was full of stupid butterflies.

"Tell that to my students. None of them seem to have grasped the basics of human evolution, let alone that the French Revolution has nothing to do with a fashion brand."

"I bet you spend a lot of time tearing your hair out," he said softly, looking at me in a way that made my knees wobble. "Noodles, you say?"

I grimaced. Or my insides did.

"Mrs Wu's on the corner? I always have number forty-two with extra egg." His voice. Goddamn.

"Oh, no. No, no, no." I laughed. "You have to have the pork. Number seventeen. Sticky honey-ginger-glazed pieces of heaven. On noodles. Probably not traditionally Chinese at all but, man."

He laughed, and my world went into soft focus. And it had nothing to do with the honey-ginger-glazed pork.

"Can I..." he began then paused. "Wanna join me for some really disgustingly un-healthy food? My shout. As...an apology."

"Thanks, but no," my mouth said. My head was screaming *what are you doing?!* "Sorry. I have a shedload of work to do. Another time, maybe?"

I had no idea why I was smiling, but he was too, and my heart skipped a beat as he threw his gym bag over his shoulder.

"I'll just have to go eat on my own then." He pretend-pouted. "Let me know if there's anything I can do. And sorry. Again."

I nodded. He nodded.

I'd never see him again, anyway. I'd have to change gyms. Hide under the duvet for the rest of my life.

It didn't matter.

"See ya!" That was me.

He walked away. Out of my life. Forever.

At least I had work to do. And I'd just stop at the corner shop and get myself a Pot Noodle on the way home. Maybe Mrs Wu's would agree to deliver across the car park so I'd never have to show my face there again. Another place I could never go back to then. Ugh. Anyway. Whatever.

THREE

Con

Today was my birthday. Today, I officially turned twenty-five. Not that anyone had noticed.

I tell a lie. *I* had noticed because my mum had, as always, called me at the arse-crack of dawn and sung Happy Birthday to me. It hadn't actually been that early, as I'd been standing by the catering trolley downing the first of many early morning cups of coffee, and the girl manning it today had joined in and sung along. A cheerful dawn chorus to set me up right for the day.

I was going to go see Mum this weekend. Have a good night's sleep in my own bed. Wake up to familiar sounds and smells. Freshly brewed coffee and toast in the garden. Small things that had once seemed mundane but now meant everything.

I missed normality. The girl wrapping my croissant in a napkin seemed to miss it too.

"I can't stand getting up at three in the morning," she moaned. "But then, once I'm here, in the middle of a giant set and getting get paid to feed you lot—you guys are even more insane than me, by the way, and the security people have been here all night, so I don't know why I'm complaining..." She paused and smiled. "Anyway, once I'm here, I actually like it."

I nodded in agreement. I felt very much the same. The early mornings would never agree with me, but I'd got used to it. I'd had a forty-minute run on the treadmill at four this morning before I got picked up. Now it was just gone six, and I felt like I'd done a full day's work already. I had a meeting with the scriptwriter, and the intimacy coordinator was currently waiting for me outside my trailer.

Happy birthday to me.

"Con-Con. Good stuff. The guy we were supposed to be filming with today...Toby. He's called in sick, so we've had to draft in a new guy."

"Ah." Fun times. Also I hated that she called me Con-Con. Like I was some kind of performing monkey. Happy birthday to me indeed. I'd spent most of Monday afternoon rehearsing with Toby, so whatever he had...

"Please don't tell me you're coming down with something too. The hair team were all sneezing this morning, and Peter has the flu. We were going to delay, but we can't. It's only a short sequence. They're swapping the schedule around, so we need to prep you both and go over the choreography."

We were filming part of an action scene today and a nude intimate scene that turned nasty in the end. Some fight moves in the buff, nothing too complicated, and Toby had been good. We'd worked through the scene a few times and both been comfortable with the set-up. Now I had to go through all that again with someone new.

"This is Alex."

I shook hands with the guy in front of me, and we exchanged polite nods. He looked nervous. Star-struck. I got that sometimes. Most of the extras were pros and knew the ins and outs of these small jobs, but many were brand new, and this guy looked greener than green.

"Con," I said, taking a step back and folding my arms. It was too early for this shit.

"Now," the intimacy coordinator said. "I want to start with some simple moves, just to get the two of you comfortable."

Her name was Sally. She was a nice enough woman, but this wasn't my first rodeo. I'd shagged on camera since my very first role. I'd been sixteen that time. The scene had been a school disco quick fumble in the toilets, and I'd almost wet myself with excitement. The girl playing my counterpart had been older and intimidatingly experienced to my totally frazzled nerves. I'd had an intimacy coordinator then too, who'd choreographed our moves down to my facial muscle movements. By the time we'd actually filmed the scene, I'd been yawning between takes.

I *still* yawned between takes and had a habit of getting a couple of minutes shut-eye in between scenes. Most of the time, we filmed these things on beds or in showers, wearing fluffy bathrobes in between takes to keep us warm in the sometimes-arctic conditions they made us work in. Erect nipples and goosebumps looked good on film, but it was actually near frostbite masquerading as arousal.

I didn't get aroused doing these things. I was working, and as fun as it sounded getting down and dirty with your co-stars, it was anything but.

"Hey, Con."

"Hi, babe." I raised my hand in a little wave as Caroline—aka Inspector Stella Rubin—rushed past, bright and cheerful with her hair in rollers, making her way towards the line for those croissants. She always made me calm, a small, steady presence in my chaotic life. I'd known Caroline since I was barely eighteen, which meant we'd worked together for seven years now, and she knew me. Intimately, but not in *that* way. We'd always been close, but not like that.

Cass Powell and Inspector Stella Rubin knew each other intimately, though, having been workmates with benefits from the start of season one. They'd shagged numerous times, their on/off relationship a big part of the show's success. We were so used to being nearly naked around each other that I knew the pattern of birthmarks on her back. She knew all the places where I was ticklish. It was a comfortable relationship as actors. As characters, those heated passionate scenes had won awards, our awkward attraction palpable on screen. Something today's scene would no doubt lack, looking at my partner for the day, loitering in the early morning sunshine, hyperventilating and treading muddy footprints into the grass.

"Calm down, mate," I said as Sally took another phone call. "It's only a quick scene. Do you want to go over the moves? Has someone gone through the full scene with you?"

"Yeah," he huffed. "OK then."

Oh, fuck. I took a deep breath. This was *not* my job, it was Sally's, and if we'd gone with Toby, we'd have been all chill about what would go down.

"In an hour or two, you and I will go on set. We're arch enemies, but I've never actually seen your face before. You've been taunting me for the entire season. I'm really pissed off with you. You hate my guts. So, to start the scene, we do our lines until you say, 'The ultimate prize. It will be right there under your nose.' You'll push me into a wall, I'll pretend to hit you, then you'll grab my shirt, like this."

I grabbed his hand, placing it on my torso. Standard move. Nose to nose. I crowded him, right there. He recoiled in shock. Yep. It would be a long...long day.

It was nearly eight in the evening when I sat in the car heading back towards my hotel. The action scene had been textbook, but we'd done so many retakes that we'd all slightly lost the plot before we wrapped up. My arm ached with the unease of those repetitive moves, but the end result would be good. You could feel it in the air sometimes as we filmed. People around us were quieter than normal, and when it was over they cheered and applauded.

I wish I could have said the same about the intimate scene. We'd done it, eventually, but Alex was clearly a straight dude with issues, and the kissing had been awkward...until I'd turned around and told him to swap places with me so I could show him how to do it.

The director had followed my lead, rolling with my intuition, and we'd filmed it that way around a few times—me going for him instead of him going for me. That had produced some good raw footage, but it wouldn't surprise me if we had to reshoot the entire scene in a week. Hopefully with Toby. Anyone but this guy, who had used a wet wipe to clean his face after every take. Fuck him.

The car turned onto the familiar verge outside the Premier Inn, where the purple illuminated logo shone to welcome me home. I stood there for a minute, wondering whether to go straight to the gym. I was knackered, and I needed a shower, food and my bed in that order.

I took a few steps forward, turned around, and headed for the gym. I had my kit in my holdall, as always, and I still needed to read through tomorrow's scene one more time. My head was fried already, some complicated choreography clouding my memory cells—

"Hey!"

Oh! I stopped. Smiled. He smiled too. Then I didn't because OMG! The guy's face!

And now I was right up there crowding him again. The black eye he was sporting was no mean feat, and his cheek was...mangled...for the lack of a better word.

"I'm so...so...sorry," I ground out in a voice that made me cringe. I'd done this. Me. All my handiwork.

"No worries."

No worries? This was not a no-worries thing. This was the kind of thing that brought on medical issues and lawyers and court appearances and charges of assault.

"Mate, are you OK? I can't believe..." I stopped myself and pulled my sleeve back, revealing the faint bruise on my wrist. It was nothing really and could easily have been covered up with a bit of make-up. I showed it to him, almost proudly, like a child. "We have a matching pair," I joked weakly. "I'm...I'm mortified."

"It's fine," he insisted. "Gave me a one-up on some of my students today. Said I'd taken up kickboxing and won my first match. Not sure they believed me." He smiled. He had such a big smile.

"You should have told them the truth, that some idiot beat you up at the gym, totally unprovoked." It wasn't funny, and I was ashamed. Really embarrassed.

"Don't worry about it." He waved his hand like he was about to walk off. I grabbed his arm because apparently, I hadn't learned my lesson to *not* assault members of the public. "I've come straight from work. Long day." It sounded like a standard excuse, but he looked as tired as I felt.

"I still owe you dinner," I said, breathless even though we were still on the street. I didn't know what it was, but there was something wrong with my head. Static. White noise in my ears.

He wasn't what you'd call a handsome man. He was just an ordinary bloke. Nice suit. ID dangling from his neck. Huge, heavy bag hanging off his shoulder. Earphones. Good ones. Curly, messy, dark hair. He had nice eyes. A good face. Expressive. And when he smiled, the world seemed to go silent.

"There's no need," he said quietly, or maybe he was shouting. What did I know? I shook myself out of my weirdness. I was so bloody tired.

"I'm Con," I said, trying to rescue my dignity. "Con...Telford."

"Matt Winston," he offered a little too politely and reached out to shake my hand. His fingers were cold. Mine were far too hot.

"Matt," I repeated like a muppet.

"Short for Matthew. But only my mother calls me that." He grimaced. I grinned.

"Look," I said weakly, "it's my birthday, and I'm starving, and it would be...really nice to have some company over food. Also, I do owe you, and it would..."

"But we don't know each other," he said, looking more confused than I was comfortable with.

that handsome to start with. My dark curly hair was probably my best feature. My ears...
Yeah. I wasn't going to go there. They were mine, and they would always stick out, like
the rest of me. Full of angles, all 'skin and bone'. Hey, maybe the extra bulk in my cheek
would add to my looks!

I showered quickly and got dressed. I hadn't even finished my workout, but I was too
embarrassed to stay. Another wave of shame washed over me because this place had always
felt safe. Nobody knew me here, and I treasured my time in the evenings, running for
miles on that treadmill, losing myself in my music.

God knew what I'd do if I ran into that guy again. He was usually here when I rolled
in, always wearing headphones and keeping to himself. He was a bit like me, a gym loner
in his own world, staring out into nothing.

And no, I wasn't a creep, but he had an aura around him. He was one of those
handsome guys, built and strong, pale skin full of freckles and lines. Perfectly messy, thick,
blond hair. Legs for days. And he had the most...I blushed and pulled my hoodie over my
head. Hood up. Eyes down.

The guy had an arse to die for. One I wanted to sink my teeth in and just... Ugh.

Out of my league. Definitely.

I'd had my fair share of nice hook-ups. Really nice hook-ups. I liked my men built. Tall,
bulky and strong. I also really...really...liked sex. But it took a bit of effort to gear myself up
for those kinds of encounters. I wasn't into clubbing and going out, so apps had worked
well for me. I had a nice flat, but that was home. So, I'd usually spring for a cheap hotel
room across the road and meet someone for an hour of casual fun, no strings attached.

Not that it was something I'd brag about. I wasn't the kind of guy people asked to
see again, and the men I hooked-up with were not the kind of guys I'd want a repeat
performance with. It was easier in your head when the parameters were firmly set. One
hour. Sex. A lazy kiss goodbye. No guilt attached.

I laughed ruefully as I tapped my card against the gate reader and headed out into the
cool evening air. The light was fading, and I paused to grab my phone from my bag. I
was starving, and my fridge was bare. I had a bunch of assignments to go through for
tomorrow, and the noodles from the takeaway on the corner were calling me like some
siren. I could smell them, my stomach growling.

"Hey!"

I spun around.

Oh...bummer.

"No," I agreed.

"You mean like a...date?" Now he was blushing, and I was squirming on the inside.

"No. No, nonono. I... Look... I'm sorry, I'm not..."

"It's fine. Us gay men take these things a little too seriously sometimes." He was smiling, joking. I got it. "And Happy Birthday!" he added, though he still seemed weirded out, but then I *was* weird. I knew that. I'd grown up in a bubble of acting and lived a skewed existence my whole adult life. I had no idea how to deal with things that didn't involve work. I didn't date. My agent set me up with people to be photographed with. I had no friends outside the *White Noise* production team. I didn't see anyone but my mum on my rare days off. It was just the way it was, and now I was being completely inappropriate with a stranger.

"Thanks," I whispered weakly, having completely lost myself in my own stupidity.

"I'll see you around?" He was walking backwards, giving me that awkward wave again and a smile, setting my head spinning once again.

I had no idea what to say or do.

So...I went to the gym, ran until I almost threw up and had the longest shower known to man before I crammed a protein shake down my neck and passed out.

Matt

"**Y**ou don't want to do this," Detective Cass Powell growled in a voice that made the hairs on the back of my neck stand to attention.

He was naked—from the waist up at least—but the camera angle implied more, as a shot of a female hand stroking his bum flashed before my eyes.

"I can do whatever I want. I'm your boss, Powell. You know that. And now I have your balls in a vice."

Inspector Stella Rubin did indeed have his balls in a vice. Not only was she seductively whispering that last line into his ear but she also now had his balls in her grip and going by the mess Cass Powell had got himself in, she knew his tricks. He knew hers too, and they were clearly doing the deed right there in the back office of their police station. I grimaced slightly and checked my watch.

It had been stupid even sitting down to watch TV when I should be prepping for tomorrow, but I'd come back from another shitty day at work, dealing with a fight and a suspension, and now the head wanted me to take on some Enterprise business venture thing that would win the school prizes, and I had a brand-new colleague to onboard onto the team. She was fresh out of training, young and green, but nice. To be honest, an hour or two on the sofa watching mindless rubbish on TV was exactly what I needed. Hence, I was two episodes into the first season of *White Noise*. I'd watched it all before, of course, but that mess of a bloke was now pretty much stalking me, with his total lack of personal space and insistence that I agree to dine with him. I shook my head in disbelief. Wasn't happening. I'd always thought he was handsome, but in real life? No.

No. Absolutely not.

There were lines in the world that should not be crossed. Ever. I, of all people, knew that. It didn't work like that. I'd known I was gay all my life and been out since I was fourteen, but I was not some uber-attractive, ripped dude who could waltz off into the sunset with the chap from the cover of *Men's Health*. Things were not going to magically change just because I'd got hit square in the face.

It wasn't that bad, the bruise on my face. It had made people laugh at work today, my colleagues ribbing me, endless stares from the students as I held my head high and stared back. I didn't take any crap from anyone, not anymore. I may have been a weak kid back when I was a student, but these days, I handled myself better. I knew when to blend into the wallpaper, and I knew when to stand up for myself and shout louder than anyone else. I'd won battles, many of them. I wasn't living in some kind of dream world, but grey had never been a colour that had suited me, and I refused to blend into the straight world and just pass.

Pride was a strange word, but I was proud of who I was. Maybe I wasn't living in the grandest house. Nor did I have a husband, dog or two-point-four children, but I hadn't done badly for myself, managing to buy this flat. It was handy for the Tube, had every convenience nearby and was far enough away from the school that I didn't have to deal with my students in my spare time. Not like my colleague Otis, who lived right next to the school entrance and had eggs thrown at his door on a daily basis, graffiti sprayed on his car. He needed to move, and he knew it.

Here, in my little second-floor flat, I was shielded from the world outside. I had my workstation, my bookshelves, a sofa and TV and a small kitchen where I whizzed up meals. Not that I was a MasterChef of any kind, but I grilled some mean burgers, and my stir fries were legendary. See? I was fine. I was OK.

I was wondering if I should bite the bullet and get myself laid this weekend. I deserved it. I really did, and it would make me feel better about everything, but every time I passed the mirror, I'd cringe and realise that getting some good dick might not happen if I opened the door looking like this. I'd give people the completely wrong idea. No. No.

Dammit. I smiled ruefully to myself. I was getting cockblocked by Detective Cass Powell. He was back on my screen, walking down a deserted road, apparently looking for an abandoned suitcase. He'd misplaced some evidence or something. I'd stopped paying attention when he'd taken his shirt off. Then the white vest he was wearing underneath came off, his hand bunching it up so he could wipe his face. Muscles bulged on those arms of his, shoulders flexing in slow motion, eyes glittering in the sun, a drop of sweat running down his cheek and over his lips as the camera zoomed in on his mouth, the very tip of his tongue sticking out before he roughly swiped the sweat away with the back of his hand and normal playback speed resumed.

Whoever cut this fine drama together knew what they were doing because *my* hand was down my trousers, my zip straining against it as my other hand paused and rewound. Here he was again. His shirt coming off. A bronze nipple showing. His freckled skin talking to me.

I stopped myself in horror. *What the...? This guy. OK Matt, get a grip.*

I could never go to that gym again, although I needed a good run with all this pent-up frustration pulsing through my veins. I also really wanted noodles. I'd been craving them for days, but Con Telford had stolen those from me too, and I'd have to take the long way back from the Tube since I now apparently got stalked by famous actors outside the Premier Inn. It would add another ten minutes to my mornings, having to cross around the back of the estate instead of walking straight to the Tube.

Not only was I being cockblocked, stalked and frustrated by this dude, but he was ruining my life.

I laughed out loud.

I was head of Year 8 in an inner-city school. I could deal with anything. Yet here I was, scared of a man who couldn't even tie his own shoelaces. What was wrong with me?

I switched the TV off in disgust and unbuttoned my shirt, chucked my suit trousers over the back of the sofa as I caught a glimpse of myself in the mirror. OK, so my face was not much to shout about, but I did have nice lips. Strong shoulders. A runner's body. That's how I described myself on the apps. I was lean with muscles in the right places. Not too little, not too much. Just right. Strong.

I didn't do weights, but I did use the rowing machines to my advantage, leaving my body to do its job, my mind blanking as I breathed and let my music take me away.

I'd hated PE at school. Now the gym opposite where I lived was the highlight of my evenings. The one place where I didn't feel out of place. It didn't matter if the other gym users had bigger muscles or ran faster; I kept a steady pace and popped 5K without too much effort. It made me feel good, and nobody actually cared who I was or how fast I ran or what I was wearing.

I grabbed my usual gear, a shirt and shorts, and tied my shoelaces. Double knot. Key. Wallet. Bag.

I kept my head down and tapped myself in through the gates. Put my stuff in a locker, shoved my card in the lining of my shorts. Grabbed one of the free water bottles. Yes, this was a posh gym, which was why I liked it. They provided towels and water in actual bottles—reusable, of course, so they were also kind to the environment. Small things, all considered, but they were important to me.

I took part in beach clean-ups. My class sponsored rainforest work in South America. I'd championed the complete removal of plastic from our school canteen. We were not there yet, but the changes we'd pushed through were substantial.

Pride. My chest was sometimes filled with it.

I ran. And ran some more, my face drenched in sweat. Then I walked for ten minutes, some Eurovision-winning song filling my head. I closed my eyes, let my body calm, cool down. More water.

It helped. Everything always felt better after a good run, and I was absolutely starving by the time I walked through the door at Mrs Wu's.

Pride. I didn't feel very proud skulking on the corner, trying to look through the blinds to make sure a certain person wasn't sitting in there, stuffing his handsome, non-bruised face with noodles.

He wasn't. The place was empty, apart from a woman in the corner browsing the menu and Wei Wu looking half asleep at the counter.

"Matt!" His face lit up. "Haven't seen you for ages! Hang on, I have a list at the back. I curated you another comprehensive masterpiece of books you really need to read."

Wei was a nice chap. He was my age, an English major and still at uni, when he wasn't working at his mum's take away. He also really liked talking.

"Hey," I said, with relief, perching on one of the stools by the counter.

"You eating here? MUUUMMMM! We need one-seventeen on noodles, chilli on the side and a Diet Coke."

"The till is there for a reason," came from the back. "Use it. It's called modern technology and produces this handy little pop-up on my screen telling me just that."

I loved Mrs Wu. She cooked like a goddess and had a wicked sense of humour. She was also snarky as anything to her son, but she loved him to bits.

"Matt!" she squealed as she came around the corner. "Your face!"

"Don't ask." I huffed. "It's so stupid, the story's not worth telling."

"No story is *not* worth telling." Wei moved his stool, so he was sitting opposite me on the other side of the counter. He clearly expected me to tell him everything. "Your insignificant story could one day make the greatest tale of all times."

"I doubt it." I laughed but gratefully sipped at the tall glass of Diet Coke he'd set in front of me. It was chemical junk, I knew, but everyone deserved a little treat from time to time.

"So come on," Mrs Wu cajoled, "what happened to that handsome face of yours? If it was those kids who hang around here at night, I'll put washing-up liquid in their meals. Give them the runs for days."

"Mrs Wu!" I gasped in fake shock.

"Ancient Chinese recipe." She laughed but then became stern. "Tell me. Who did this to you?"

"I had a bit of an altercation with some gym equipment." I didn't want to get into this. Not again. "And some guy attached to it."

Wei rolled his eyes. "And...?"

"And nothing. He tripped. I was in the way." That was the truth. Kind of.

"Ohhh." He sagged. "I was expecting some grand romance."

"Ah, but it could be," Mrs Wu said mystically. She pulled up a second stool and sat beside her son. Now they were both staring at me in anticipation.

"Aren't you supposed to be cooking me noodles? Topped with the best fried pork known to man?"

Mrs Wu just waved her hand in frustration. "Gossip first. Food after. Spill the oolong."

"It's tea, Mother. That...that..." Wei circled his finger in front of my face. "That bruise looks nasty. You have a black eye. There must have been more."

"No, honestly. The guy apologised. I'm fine." I was.

"Now I'm disappointed." Mrs Wu slumped forward and thumped her head on the counter. "I will put all this disappointment into your meal, Matt. Disappointed pork with even more disappointed noodle. You'd better come up with a better story for when

I come back. I asked for oolong. You gave me lukewarm, disappointed water." With that, she winked and disappeared out the back.

Wei pinned me with his eyes. "Were you hurt? Did you report it?"

"I wasn't hurt!" I sighed in frustration. I'd known Wei since I moved in here but had no intention of telling him my life story.

"You might not have been physically hurt—well, you were—but you're butthurt. It would help to talk about it."

I eyed him dubiously. He shrugged.

"I live my whole, boring life in this small room, evening after evening. I need the full story, warts and all—did the guy have warts? I hope he did, doing that to you."

"He did not have warts." I laughed and gulped down more Diet Coke. I'd showered, washed my hair and dressed in clean clothes, but I was getting hot and bothered, and I was hungry. I just wanted to go home, eat and treat myself to another episode of that naked idiot detective losing most of his evidence and shagging his boss, then sleep. Long day tomorrow.

"Come on," Wei persisted.

I sighed. "Fine." He wasn't going to let this go. "Does the name Con Telford ring a bell?"

"Overrated soap actor?" he said.

I burst into laughter. "He's won quite a few Baftas, and he's *GQ*'s Man of The Year..."

"Matt, I'm an English major. I take scriptwriting. I know a thing or two about decent storytelling, and you're treading on my delicate toes here. He's a British soap actor. Overrated. Celebrated for no reason."

"I like *White Noise*," I protested.

"You also like *EastEnders* and think the Marvel Universe is culture."

"Don't mock my tastes."

"I'm not. I'm also very impressed with you reading my recommendations. Some of the ones on my new list are trailblazers in the industry. Watch this space. One day, Wei Wu will be up there with his very own works of perfection." He bowed and sprinkled imaginary stars onto the counter.

"I'm sure he will," I said, and I meant it.

"What about Con Telford, anyway?" he asked.

"He's the one who whacked me in the face."

"Oh God. And now you're in love with him?"

"*Wei*!" I shouted, horrified. "I'm not! It was just a stupid thing."

"But it *was* a thing?"

"No." I took a deep breath. "It's not. He was on the treadmill, and his shoelaces were undone. He fell off and whacked me in the face."

"And you're telling me this because...?"

Sometimes Wei was annoying as hell.

"Because you asked!"

"No. You're telling me because you know he comes in here, and you're hoping *I* will spill the tea."

"Absolutely not!" I groaned.

"He orders number forty-two with extra egg. That dish is an abomination and an insult to the food it contains."

"I know. He told me."

Wei grinned smugly. "Aha! There *is* more to this story."

"There's not." See, this was what happened when I talked to people. Well, when I talked to Wei. I'd spent a lot of time in this fine establishment talking to the guy...who was now looking suspiciously sympathetic. He had more to say, and I got the feeling I wasn't going to like it. "Go on," I invited reluctantly.

"Con Telford may be some kind of gay icon, having shagged men on that show of his, but to be very, very brutally honest here, Matt, he's the straightest guy I've ever laid eyes on. And by all accounts, he's a bit of an arsehole—I read up on him online. I know we don't believe all the gossip in the tabloids, but he's apparently dating that new supermodel. You know? Tara Marie. They were photographed together getting coffee. In the morning. I mean, we all know those event photos are staged, but when people get coffee early in the morning together, you've got to admit it's suspicious."

"I'm not interested in Con Telford," I insisted.

"He lives in the Premier Inn across the road. Right over there. We deliver to him. I even know what room, should you need it to deliver threats or give information to the police or something."

"I *don't* need it."

"Suit yourself. But I still don't get it. He beat you up?"

"No!" Why was I shouting? And here came Mrs Wu with my food, steaming hot and on a plate when I would have preferred it to go. She stuck a pair of chopsticks in my hand and resumed her seat next to Wei.

"So, you got beaten up by that actor? Do I need to put washing-up liquid in his dinner?"

Ignoring her, I tucked into my food, breathing a huge sigh of relief when a bunch of kids walked through the door.

So, Connor Telford was straight. Of course he was. They almost always were—the hot actors playing gay and bi characters. There'd been some big debate about whether only gay actors should play gay roles and so on, but I hadn't really paid attention. It had nothing to do with me, anyway, because I would never see him again.

Con

T his week had been painful, and I wasn't just talking about the bruises on my knees. We'd wrapped up on Friday with an almighty simulated car crash, and believe me, getting thrown out of a moving car wasn't as much fun as it seemed on screen. Not that I'd actually been thrown out. My stunt double Justin had taken the hits, but I still had to hurl myself onto a mattress with four wind machines in the background. Even when falling with textbook grace, sliding across that mattress was like the worst carpet burn.

I'd also spent an insane amount of time in the make-up chair, getting my face done up to look like I'd truly been run over by a car. I'd snapped a photo to show...Matt. I hadn't forgotten his name, but I didn't have his number so I couldn't send it to him. If he thought his face had looked bad, mine looked positively terrifying. Except, of course, it wasn't real.

At least I had two days off, so here I was, sitting at my mum's kitchen table, showing her my selfies, and she was half hiding her face in horror, half laughing.

"I can't believe what they did to your face!"

"They had to do it twice because Justin looked just as bad."

"Oh, I remember Justin. Scottish guy?"

"No, that's Hamish—my body double."

"Oh, yes." Her laptop pinged with an incoming message. "I never know the difference," she said, pushing her glasses up her nose.

"Justin does my stunts, saving me from getting myself killed. Hamish is me when I don't need to be on set."

"That's right." She hadn't heard a word I was saying, too busy sighing and scowling at the screen.

Still, it was nice. I loved being home, sitting in my T-shirt and boxers at the table, drinking coffee, no pressure. Not even the sound of the kettle boiling dry could snap me out of my zen. This was how Mum and I rolled. Existing here in peace and quiet, doing our own thing.

"Sweetheart, fill that kettle back up and make me a cup of tea, will you?"

"I'm not your slave, Mum," I mumbled but did it anyway. I loved my mum, more now than when I'd been a grumpy kid. She was kind of cool.

"You look tired, sweetie. You need to take some time off," she said, turning a paper over and putting it back down. "You work too hard."

"Look who's talking!" I shot back at her. She worked as much as I did, and it was the same every Saturday—me complaining about making the drinks, her with her paperwork spread around her and her laptop open. I gestured at it all to make my point. "You're the one who taught me all about work ethic."

"Yes, but you're young. You should be out partying, travelling, having wild weekends in Ibiza."

"Not for me, Mum. Just because you were some wild party girl who got yourself knocked up on a night out, it doesn't mean I have to."

She laughed, and so did I. My conception was no secret, and I liked hearing Mum laugh. She'd done some wild things in her youth before she'd settled down in this house, got a degree, built up her business. Raised me.

"When are you wrapping this season again?" she asked, still tapping on her keyboard.

"Four more weeks. Then I go straight into rehearsals for *LA Boys*."

"That the theatre thing? That play with all the nudity?"

"Yeah, Mum, and you and Aunt Trish will *not* be coming to see it."

"Of course we will! I already emailed Lucia for tickets. She said the whole run is sold out, and they haven't even officially started promo."

"Yeah." I sighed. The pressure was on. I'd done small, backstreet plays before, and this was...still a small backstreet theatre, but the hype had been insane, and Lucia—my agent—was once again begging me to take an interest in my social media, which would only mean more sleepless nights worrying if I could actually pull this off.

"It's a good play," I said. "I'm excited about doing something new. Different."

"Yes, and then as soon as that wraps, you'll go off to America again to meet with another round of casting agents, and then you'll be on another project before you've even got a splash of sunshine on those cheeks. You do realise that everyone will have seen those cheeks?"

"Everyone has already seen these fine cheeks, and anyway, I'll be getting a spray tan for the *LA Boys* run. It's set in Los Angeles, and I can't be looking all pale like this."

"You'll be brilliant." Mum smiled, for a minute stopping and grabbing my hand. "But you need to take care of yourself too. Look after your needs. Hang out with your friends. Get yourself laid. Meet some new people. Find that special girl. Or boy. A friend. Person."

That was Mum in a nutshell, always choosing her words carefully, ensuring she wouldn't offend. The fact was, I had no friends. I hadn't seen the people I'd gone to school with for years, and yeah.

"You know, Mum, it's not real what you see on TV. That's not me."

"I know, sweetie. I know. I'm your mum, and I understand these things. But you need to be happy, and right now, there's something lacking in your life. Something quite important. I can't be there to hold your hand and tuck you into bed anymore."

"Mum," I groaned, and she laughed.

"Think about it, yeah? You need someone special. Someone who will look after you. You can't just work and not live."

"I *do* live, and I will have some time off...at some point." I wouldn't. What the hell was I supposed to do? Go off on a singles tour of India and learn to meditate? Lucia would have my balls on a plate, and I kind of knew it. I loved her and knew she always had my back, but I was pushing this as much as she was. She'd offered time off, even forced me to take a few days a couple of months back, then we'd both agreed to cancel them when the booking for the cover for *ELLE* had landed, and instead I'd spent three days in some fancy studio with a supermodel called Tara. Who was nice enough, but...

"I hate photoshoots." Random, but so was my mum, and she would know where my thoughts had gone.

"I hated that cover you did," she said. "What was the magazine again? *Masculine*? That was it. It didn't even look like you. What did they do? Cut your head off and paste it on someone else's body?"

"It's called Photoshop, Mum."

"I know about Photoshop, sweetie," she replied snarkily as her phone went off with a shrill, loud tone that broke our peace and quiet.

I grabbed my cup and phone and went out in the garden, flopped onto one of the garden chairs and scrolled through my pathetic Instagram account, grinning at pictures of people I no longer knew.

The photo I'd taken the other day popped up, and I suddenly had a thought. Hmm. I wonder...

It was perfectly acceptable to look up people on Instagram. Lucia did it all the time, showed me the glossy accounts of up-and-coming influential names, pretty faces in fake situations. I'd done those too; they were plastered all over my own verified Lucia-controlled Actor Connor Telford account. I'd be carted off to stylists, who'd dress me like a paper doll, and then I'd get wheeled out to events so people could take photos. I didn't mind when I went with Caroline, but she was now dating another actor, and now the two of them got carted out together, usually in matching outfits. Ties to match handbags. I sighed to myself.

I was booked in for an event next week with Tara. The supermodel. She was very nice and had actually spoken to me like I was a human being and not just a prop. We'd even snuck out for coffee, and I'd very briefly met her girlfriend. At the time, I'd gladly agreed to be Tara's date for next week's Gucci event. I regretted that now, but Lucia would have my head on a plate—again—if I dared to cancel.

His name was Matt. Matt Winston. I remembered. I popped it into the search bar on Instagram and got loads of hits but nobody that looked anything like him. Yes, I feel you, Matt. If I was a teacher, I wouldn't have public social media either.

In case I'd misheard, I tried Matt Waters. Walton. Window.

Nope.

Next, I tried Matthew, and there he was. Matthew Winston, from Maidenhead. His profile picture was sleek, well dressed. He looked younger on there.

I pressed follow. Private account. Of course. But I could message him.

What the fuck was I doing?

Message.

Matthew Winston.

Hell.

Hello!

Sent. Fuck.

I had no idea how to do this. And why was I messaging him in the first place? WHERE WAS THE DELETE BUTTON? How do I unsend?

Who is this?

Dammit. I didn't think. He'd have no clue who Connor Kincaid was. I'd changed my Instagram last name to my sperm donor's name a few years back. Some of my old mates had been inundated with weird followers, and I'd temporarily deleted my account. Deleted some of those mates as well. Wankers.

It's Con. Connor.

Teacher Matthew Winston probably knew at least five hundred Connors. I was an idiot. I tried again.

Con, from the gym.

I should just throw myself into the garden pond, headfirst. Right now. Or not. Mum would kill me. We had tadpoles, and I wasn't even allowed to walk near it.

I sent the photo, studying it again on the screen. It was a particularly gory one in which I looked half dead with those unrevivable injuries painted all over the side of Cass Powell's face.

Don't worry, It's just make-up.

I had no idea how to make friends. Did I want friends? Why the hell was I texting this near stranger?

I was a creep. It was official.

You deserve it, after what you did to my face.

I cringed, my lungs burning with guilt. I hated this. I was a decent person. A good person. I was not a person who...did shit like this.

I was typing out some longwinded, crappy apology when the next message came in.

It was a photo of his face. He looked like shit.

I just sat there staring at it. Blues and greens and yellows all down his cheek like he'd been the victim of a child's finger painting.

Just kidding. I'm absolutely fine. It's fading nicely.

Hope your make-up came off. Looks messy.

Is that your real name then?

Sorry, shouldn't ask. I know people like you value your privacy.

I did value my privacy, and I should not be doing things like this.

~~*I still owe you dinner.*~~

I wiped it out. Tried to do better.

Sorry again. I had no idea you were there. Honestly. If you see me at the gym again, you have my full permission to whack me in the face.

I wasn't thinking straight. What on earth was I doing? But there was his response. In black and white on my screen.

I don't have a violent bone in my body. Anyway, it was my fault. I was trying to get your attention to tell you that your shoelaces were undone. That was it.

My shoelaces had not been undone.

Or had they?

So you see, it was my fault. All good. Clean slate. Hope your film work is going well. Nice to talk to you.

Nice to talk to me?

I still owe you dinner sometime, I tapped out in a panic. *Maybe if I see you at the gym, we can grab a bite after?*

I closed my eyes, let the sun warm my face as my stomach dropped. The click of the reply thundered in my head. I didn't want to look. Perhaps with one eye?

X

What the hell did an X mean? Perhaps it was code for something. He'd mentioned something about being gay. Maybe it was gay code? Like a 'no thanks, you're too ugly'? What did I know? Peter, my hair guy, was gay. I could ask him. A lot of people on set were gay too. Why did I not know these things? Fuck it.

I was not asking him out on a date. I thought we'd already established that.

I sent an X back. Because I could.

"Connor, sweetie, do you want another coffee?" Mum called.

I needed to stop this.

I sent another one.

X

X

Then I slammed the phone down on the table and stretched out on the chair. I didn't need this. This was my day off, and I was going to just forget about the real world. Be me. Here. Safe.

He could take his X and shove it.

Matt

X

He'd sent it twice, and it made me smile.

We barely know each other.

I'd meant it as a little joke. I mean, I wasn't saying anything that wasn't true, and now he was sending kisses like we were boyfriends.

Kisses. Deep sigh. It was my fault. I'd sent one first, and I hadn't meant to. It had been a muscle twitch. An impulse. I wasn't the kind of person who sent random kisses to men I didn't know.

I did not have a thing for Con Telford. Nope. Not me.

I groaned at the paused TV screen in front of me, where his handsome face was twisted in pain. Well, not him. Detective Cass Powell had just been stabbed in the guts at the end of season three, and Inspector Stella Rubin was holding his face as he writhed in pain.

He'd survive. I knew because I had season four queued up ready to go, after I'd made myself another cup of tea.

God, I was a boring nerd. It was the weekend; I was caught up with most of my lesson planning but had ample work I could have sunk my teeth into. Instead...

Yes. Cass Powell had once again turned out to be a nice distraction. A very nice distraction. No wonder human beings around the world grovelled at his mud-covered feet.

Which made me laugh because how had he lost his shoes? He had nice feet, though. Gorgeous legs, even covered in blood and gore.

FML.

My kitchen was clean and tidy as I toddled out there in my sleep socks. Don't judge me. I got cold at night, and sleep socks were one of my few guilty pleasures. Fluffy warm little things of happiness that screamed comfort and home. So was the knitted cardigan I tended to live in at the weekends, bunched up around my waist as I adjusted the string holding my pyjama bottoms up over my hips.

I didn't really have hips. Nor did I have a bum, and clothes tended to just hang off me like I was some kind of clothes hanger.

Not that I cared. Not really. I'd come out of my box just like this, and there had never been anything I could do about it. I was Matthew Winston, and if people didn't like that, they could do one. I'd grown up not caring, and I was not about to start now.

My phone chimed from the sofa as I crawled back up there, burying myself under my blanket.

Connor Kincaid. Two new messages.

Cringe.

Double cringe.

Connor Kincaid posted on Instagram.

Infinite cringes right there. I'd followed Connor the actor. Then I'd followed the real him. He'd followed me back. How stupid was I?

I didn't want to look. I didn't want to get myself more involved than I already was. He was a major television star. An influencer. A bisexual icon.

And I was...

Me.

I still looked. It was a nice picture of him curled up on the sofa, perhaps at home.

Messages: two. Just as the notifications had said.

I like that you're open about yourself. It makes things easy to relate to. I feel we kind of know each other a little.

Despite you sending Xs at me. You can always block me if you think I'm annoying, but I think we should be friends.

I didn't know how to feel about that message. I got a sudden pang of guilt. Con Telford was a star, but Connor Kincaid was obviously lonely. A sad lonely bloke who probably just needed a hug.

I did *not* want to hug Con Telford.

I moaned into my sofa blanket and threw my phone onto my little coffee table. Then I turned notifs off and left it face down. There. No distractions.

I had umpteen union emails that I really should deal with. I was part of my Teachers' Association Pride committee, and I still hadn't started on getting our float registered for next year's London Pride. This year's plans also needed attention, and I needed to send emails, make phone calls, draw up basic plans, write lists.

I switched on BBC1. *Antiques Roadshow*, where some pensioner was getting his mum's old wall clock valued. I sighed.

BBC2. *Songs of Praise*. I switched the sound off. Sighed some more. Picked my phone back up. Typed.

Dinner Monday? After the gym. My treat.

I pressed send. Then I screamed at the screen.

No can do. Shooting until midnight Monday. But I can do Tuesday since it's a day off. Have a meeting with my agent in the morning but can definitely do after the gym. 8-ish?

What was I doing? Setting up a date?

8-ish is fine. See you at the entrance or something?

He replied straight away, like he had nothing better to do in his celebrity world than sit around texting with me.

Looking forward to it. C

My hands were shaking, trying to figure out how to reply. It really wasn't that difficult. All I needed to do was to write something cheerful and positive.

Except I didn't feel very cheerful and positive. I had no issue meeting up with complete strangers to get naked and do the horizontal tango. I was quite happy to stick my dick in people. Even happier letting people stick their dicks in me. I liked a good blowie. I liked...

There it was. Another moan coming out of my mouth. He was just a bloke. A nice, normal bloke. Very much my type. I liked the fringe he had going on. I liked the way his shoulders went from smooth into all those curves of his muscles. I liked...

"FUUUUCK!!!" I shouted at the children's choir mutedly singing on the TV. Why the hell was I watching this?

I turned it off and drank my tea. Scrolled the news on my phone. Tried to ignore any social media apps. I did not google Connor Kincaid. Turns out he only seemed to exist on Instagram.

Where his last message still sat unanswered.

So, I did what any self-respecting human being would do. I loaded episode one of season four of *White Noise* and half cheered when Detective Cass Powell's face filled the screen, a little worse for wear, a little older. His shoulders filled out his shirt—like he hadn't just spent six months recovering from a gruesome stabbing to his midriff—as he lifted up his daughter and kissed who I supposed was her mother. Such a respectable, responsible human being. Cass Powell had his life under complete control, despite the fact that his daughter's knee was right in his stab wound. If that had been me—

I was overthinking this and far too involved in a television drama where characters magically healed from life-threatening injuries between seasons.

I spent Sunday marking papers in a panic, having made it all the way to season five. Not good. I then fretted the night away, dreaming that I was being chased through tunnels by Inspector Rubin, who wanted to stab me in the guts.

I was losing it. Fast.

At least Monday kept me on my toes, running around sorting out things that had never been mentioned at university. Want to be a teacher? Want to spend most of your days dealing with social services? Want to be on a first-name basis with your local community officer? Want to know more details about your students than are strictly good for your own mental health?

It wasn't all doom and gloom though, I acknowledged with the usual pang of guilt I got when things like that popped up in my head. I'd been sent a bunch of flowers from a former student who had been accepted to his university of choice. I'd run a very, very, *very* successful intervention group meeting in which we'd come much further in our discussions than I would ever have dreamed. My students were exceptional, in so many ways, and the pride that filled my chest just thinking about it was...embarrassing at times.

I'd also set up a new intervention team with Sadie, the new colleague. She may have been green and fresh out of training, but she was exactly what we needed. New blood. New ideas. Perhaps quirky ones, but definitely ones that had worked today, bringing out the very best in our students. Sadie was sharp and direct and pushed boundaries—within the limits of the classroom. She'd been quick to tell me that her personal life was private and to not ask questions. I was more than comfortable with not going anywhere near discussing my own chaotic private life or anyone else's.

I needed a break from work. I needed a break from sitting at home watching stupid TV. I needed to get out of my head. I needed desperately to get laid and get all this frustration out of my body.

Not that I was frustrated. Not that I had wanked last night. OK, maybe I had. Again. That scene where Cass Powell got royally pegged by the dead prince's protection officer had not only completely blindsided Inspector Rubin, but...well...

It wasn't real. *Nothing* was real. My life had become completely surreal, and I didn't know how to cope with it.

I skipped down the stairs and tapped myself out of the school office, setting off at a brisk pace.

I was OK. My life was OK. Fulfilling. I was happy. I had brilliant colleagues and great students. I had a union meeting on Friday and plans for the weekend. Good things were happening.

Yet my phone pinged again, and my heart set off in some kind of stupid dance beat.

Actor Connor Telford posted on Instagram.

I needed to cancel this stupid dinner date. I was not going on a date with Con Telford. I was not.

Tomorrow is not going to be a date. Right?

I sent it in a panic. And now I was panicking even more.

What the hell was I doing?

Con

"We are concerned."

That was Lucia. She always spoke like she was doing so on behalf of the entire team when it was actually just her in the room. It usually made me laugh, but this time it made me sigh. It wasn't that bad. The proofs from my recent photo session were spread over the table between us, and I thought they were rather good. Steamy? Yes. My palm was on Tara's breast in one of them, and Tara looked scandalised yet suitably aroused over her slight wardrobe malfunction. But Lucia was right. In one photo, I was doing a total cum-face. So sue me. I was a professional actor and that face? Perfection. Well, I would rather they didn't use that one specifically, but *ELLE* magazine was keen to keep things family orientated, and the photos were all...

"They're all filthy, Con."

"Yup." What could I say? The photographer had asked for steam. We had delivered. I also remember having laughed a lot during the session, yet none of the pictures depicted us looking even remotely happy. We looked like we were... Ahem.

"It's an image we're trying to get away from for you. If you're to land more diverse roles, we can't go with these. I would like to veto some of the shots—you said you did different poses?"

"Well, there's different and...different." I sighed. "There were a few we took where I was kneeling between her legs."

"Con!" Lucia groaned. "Was there not a single picture of you and Tara Marie looking elegant and ready for a night out, toasting with champagne instead of her pouring bubbles down your trousers?"

"The brief was simple." I shrugged. The photos were really good. Tara looked incredible, and the one where my tongue was suggestively licking down her cleavage as she poured champagne into my mouth was actually pretty clever. Not real champagne, of course. Sparkling water. They added the colour post-production. After all, we couldn't ruin the clothes, and most of the shots had been done with an empty bottle. The end result was...well...I wouldn't call it porn, but...

"The brief was a sexy look at today's up-and-coming stars of stage and screen. Tara's first movie is out in a month, and this—"

"Will sell," I interrupted. "The click rate will be through the roof."

I wasn't born yesterday, and I did understand some of what Lucia was saying. The photos were truly scandalous and would either break us both or my social media following would shoot up like a rocket.

"Oh, Con." Lucia slumped onto a chair, her head in her hands. "It's a massive risk. I'm not sure."

"There are already rumours of me and Tara dating. There were those pap photos of us buying coffee, and yes, I know you hired him. Sneaky. Same guy you used last time."

Lucia glanced up but said nothing while I rambled on.

"And we'll be at the Gucci party next week. This is just the natural follow through. These pictures invite the public into our imaginary bedroom. End of. Then you can have the fun job of announcing that we're *just good friends* and that our commitments are keeping us apart. Some bullshit like that. You're good at those trivial little lies."

"Tara is queer, a very outspoken, proud lesbian," Lucia pointed out. "Her publicist has done a fine job of curating her image, and Tara's team is keen to get these photos approved to broaden her appeal."

"Does that matter? No," I answered for her. I was so sick of all of this. The expectations. The branding. The image. The perception people had to have of me. Lucia wasn't done, though, and she continued to lecture me when all I wanted to do was forget all of this existed.

"I know you're not keen on having those kinds of personal statements about yourself out in the public eye. But if you need me to put anything out there, you know I will always support you."

"I still don't feel it's something I have to...explain," I said quietly, finally allowing myself to breathe. I'd toed that line since my teens. My sexuality wasn't something that had been shoved down my throat despite the rest of my life having been micromanaged and scripted. I'd just been *that* kid. The one who was too scared to figure things out. I liked girls. I really liked girls. I'd kissed my first boy in a soap role at seventeen. He'd been gay, and I'd been so bloody green. Our on-screen chemistry had been off the charts, everyone said, and he still kept in touch. George, his name was. Nice guy. Had a boyfriend.

He'd been a good kisser and had taught me some tricks. I'd never been so embarrassed in my life, but they'd been good tips. I was a good kisser now too and rarely needed choreography to adjust my moves. I liked kissing. I liked when things felt good. Not that I ever allowed myself to think that way because it was all work. Nothing was real. Ever.

"Approve them," I said quietly. "The photographer was very professional. He knew exactly what he was doing, and these shots are scorching. I think, if anything, the magazine will face any backlash. We're just actors."

"The public don't see it that way," Lucia argued.

"I don't care." I was tired. Really, really tired.

"This one," I said, pointing at the photo where Tara looked like she was in the throes of orgasmic bliss and my hands were up her skirt. "This one should go on my social media. Tag Tara. It'll make her laugh."

"Seriously, Con. You'll be the death of me. The US will take a step back. It's too much."

"It's pure filth," I agreed.

"Not the image we are trying to portray."

"Well, that's all I know how to do. I can get into fights and run and roll in the mud all I want, but that's not what people remember. And we already have the play. Ties in nicely. Then we'll start filming that BBC period drama afterwards, right? That's still on the cards. I have a varied schedule coming up. If the US pull out, then so be it."

"Ambition, Con. We're not aiming for mediocre here," Lucia scolded. "I'm still not sure if you should sign up for the BBC drama. It's not...quite you. And I have another client in mind." She managed some huge names. I was lucky to have her, and I certainly didn't want to piss her off or turn down her advice or whatever she was offering, but I just wasn't feeling it today. I wasn't feeling anything.

I was driven back to my hotel, the plain room greeting me with its usual dullness. I had all my stuff spread messily over the table. The bed was unmade. The cleaner came in every Friday to change my sheets, but the rest of the time, I slobbed around in a state of slight chaos. I didn't care. I didn't spend enough time here anyway, and once I started rehearsal for *LA Boys*, I'd move all this crap to a different hotel closer to where I needed to be. This one was just a short hop from the current set; hence, this was currently home.

Home. I laughed bitterly to myself and flopped down on the bed, grabbing my phone.

Matt. I still hadn't answered his text. I had no idea what to say. This was definitely not a date. Nope. Absolutely not. We were just going to hang out and have dinner. A quick bite. A brief, cheerful conversation. Behave like normal people because Matt *was* normal. I needed to learn how to be that too.

I sent a text to Tara, gingerly asking if she'd seen the photos.

She replied with a string of fiery emojis. She was happy. That was all good then. Had she not been, I would readily have gone with Lucia and vetoed the shit out of them.

I tried to nap. Tried to look at next week's scripts. Scrolled back to Instagram where, for the umpteenth time, I stared at Matthew Winston.

I couldn't help it.

I had no idea why.

I managed to survive until five-ish, when I gave up and rolled down to the gym. Did weights until my arms screamed. Ran with my lines thundering through my head. Went over some choreography for a fight scene using the punch bag as my prop.

I tried not to look for him, knowing full well he was probably right here in the room. I wasn't going to make things weird. Things weren't weird anyway. Were they? People went out for food all the time. Friends went out and had chats.

I'd punched him in the face.

Old news. We were over that. Weren't we?

I was going nuts, and I knew it. I went and had a good, long shower. Sat in the steam room. Stewed in thoughts I didn't want to think. My normal gym routine usually perked me up, yet all I wanted to do was close my eyes, go to sleep right here on the bench with a towel around my waist.

My head lolled, and I shivered as I tried to stand up, only to half faceplant into a wall.

I saved myself at the last second and carefully straightened up, taking long, slow breaths to try to get some oxygen to my head as I walked as normally as I could to the changing room. Fuck. I was not doing this. I was not coming down with something.

"Hi!"

Matt. Of course. Towel around his waist. Hair wet. Looking...

"Hey." My head swam. My wet body broke out in goosebumps as I tried to drag on a shirt. My hands shook, and my mouth was bone dry.

"Here," he said, tugging my T-shirt down over my shoulders. "You OK?"

I was usually the one too much in people's faces, but here he was, right next to me, his hand on my forehead.

"You're burning up. You're not OK, are you?"

"I don't know," I mumbled.

He was too close. I was a mess. My eyes were too heavy to keep open, and I was cold. So bloody cold.

"Con? Look. Get some clothes on, and I'll get you some paracetamol, I have some in my bag, I'm sure."

Clothes. I grappled something out of my bag, but I couldn't get my body to cooperate. I felt like death. Truly.

"I don't..." I started. "I think I need to go home."

"You're not going home," Matt stated, holding up a blister packet of pills. "Here. Two of these babies should have your temp down. It's just paracetamol. You're not allergic, are you? Any health issues?"

He was holding up the packet, but my eyes wouldn't focus.

"I can't...go out...like this. Dinner..."

"Hey," he said, again, but quietly now, his face so close to mine, a faint flash of bruising still visible on his cheek. I reached out and stroked it.

"You don't need dinner. You need sleep. Period."

"If I can just..." I couldn't even speak. What the hell was happening to me? There were bitter pills in my mouth and water being forced down my throat. I drank it. Then I felt sick.

"Is he OK?" Someone else in my space.

"He's fine. He's just overdone it."

Matt pulled a hoodie over my head. I wasn't wearing any underpants. Or was I? There was a sock in my hand, and I managed to put it on. Then a shoe. Someone tied my laces. Dark curls under my fingers as I tried to steady myself.

I hated being out of control. I hated being sick. Everyone on set had been sick, and now it was apparently my turn. I tried to stand up.

"Whoa, big boy, take a seat. One more shoe."

I liked Matt. He was nice. He looked after me.

I just wanted my bed. A cool pillow against my face.

"Done. Now, just sit there so I can get dressed."

I leant my head against the wall and watched hazily as Matt dropped his towel, slipped that arse of his into a pair of tight, cotton briefs. Hoodie over his head. Joggers. Shoes.

I closed my eyes. Tried to breathe. Just kill me. Now.

No. Let me curl up right here and sleep this off. Just an hour and I would feel human again.

Fuck. Head. Swimming.

I was not going to pass out. Nope. Not me. Not here. Not in the gym.

And there he was, palms on my cheeks. My vision was still blurry, but the water he once again forced me to drink helped a little.

"Come," he said, pushing my fringe out of my face. "I'm taking you home."

Matt

OK, this may have been one of the stupidest things I'd ever done in my life, and I really, really wasn't a stupid person. Normally. I had no idea what came over me, dragging an award-winning famous actor across the road and bundling him inside the lift. Not only that, but I'd also frogmarched him through my front door and tucked him into my bed.

Were you following the stupidity yet? Oh, but wait for it. There's more to come.

I lived in a small studio apartment, which meant I spent the rest of the evening trapped like a caged animal, sitting on my sofa not daring to make a sound. I hadn't even moved. Barely managed to breathe.

I should have taken him back to his hotel. There'd have been a key in his bag or something, and the hotel staff could have taken him up to his room. I didn't know his room number. Figures, since we were back to the fact that he was a famous actor, and I was not anywhere near that kind of status.

I should have texted my friends for advice. But then no. This was not the kind of situation where I'd snap a picture of an unwell man and post it to Instagram for health advice.

I couldn't even text my mum, who would gladly have pitched in her thoughts on me dragging strangers back to my flat to entertain.

I was not entertained, and neither was Con Telford, I'm sure.

He'd been out cold, then awake three hours later, tossing and turning, shivering with fever. I slept on my two-seater sofa, another thing to add to my list of seriously questionable life choices.

I was six feet tall, and my sofa was barely long enough for my upper body, leaving my legs dangling off the end like two pieces of spaghetti. Stone cold spaghetti.

Hence, once I'd force-fed the famous actor more paracetamol, in amongst a flurry of silly apologies, he'd gone back to sleep, and I'd sheepishly tucked myself under the covers and stayed there in my bed. Next to Con Telford.

The Con Telford.

It was one thing being on a casual *Hello, how are you?* basis with him. Another thing having some kind of juvenile sleepover.

He woke me up at silly-o'clock, trying to hold a conversation over the phone with someone who was mostly shouting at him. I was impressed at him keeping his cool throughout that stilted exchange, during which he was told to bundle his arse in a taxi, pronto. I heard the words quite clearly—that was how loud the other person was shouting. Con insisted he couldn't stand up long enough to make it to the toilet let alone get into a taxi.

He hung up, and I delivered more paracetamol and apologies, mostly concerning the fact that he'd woken up with me in the bed. He muttered something about not being stupid and went back to sleep.

I didn't go back to sleep. I got up and went to work, leaving him in my bed.

Told you my life choices were all slightly off.

He was a stranger. I was a responsible human being, and I was quite sure my home insurance wouldn't cover being burgled by famous people and blaming a random act of kindness or whatever.

Anyway. He hadn't messaged me or called. Not that I'd expected anything, but I had left my number on a note next to his phone, which I had put on charge. I'd even put out some more paracetamol and a tall glass of water. And a key—evidently, I'd eaten stupid flakes for breakfast as well—in case he had to go out and couldn't get back in. I couldn't even explain to myself why on earth he would want to do that.

He would have felt better and got up and left. That would be it. End of a beautiful, temporary friendship.

I had no idea how I managed to get through the day. More than that, I tried to repress the last twelve hours of my life, quietly hoping I would return home and find that everything had been a dream. Those kinds of things did happen on TV shows and stuff, and I was willing fate to go my way for once.

Instead, I sat through another intervention meeting, gratefully letting Sadie take the lead since my brain was too muddled to function. She called me out on it, asking if I'd been hit over the head or if I actually knew how to speak in comprehensive sentences. I wasn't ashamed to admit that I was a bit of a mess. Afterwards, I changed my clothes at work and headed to my union meeting, where, amazingly, I managed to speak like a grown-up, pay attention and not completely lose my mind.

It was almost six in the evening when I stumbled off the Tube and headed home, quietly praying for everything to be normal. I wasn't geared up for confrontations. I didn't fancy company. Didn't know how to explain.

I stuck my key in the door and carefully slid it open, putting my bag down on the floor before peeking around the corner to find...

Con Telford sitting up in my bed with my TV blanket tightly wrapped around his shoulders and a panic-stricken look on his face.

"I tried to leave, honestly," he said quietly. "I'm so sorry. I got up to get dressed and ended up...disgracing myself in your bathroom. I've tried to clean up, but I couldn't find more kitchen roll, and I didn't know where to put the bin."

"Don't worry," came out of my mouth, but *I* was worried. I sat on the edge of the bed and put my hand against his forehead.

He was warm but not burning up anymore.

"I took all your paracetamol," he said. "Every four hours. I'll replace them, I promise."

He looked weak, sad and deathly ashamed, which I just couldn't bear.

"Have you eaten?"

He shook his head, then nodded, embarrassed. "I stole that blackberry smoothie from your fridge and ate some cereal. I was starving. Turned out I couldn't keep it down, hence the mess in the bathroom, and now I just want to lie down and close my eyes, and everything...hurts."

I could imagine.

He wrapped the blanket tighter around himself and leaning awkwardly towards the headboard.

"If I make some toast, do you want to give it a try?"

He coughed and shuffled down a little. I stroked his fringe out of his eyes. It was instinctive and too much. I was as bad as him. I couldn't help it.

"Matt?" He feebly grabbed my wrist as I tried to get up. I sat down again.

"It's fine," I said, trying to anticipate what would come out of his mouth.

"I really appreciate...all this. Work's insisting I go in tomorrow, but I—"

"Don't be ridiculous," I grunted out. "You can't go to work like this."

"A breach of contract and a major production delay and having everyone on set hate my guts? I'll have to."

"Con." I wanted to stroke his hair again. What the hell was I doing? He wasn't a child or one of my students, not that I would have stroked a student's hair, but I dealt with sick youth. Distressed youth facing end-of-the-world kind of issues that required gentle words and compassionate strokes of arms and small gestures of comfort. Again, Con was no child. "You look like death," I said.

"Yeah." He attempted a grin. "I looked even more like death earlier, puking my guts up. Not my finest moment. If you have any more paper towel, I'll clean it up better."

I shook my head at the thought of him doing anything physical in his state.

"I owe you for dragging you here instead of dumping you at your hotel. In my defence, you could barely walk, and this place was closer."

"I have no idea where I am." He laughed, looking a little bewildered.

"Back of the gym, down the alleyway. Cardiac Road. Stupid street names, I know, but the gym and all these apartments were built on the site of an old hospital. The road outside the gym is Lung Street. This is 4 Cardiac Road. Second floor."

"Oh. Still not sure." He was trying hard to smile, confusion written all over his face.

"So I am truly holding you hostage here. Just like in that show of yours." I smirked.

He did smile at that one. Thank God.

"You've watched it? Load of bollocks."

"It's won awards."

"It's not real. You know that, don't you?"

I took a deep breath because there was something about Con Telford that calmed me. He looked so much younger than he was, lying in my bed, his face pale against the pillow, and then he was ripping off the blanket and almost kicking me off the bed in his quest to get to the bathroom.

Yeah. And that was me, running after him like the idiot I was, holding the hair out of his face and muttering words of comfort like I was his mother. I couldn't control it around him, and I was secretly, appallingly glad that he was still suffering. If he was still sick, he wouldn't leave me.

But I wanted him out.

Didn't I?

"You're not going anywhere, Con," I said sternly, surveying the damage to my usually sparkling clean bathroom. The same one where he was ripping his shirt off and trying to clean the wall with it while hurling up his guts.

"I'm so sorry, I don't know what to say," he grunted into the toilet bowl.

"I'm going to go get you a bucket. Do you think you can manage a shower?" There was vomit all over his arms.

He didn't reply, retching violently, his forehead pressed against the toilet lid.

Yup. All my fantasies were definitely coming true here. NOT. I stumbled out to the kitchen and raided my under-sink cupboard.

Returning with a bucket in my hand, I expected him to still be hugging the bowl, but surprisingly he'd managed to mangle himself into my tiny shower cubicle, dropping his trousers in the process and kicking them out before he shut himself in.

The floor was in a bit of a state, I had no more toilet roll, and the room stank of bad days. Horrible days. I hated being sick. And now I was retching myself as I flushed the toilet in disgust.

All my rose-tinted dreams of having Con Telford naked in my shower were coming true. Because my shower screen was made of clear cheap plastic, I had a full-frontal view of him shivering under the steamy spray, asking if I had any soap.

I'd give him soap.

I didn't know where to look as I pulled the screen open and handed him my pathetic piece of human cleanser.

I left him to it and got on my knees with a hand towel and bathroom spray in a sorry effort of cleaning.

It wasn't that bad. A few wipes here and there. The towel could go in the bin. I threw a clean one on the floor in time for Con to step out of the shower, white as a sheet, still shivering and not even attempting to cover himself up.

"Nothing the whole world hasn't seen before," he mumbled.

"True." I coughed the word in embarrassment and scrambled out in the hallway trying to find...something. Shit. Dressing gown. There we go.

I stuck my arm in through the door, and he grabbed what I was offering before making a beeline for my bed, leaving a trail of wet footsteps across the floor.

There were reasons I lived on my own, and I hated that I immediately followed him with my pathetic hand towel trying to wipe up his drips.

With him safely back on the bed, I returned to the bathroom, cleaned up properly and had a shower myself. Unsurprisingly, he was out for the count by the time I emerged, clean and starving. I made myself a bowl of soup. Ironed my shirt for tomorrow.

Stared at Con Telford sleeping.

Checked he was breathing.

Unpacked my empty lunch box. Made a new one. Smiled at the empty smoothie bottle in my recycling bin. He'd even rinsed it.

Stared at Con Telford sleeping again.

Questioned my life choices.

Found a spare charger so I could charge my own phone since he'd stolen mine.

There were reasons I lived on my own. Especially since Con Telford was now snoring, hugging both my favourite pillows in his arms.

He looked pale, but he looked peaceful.

I finally summoned up the courage to carefully slide into my side of the bed. Well, Con Telford was sleeping on my side of the bed with all my pillows. I grabbed a lumpy sofa cushion and tried to get comfortable.

It was going to be a long night.

Next thing I knew, my alarm was going off and the bed next to me was empty and cold. It was six-fifteen, and he wasn't here. I sat up in bed, staring at the room in disbelief.

He was gone without a trace, and I did wonder if it had all been some cruel, horrible, stupid dream.

NINE

Con

My head was a little foggy, and I struggled to stand for more than a few minutes, but these things didn't matter when there were hundreds of thousands of pounds at stake if we didn't wrap this season on time.

I knew that, and the production team and the set manager and the director and everyone else within earshot had reminded me of my responsibility when it came to safeguarding the budget and schedule and all the other big words that had been thrown at me this morning while my body was struggling to function.

I'd been seen by the on-set medic, who'd muttered about the damn Norovirus and some kind of twenty-four-hour bug that had swept through the set like wildfire. No wonder I'd gone down with it since everyone around me seemed to have been out at some point in the past week.

I wasn't hungry and didn't dare eat anything, but I was shaky and slow, so I sipped water, the bottle rattling in my nervous hands, before being caked in make-up to ensure I looked alive and assure people I was only playing dead. I might as well have been dead, as we were filming the aftermath of the car crash, and I spent most of my time in a hospital bed on a side set masquerading as an intensive care unit. People got themselves hurt in this series, and we'd used the same hospital-corner set since season one with the same rickety bed. The only thing that changed was the colour of the curtains and whoever they'd dragged in and dressed up as a nurse. Today's extra was a bloke in his fifties who actually looked like a proper nurse. There would be a female nurse too—a recurring cast member who I would try to kiss at some point. Cass Powell had no shame and still had game, even if this wasn't the first time and wouldn't be the last that he was tucked up in this bed, looking ready to be claimed by the Grim Reaper. So, while I did understand the producer and director's concern, I could probably have won more awards for my realistic acting of a man dying seeing as I was half dead for real.

Still, at least they'd all stopped shouting at me. They were now readjusting the light so the set would go from daylight to nighttime and poor Cass Powell could receive a heart-wrenching visit from his daughter.

We'd rehearsed it already, and I was lying here like a lemon with my on-screen daughter perched on the floor with her iPad. Normally, I would have struck up a conversation, but I was too tired. I was also a little preoccupied with thinking about...

Matt. Bloody Matt. The guy who had flung himself into my life. Or, should I say, he flung himself into my wrist and God knows how that had happened. I had a lot of questions because I remembered the things he'd said, and he was gay and now I had spent two nights sleeping with him.

Yes, that made no sense in my head either.

The thing was...

I took a deep breath. I was lying here talking to myself and I wasn't even ashamed to admit it. Someone needed to have a word with me before I went totally nuts.

I wasn't gay or bi or pan or demi or anything like that. I'd been groomed into this character and built a very successful brand playing the part of a man who didn't exist. I'd always been careful not to blur the lines into my real life.

Who was I kidding here? My real life didn't exist either. I lived in hotel rooms, and when I didn't...

I was playing house with a man called Matt Winston.

I groaned in frustration and tugged at the hospital sheets.

"Are you really sick? Not just acting?" The little girl on the floor peered up at me in concern.

"I'm OK," I assured her. We weren't even filming, and there were at least ten people laughing at me. The cameraman above my head dangled from his harness and shot me evils as I once again shifted uncomfortably on the bed.

"Do you want a break?" the AD asked begrudgingly as she drew up next to me with a clipboard. "We're doing well timewise. We shot this scene twice with Hamish, but..." She grimaced.

She didn't have to say it. I knew. I'd fucked up twelve hours of incredibly valuable production time, and I would have to shoot off a grovelling email to Hamish to thank him for getting up at some ungodly hour to pretend once again to be me.

Hamish had a real job. It was just his luck that he kind of looked like my twin from a distance. Up close, he was some normal bloke, and I bet he was getting tired of getting dragged in whenever *White Noise* decided I was too expensive to keep on set, often being replaced with minimum notice by Hamish.

All Cass Powell's costumes existed in at least two versions—one in my size, one in Hamish's size, one for the stunt double and sometimes even more.

I was expendable, I knew that. I also knew that two new characters were being introduced in the last two episodes, and the rumour mill was rife. Caroline and I had had our heyday, and new blood would be needed to keep the viewing public interested. There was not much more they could do with our storylines. Well, apart from killing us off.

I shuddered again, feeling suddenly cold.

"And positions!" the AD called, fanning the clapboard in my face.

The space fell into that eerie silence, as I quickly adjusted back into position, face blank, pretending to be asleep.

I wish I could go to sleep.

"And... action!"

I lay there listening to the dialogue between Pretend-Nurse Dude and Cass's ex-wife, as Cass's daughter ran to my side grappling with my hand as the pretend machines beeped alarmingly in the background. It was slightly ridiculous, but once it had been cut and filtered and dramatic music added, the public would be crying ugly tears as Cass struggled to breathe.

And there was the pretend mask being jabbed onto my face.

"Cut!"

"Make-up!"

The make-up team shoved blush all over my face because I looked weird and dead. The director's words, not mine. On the plus side, I had no dialogue since I was apparently unconscious.

"Con, can you relax the muscles around your eyes? You need to look totally relaxed, despite breathing."

Welcome to the acting world. Play dead. Don't breathe. Breathe! No, you're breathing too much. Too little. You're unconscious. You're dead. No, you're not.

I was half giggling under the make-up brush assault before the AD called it again, clapping the damn clapboard in my face.

"And... action!"

I was once again unconscious and let my mind wander. Matt. OK. There was something weird with Matt. Whenever I spent time with him, I behaved like a creep. I was constantly touching him. His face. His arms. And the things that came out of my mouth were totally off the wall. It was like there was static everywhere and my head was filled with white noise, erasing every coherent thought.

He had really nice lips. See? I needed my head examined.

I'd never had feelings for a bloke. For girls, yes. So many crushes. I'd even had a long crush on Caroline before she put a swift end to it, which was why I still adored her. She'd always been blunt with me and seemed to love me despite my terrible traits.

I liked when people were direct. It made expectations easy. Like with Tara Marie. She'd grabbed my chin—my slightly drooling chin, as she was bloody gorgeous—and told me to rein it in because she had a very, *very* jealous girlfriend, and if I said or did anything inappropriate, she'd have my arse kicked. Her girlfriend was lovely, but the two of them together had been quite intimidating, making me back away with my hands in the air. Which was why Tara and I had hit it off and had produced that ridiculous pornographic excuse for a fashion shoot. I'd asked Lucia to email me the shots—for my private collection. They were absolutely *not* the kind of material I'd hang on my mother's living room wall. Mum had all my headshots framed in the hallway. Action shots from *White Noise* adorned her office. Film stills from random projects were dotted all around the house. I should have one printed for Matt. A signed picture for his office desk perhaps? Like a thank-you. The thought made me smile and—

"Cut! Con, for fuck's sake, what's up with you today? That take would have been perfect, and then your cheek muscle spasmed! Get with the programme here! And again!"

Back in the room. Fuck. They should just go with the shots of Hamish. I bet he'd nailed this shit on a first take, whereas this was going to take me all day.

"And... action!"

Dead again. Slow, shallow breathing. Relaxed face.

Matt.

I wanted to shout at him. Tell him to get out of my head. But instead, I was remembering his hands on my back, soothing strokes, telling me everything was fine.

Nothing was fine. I was not...

Fuck. I'd done it again.

"CUT! Con! Another grimace! What the hell was that?"

And now I was getting on everyone's nerves—even the child actor was staring at me with an annoyed look on her perfect little face.

"Sorry, I needed to cough." I didn't, but I was fucking this up.

Everyone was giving me evils, and I shuddered as I tried to get myself back in the zone.

The day got better; it actually did. Once I was out of that bed and in and out of make-up again, I managed to deliver the next scene, which made no sense. I was once again made up like some supermodel, not a sign of car crash on my face, and back in the hospital suite, now with different curtains and a different fake medic. A professional medical model was splayed out on the slab, laughing as make-up was applied to her ample breasts.

Yeah. I delivered. Thank God for that because actors had been killed off for less, and being unprofessional on set was not something I was proud of.

At lunchtime, I managed to keep down my lunch, munching away alone in my trailer. Not thinking of Matt.

Matt.

FUCK!

I screamed—on the inside, as one of the runners was passing by my trailer.

"Hey, Aisha?" I cringed as I called out to her. I never did things like this. Ever.

"Whassup?" She came over, shifting the box in her hands to adjust the radio clipped to her utility belt. I cringed again. She was obviously busy, but she was a nice person and had stopped anyway.

"Any chance you can get your hands on a couple of boxes of paracetamol?"

She took her earpiece out of her ear and examined me. "You OK?"

"Yeah, just need a few boxes."

"You trying to kill yourself?"

"What? No!"

"Like, dude, one box is enough to kill you." She rolled her eyes.

"It's not like that. I used..." Fuck.

"Normal people just pop into the corner shop and buy a box if they need one. I'm not your slave," she sassed.

OK, I lied. She was not a nice person.

"I...I'm on set until late," I tried, feeling stupid.

This was my life. I'd lived like this since I was thirteen, and I had no idea how to actually manage the normal things like shopping, keeping supplies in my bag, ordering shit off Amazon. I didn't even know if you could order paracetamol off Amazon, and in all honesty, I just wanted something that I could use as an excuse to go back to Matt's tonight.

He may be sick. He may need some.

Matt wasn't sick. He'd have texted me and told me.

He didn't have my number.

I scrolled my phone in a panic as Aisha sighed loudly.

"Dude. You're bloody hopeless. What do you need? No illegal shit. I don't do that."

"God, no!" I was going to have to tell her the truth. "I used up a friend's supply of paracetamol and drank his blackberry smoothies and ate some kind of cereal he had."

"Good hook-up then?" she teased.

Definitely *not* a nice person. I regretted even opening my mouth, despite her face softening as she shook her head.

"Chill, man. I'll get one of the drivers to grab some. What cereal?"

"I have no idea," I admitted. "Green box? Maybe blue?"

She rolled her eyes so loudly that I recoiled from my own words.

"You actors are nuts," she said. "Was it muesli? Or kids' stuff? Big tiger on the front?"

"I don't know," I whined.

"So, Aisha's choice of cereal then. Got it. I'll bill Production and blame you for any fallout. Good?"

"Perfect." I sighed. "And can you add a bunch of nice flowers with that?"

She stared at me.

"For my mum!" I shouted.

"Sure." Her face was pure evil. "For your mum."

"*Yes!*" I shouted. Fuck, what was it with all the shouting?

I survived the day with some of my dignity intact. Barely. My driver took me back to my hotel, along with a bag containing stuff I didn't dare look at and a huge bunch of flowers. Not the supermarket kind. The expensive kind. The sort flower companies sent you when they wanted shit from you. Influencer kind of flowers.

I hated them already. Matt would hate them too.

I was *not* giving Matt flowers.

It was the proper thing to do, wasn't it? As an apology for completely being a dick and getting sick and squatting in someone's home and all that.

Matt probably never wanted to see me again.

I felt sick just thinking about it. Even more so at the thought of actually walking over to where he lived and attempting to see him again.

The truth was I wanted to. Even though the idea of faceplanting my hotel-room bed was tempting. But I knew if I didn't do this now, I would lose my nerve.

Never. I was going to bed.

I got out of the car and thanked my driver. Slammed the door and walked into the lobby carrying my wanky flowers and the shopping bag.

Then I turned around and caught a glimpse of myself in the glass.

I was still wearing Matt's clothes from yesterday. Joggers and a stripy T-shirt that was far too tight for my frame.

I looked ridiculous. Utterly ridiculous. I was officially a clothes thief. In my defence, I couldn't find my own clothes this morning, and I'd woken up wearing a dressing gown. I'd just picked up stuff from the floor, got dressed and left.

I turned around again. And again. And next thing I knew I was stomping down Lung Street with determination in my step. Ridiculous or not, I needed to do this.

It was the polite thing to do.

See Matt just one more time so I could finally put this insane crush to bed, and anyway, I was wearing his clothes.

FML.

It wasn't a crush.

I was not gay. Or was I?

Honestly.

Matt

The doorbell going at ten o'clock at night wasn't the norm around here. Especially not when I'd been casually sipping chamomile tea, scrolling Instagram and just found the courage to comment on one of Con Telford's photos. Which was stupid. I wasn't that kind of person, and he had, like, billions of followers or something. That photo, though? I'd been daydreaming. Stupidly so, but this was my home, and I could do whatever I wanted, thank you very much. The building was quiet and civilised, full of professionals on the inside and the road outside was silent. That was how I liked it, and the shrill of the doorbell gave me palpitations.

Lucky for me, there was nobody standing outside my front door because the doorbell was for the intercom, which allowed me to talk to people downstairs and decide if I wanted to let them in, like the pizza delivery man, the person delivering my Amazon purchases, the guy in the Yodel van...

And apparently Con Telford.

This was unexpected, kind of, despite me having just hung his clothes up on my tiny drying rack in the bathroom.

"It's me," he said when I hollered down the line, as if I'd know who 'me' was from his voice alone, which I did, surprisingly, since we could probably count the words we'd spoken to each other on one hand.

Instead of doing the sensible thing, I'd buzzed him in and then stomped around in frustration wearing my pyjamas.

Yes. Pyjamas and sleep socks. It wasn't like I entertained at night, and...fuck.

There he was. In my doorway.

I exploded into a fit of giggles. I needn't have worried about the pyjamas and sleep socks because he looked ridiculous.

"Please tell me you haven't worn those all day."

"I have. Couldn't find my clothes, and these were in your laundry basket." He grinned and held out a bunch of flowers. "For you. A very feeble apology for...being me. And stealing your clothes."

"Those are obscene." I didn't mean to say it, but I was in shock. Honestly. I wasn't always this rude, but the man in my doorway made me nervous. And the flowers...

"I know," he sighed. "I didn't choose them. My runner did, and if anyone is insane, it's her. She also got you this."

Looking embarrassed and a little terrified, he stepped into my hallway, trying to hide behind the flowers. My T-shirt was several sizes too small for his bulky frame, and those were my cleaning joggers, the ones with a paint mark on the thigh. Also? He offered me the flowers again, along with a shopping bag.

"Con. You don't need to give me presents." I had to stop and take a deep breath because this situation was out of control, and I couldn't just stand here in my flannelette bottoms and pretend my life was fine. Right now, my life was as inconceivable as those flowers, and Con looked like he was about to faint.

"Come on," I said, taking the flowers from him. "In you come."

I sounded like my granny, and not in a good way. Next, I'd be calling him poppet and force-feeding him stale sweets from the eighteenth century.

He closed the front door, toed off his shoes and followed me to the kitchen, where I dumped the flowers in the sink.

"I don't own any vases." I cringed. Way to go, Matt.

"Bucket?" he suggested, holding up the puke bucket still sat in the middle the floor. It was clean, as were the sheets on my little kitchen table.

"Classy." I grinned.

He smiled and brought the bucket to the sink, filling it from the tap as he carefully unwrapped the greenery.

Five minutes later, there was a yellow bucket on my kitchen table, full of huge, showy flowers with green sprigs sticking out from every angle.

"I've never bought anyone flowers before." Con grinned. "And you're right. They are...a bit over the top."

"Funny, though. Especially in a bucket. We could start a new trend. Bucket vases."

He laughed, while I was internally screaming. I was officially a total nerd, unable to hold a proper conversation.

"Sorry," he murmured.

"God, don't be. I love that you bought me...these."

"I didn't even buy them. Aisha did. My runner."

"You have a runner? Like a slave?"

"Yup."

He grinned again and reached out and stroked my cheek. I tried to ignore how ridiculous he looked in that T-shirt, the fabric straining over his muscles.

"Your bruise is almost gone. It's almost strange seeing you without it. I've never known you without my wrist imprinted on your face."

"I should've had it tattooed. I could have become quite popular in your fandom...or something."

"Don't." He smiled. Funny how I liked it when he smiled.

"Do you want anything to eat?" I offered. "I mean, I've eaten, but I've got..." I rummaged around in the shopping bag he'd brought. "Blackberry and beetroot smoothie. Nice. You didn't have to."

I was rambling and my hands shook as I placed two bottles on the table.

"Sorry it's not the right cereal. I couldn't remember the brand."

I didn't know what he was apologising for. He'd obviously been shopping—or his runner had—at some uber-posh farm shop or something. Cereal milled by hand by the self-proclaimed Duke of Fibre.

"I always buy Sainsbury's own cheap crap muesli. This is like organic, award-winning...probiotic goodness of some kind."

I stared at the box. He stared too.

"Too much?"

"Nah." I giggled. "You can do my shopping, anytime, if this is what you buy me. And look. Paracetamol." I held it up like it was a prize.

His fingers had dropped from my face, and now his hand weighed down my shoulder.

"Sorry for eating all your stuff. Sorry for puking in your bathroom. And squatting in your bed."

"You can squat in my bed, anytime."

Matt!!!!! What was I saying?

"Is that an invitation?"

"Dude!" I hated that word. Never used it.

He let his hand drop. I wanted to bite off my bloody tongue.

"Con, I'm a totally normal, red-blooded gay man. If I didn't know any better, I'd think you were flirting. But this is...it's not a date. It's a very lovely friendship and I appreciate all this and—"

"It's nice to have a friend," he said quietly, and there it was again. The way he stared at me.

"Yes." I had no other words.

"I really like that you're so...direct with things, Matt. Most people don't tell you anything about themselves. You just blurt out your life story the minute you meet people, and I like that. It makes you easy to...be friends with."

"The gay stuff, you mean? Look, I went to a really crap senior school, and I got outed and bullied and bloody crucified. And on top of that, when you spend your teens carrying around this big secret, it feels like a tonne of weight has come off your shoulders once you realise that you don't have to lie anymore. I learnt that the hard way. I'm me. I'm a teacher and I'm gay. It's just easier to be upfront with these things. Saves rumours and misunderstandings and...such."

"You have a boyfriend?" he asked, sitting himself down at the table.

"Nah." I pushed a bottle of smoothie towards him, grabbing the other bottle for myself. "I've never met anyone I wanted to share my life with. I like living on my own, my own space. Peace and quiet."

"Sorry." He was looking at his hands.

"Until I met you." I was desperately trying to save this because I was not only being unfriendly, but I was also now being downright rude.

"You don't have to be polite. I know I'm a lot."

"You're not a lot. You're actually, truthfully, nice."

"Even my mum thinks I'm an antisocial tosser. I don't do anything but work and work out. And I have no friends. Never even had a relationship."

That was a lot coming out of his mouth, and he was staring at me again with that look that said he regretted ALL his life choices.

"Neither have I," I said. "Not the end of the world. Not everyone meets the love of their life and gets married and has kids and lives happily ever after."

"Is that what you want?" He unscrewed the lid of the smoothie and tapped the bottle against mine, like we were toasting. This wasn't a date.

"Don't we all? I'd love to have someone to love. Kids would be awesome. But life is sometimes...complicated. I work too much too." I took a deep breath. "What about you? Things going well with...what was her name? Tara? She looks lovely."

"Tara is fabulously..." He shot off a grimace, pushing the smoothie bottle away from him. "Tara is a lesbian. And that smoothie is rank."

I took a cautious sip of mine and swallowed carefully.

"It's..." I tried to read the label. "Organic beetroot-based vegan drink with nettle extract." It *was* rank. Totally. "Not...quite blackberry smoothie."

"We're doing this all wrong. We're supposed to have a nice quiet drink in the evening. Isn't that what normal people do?"

"Who said we were normal people? We can do whatever we want. And who am I to argue if you like having a nice drink of nettle extract before bed?" I winked. He winked back.

"I should have got my slave to buy you champagne."

"She's not your slave."

"No, she's not. She's actually quite rude and probably bought these just to piss me off."

"Rightly so, I guess."

We both smiled. We were ridiculous.

"So, since you're here, wearing my clothes and your smoothie is undrinkable, do you want to help me put these sheets back on the bed?"

"Well done for washing them. I wouldn't want you to catch whatever I had. It's been all around the set. Everyone's been ill."

"I've got a rock-solid immune system, promise. I deal with hundreds of teenagers, every day. If you remember what it was like being a teenager, they never wash their hands, live off junk food and think hygiene is a dirty word.

"I never smelled. Not even as a teen," he said, matter of fact, and grabbed the pile of sheets. "My first make-up artist used to force me to use body spray. I was thirteen, and the show I was working on was sponsored by Love Mist. You know? That cheap nasty perfume stuff. We didn't smell. We all stank. Vile stuff."

We made the bed, chitchatting about nonsense from our youth.

I had officially morphed into my grandma.

I didn't know what it was with him, but he made me nervous in a way where I behaved like...I didn't know any better. I was a fully-fledged adult and knew perfectly well how to entertain. I'd had colleagues over for drinks. I'd had small, intimate birthday parties. My brother sometimes came and stayed over with his friends. Those kinds of things, my hosting was immaculate, but with Con, I ridiculed his kind gifts and made him take on my domestic chores.

"Your bed is nice. Very comfortable," he said.

"Should be for the price I paid for it."

He stared at me. Wringing his hands.

I stared back.

"I really like your flat. I like that it's small and cosy, and it's...it feels safe."

"The area isn't always the best, but I've never had trouble here."

"That's what my agent said when she booked me into that hotel. It's not very comfortable, to be honest. Cheap and cheerful, and everything on the inside is purple."

"Must drive you mad, staying there."

"Yeah, it does. I keep thinking I should buy a house, but then I move around for work all the time, and I'd never stay there anyway, so it makes no sense. But I miss having a base. Coming home. Being able to wash my own clothes. The little things."

"Like a comfortable bed?"

"Yup, and your pillows are awesome."

"You staying then? Your clothes are drying in the bathroom, by the way. And you left your bag next to the sofa."

I meant it as a joke. Truly. Perhaps with a very small bit of flirting in there. His fault. He'd started it.

"Would that be OK?"

"Yeah, yeah, all right. But no stealing all the pillows."

"Sorry!" He smiled.

FML.

"I could do with a shower. Sorry about your clothes. I get picked up at seven tomorrow, so I'll be out of your hair early."

"I leave at six-fifteen."

"Cool. I still have your key. I'll lock up when I go."

"Fine, keep hold of it."

Keep hold of it?

I wasn't sure if I was head over heels in love with him or...

This wasn't what it looked like. I knew that.

And now he was staying over. In my bed.

In my bed.

With his obscene flowers and twatty smoothie and bloody macrobiotic cereal.

I secretly loved that he'd brought me gifts.

Like it was a date. This was not a date.

It was an apology. Not a gift. Not a date.

And now he was staying.

I hated my life.

Fuck him.

The shower started running, which could only mean one thing. Con Telford was once again naked in my shower.

Which meant there was only one thing left to be done.

I faceplanted myself onto my bed and screamed into a pillow. Silently, of course.

Con

"Hey, Aisha!"

It was nine in the morning, and I was back in the hair and make-up trailer having my face transformed into Cass Powell post car crash but with some bruising this time. We were jumping the timeline again, and Aisha was delivering the freshly rehashed script with line changes that would not trip me up today. I was on form. Three croissants sat comfortably in my stomach, and I'd had a good night's sleep—despite that sleep being only a few hours.

"Hey, flower man. Did your...*MUM* love her flowers?"

I hated her. Truly. I should probably exercise my powers as an important member of the talent and demand to have her moved to a different production, but I wasn't an arsehole. I was a nice guy.

"Yes. *He* did."

I blushed like a child, but I'd been thinking about what Matt had said. Lying destroyed your soul, so I wasn't going to lie. About anything.

"Oooh!" Aisha teased.

"Did I hear that right?" Peter asked. He was the master of my hair, and there was no way for me to escape.

"I like him, OK? But it's not going anywhere. He's a friend. A good friend."

"The best kind of friendships..." Aisha singsonged. She needed to leave.

"I agree," Peter said. *Shut up!*

"Aisha, can you do me another favour?"

"I told you. If you want drugs, you need to speak to someone else. This girl does *not* provide anything like that." She smirked. I smirked back.

"It's nothing illegal, although the smoothies you bought yesterday should be. What were they again? Beetroot and mushroom? Totally rank whatever they were."

"We're in the middle of nowhere, Con. It's not like we have a handy Tesco in the next field. Hashim was very kind, going out of his way to find you a local organic farm shop. I'm not sure I can bribe one of today's drivers to go shopping for you, though. They're all a bunch of tossers. Even that Dave who drives you. He asked me to bring him coffee and then left it on the verge and drove off. He can get his own bloody coffee from now on."

"Sorry about that." I didn't know what was wrong with me today, apologising for shit I had nothing to do with. I could do with another coffee, but I didn't dare to ask.

"Whaddya need? Another silly gift for this man of yours?"

"What man's this?"

Fuck. Now Zara, my make-up artist, was here too, trying to get the low-down on the conversation and shoving her brush in my face. I swatted her away like the dick I was.

"Are we trying to impress him or just show friendship?" Peter was the king of the gay lifestyle and would usually have been telling me one of his longwinded stories about his latest squeeze, some insane nightclub he'd attended or a party full of sexy men dancing naked on the tables.

"You never talk about anyone. Who is this guy?" Zara demanded.

Shut up! Please!

"I thought you were shagging that Tara Marie." Aisha was never subtle, and it was a trait I admired, but right now, I wanted to go back to my trailer and silently die.

"He's just a friend!" I snapped. "A good friend who's been helping me out."

"I'm sure he has," Peter murmured.

"Ohh!" Zara nodded knowingly. "*That* kind of friend then. The helpful kind."

Cue laughter. I was tempted to look around for a hidden camera.

"So, you want to impress a gay guy?" Peter asked. "We'll need more information if we are to advise you properly."

"Who said he was gay?" I shrieked. "All I want is a damn coffee!" Not that anyone was listening.

"If he's someone you're buying gifts for, then it's kind of obvious that the guy is gay or bi. Or pan maybe," Zara said. Ugh.

"Or demisexual? Months of slow pining before finally taking your beautiful friendship to a higher level." Peter was obviously a failed scriptwriter with a vivid imagination, who'd found his passion in the art of make-up.

"Champagne is *so* last year," Aisha chimed in. "If I were you, I'd buy him a bottle of bespoke, handcrafted gin, some posh tonic, fresh organic lemons and a sprig of mint."

My jaw hung slack. They were literally planning my life.

Aisha shrugged. "What? I spent eight months running around after that Zach Kwan on my last set. He had some expensive ways of getting into people's beds. Always said he was buying gifts for his mum, but I wasn't born yesterday."

Cue eyeroll and laughter all round.

"To recap," I said, seizing back control, "if I want to buy a guy a drink for a night in, I should get him all the ingredients for some bollocks gin and tonic? You can buy them ready mixed in a tin. My mum gets those."

"Oh God, No!" Peter said, scandalised, accompanied by a gasp from Aisha and Zara clicking her tongue.

"Aisha, honey, whatever you're buying, double it up and send it express to Con's mum. We can't have poor Mrs Telford drinking substandard cocktails from a tin." Peter shuddered in total disgust.

"Sure." Aisha got her radio out, yapping instructions into it like whoever was on the other end would understand a word. Those radio conversations were full of static and codewords; even after years in the industry, I had no idea what half of the terminology meant.

Aisha put away her radio and grinned at me. "Hashim is on the job. Two set-ups of uber-fancy G and Ts, organic lemons and fresh mint. One to be shipped to Mrs Con and one to be wrapped in rainbow glitter for this guy to get impressed. Anything else?"

"You bought him flowers?" Peter asked, tugging at my hair.

"Yeah."

"Is he a flowers kind of guy?"

"I don't think so. It was a mistake, wasn't it? He didn't have a vase, so the flowers are in a bucket on his kitchen table."

"Oh, so we stayed the night." Zara narrowed her eyes. "That's serious."

"No, Zara, it's not. We're friends. I popped over for a drink, that's all."

Peter was tutting too loudly for my liking.

"The G-and-T idea is solid. He drinks, this boy of yours?"

"He's not my boy, Peter."

"Keep telling us that, mate," Aisha muttered. "Anything else before I go and bang my head against some trailer wall? I have things to do, people. Seriously."

"A coffee?" I suggested weakly.

"Big night then."

"No, it was not a big night. Stop it! I'm trying to do a nice thing for a friend."

"Sure you are. One coffee."

"Bring him two. His face is a mess." Zara winked.

"At least his hair's good." Peter mussed it for effect. "You still sleeping on that silk pillowcase I got you?"

I wasn't. I had no idea where it had gone. I had more pressing matters in my life than keeping an eye on some slinky piece of fabric that was supposed to be good for my hair.

"Yes, of course. I live in a bloody hotel, Peter."

"Handy." He sighed.

I sighed even louder.

The day rolled on. I had a bit of a laugh with my pretend daughter, delivered my lines with conviction, and then my Saturday off was cancelled as we had to reshoot the intimate scene with Toby. I was pissed off but at the same time relieved because nobody had been happy with the shoot the other day, least of all me. I was still salty about that actor. I knew that with Toby, we would deliver, and I would hopefully be back at the hotel in time to get in a good afternoon workout. My body was aching for weights and movement after I'd neglected everything over the past week.

I needed the gym. I needed to go spend the weekend with my mum and get my head screwed on straight. I needed to go to this bloody Gucci thing tomorrow night, but most of all...

After I was dropped off at the hotel, I went up to my room and stood there, surveying the familiar mess.

I was wearing Matt's clothes again. An oversized hoodie, which was skin-tight on my upper frame, and the same joggers I'd worn yesterday. The waistband was cutting into my hips, but I didn't care. The clothes smelled nice. Clean. Well, they'd been in his laundry basket, but there was honestly nothing wrong with them.

I had no idea what I was doing.

But what I did know was I couldn't stop thinking about him.

I barely knew the guy. Seriously. Yet I'd had a shower at his place last night and then walked around naked, telling him some story from school when I'd tried to be friends with someone, and they'd completely destroyed me by telling the whole school I was gay and in love with him.

It had been a horrible time in my life. Not the whole school thinking I was gay bit. That shit didn't bother me, not even back then. I'd been working on another teen show at the time, playing a gay guy. The whole bloody country thought I was gay. What was new? No, what did bother me was the complete betrayal of trust by someone I'd thought was my friend.

That had bloody hurt.

Matt had sat in bed in his fluffy pyjamas, laughed at me and said no wonder my friend hadn't wanted to be friends if I was walking around naked at his house all the time.

Which was why I adored him.

I blushed even thinking those thoughts. I knew I was...kind of damaged from years in the acting industry. Nudity was normal. In some situations. I wouldn't walk around on set with my junk hanging out. Come on. But at home, I always ran around the house in the buff. My mum used to come down and pop the kettle on just wearing her shower cap.

But I hadn't been at home. I'd been in Matt's house. Yeah. I could see the issue there, but then Matt hadn't batted an eyelash. He just pointed at the dressing gown and offered me a choice of pyjamas but banned me from wearing his underpants.

I'd slept naked in the end.

Matt had muttered something about breaking into my hotel room and retrieving my clothes, should I continue to steal his. He used some funny words. He was sassy. Smart. Sarcastic as fuck.

He also took me for what I was—hadn't even reacted when my naked arse had pushed up against his thigh. Well, he'd lightly slapped my hip and told me to get my butt back on my own side of the bed, but he'd been laughing as he said it. I'd laughed too.

It had been a long time since I'd fallen asleep with a smile on my face.

The key for his flat dangled between my fingers. I'd left my gym bag there.

Not on purpose.

OK, maybe a little on purpose.

I chucked a few things from the wardrobe into a laundry bag and grabbed Aisha's gift bag, which she'd delivered to my trailer with a very cheeky smile on her face. It was a woven jute monstrosity proclaiming to save the planet, inside it a very pretty bottle of pink gin, some rainbow-edition posh tonic, herbs of some kind and two rustic glasses. Whoever this Hashim was, I was definitely going to ask Aisha to use him for all my future gifting needs.

I really needed to figure out how to go shopping like a normal person. Visit stores and pick out appropriate gifts, not have Lucia send my mum birthday presents, even if Mum did order mine off Amazon and have them delivered to my hotel. Whatever. She'd bought me another hundred pounds' worth of gift cards to stick on my Kindle. I'd swiftly loaded up a brand-new sci-fi series and already ploughed through the first two books. She knew what I liked.

I had no idea what Lucia bought her. Flowers, usually, I think. Plus, I'd paid for Mum and Aunt Trish to go to Italy one year.

Dammit. Get a grip, Con!

I'd walked the route on automatic with my stuff slung over my shoulder and a cap on my head, and now I was letting myself into someone else's block of flats like I lived here, sticking my key in the door and...

"Hello?" I called, finding some manners at the last second.

"Hiya! Come on in! I wasn't sure when you'd be back. Lucky I made enough stir-fry for both of us—*what* are you wearing?"

He was in the kitchen, wearing an apron with *Kiss the Cook!* printed in big, showy letters.

"Am I supposed to do that?" I asked, laughing. Stupid. I was so bloody stupid.

Matt pouted before shoving a fork in my face. "Spicy enough?"

I took whatever he was offering me. Noodles. Their spicy warmth tingled on my tongue.

Matt continued stirring. "Mrs Wu does it better. She told me what to put in, but I'm still struggling to get the quantities right."

"I like Mrs Wu." Her takeaway was one of the few things I would miss when I moved on from this area.

"You need to start wearing your own clothes, Con. We're not the same size."

He smiled. I love that he smiled so much.

"I actually brought some of my own clothes with me this time. And this."

"And stop buying me presents! It makes me feel uncomfortable. We're friends."

"You're cooking me dinner. The least I can do is bring the cocktails."

"Drinks before dinner?" He smiled again. "If you've brought me more nettle juice, I'll kill you."

"Then you need to kill someone called Hashim. He's one of the production company drivers and apparently and expert on shopping around our remote set. This gin is hand-crafted from shit grown in a Berkshire field outside Slough."

"Delightful." Matt grimaced. "Go on then. There's ice in the freezer."

"Yes, dear."

"I didn't even get that kiss you offered." Matt pointed at his apron, prompting me to press my stupid face against his cheek.

"We're like an old married couple," I muttered on my way to the freezer.

"Nah. We're like friends."

"Friends?" I laughed. Using my hands to scoop ice cubes out of a shop-bought bag, I sprinkled them into the glasses while Matt cut up the lemons.

"Two dude-bro friends just having dude-bro cocktails on a Saturday evening," he carried on. "I've already been to the gym, by the way. For future reference, texts are good. You know, for saying things like, 'Matt! I'm coming to stay again! I need feeding, and I'm bringing very...pink drinks.'"

"It's the Pride edition," I blurted out.

"It's..." He lifted up one of the glasses and sniffed it. "I usually stick to white wine, but this smells...pleasant."

"Hashim said it was top notch. I usually don't drink at all. I'm supposed to be on some calorie-controlled diet to keep my body looking the same all the time. Keeps me healthy and my head clear."

"Oh." Matt took a small sip. "Well, the stir-fry is healthy. Ish. Sesame oil and noo-dles—probably not what you usually eat. Not a macrobiotic piece of tofu in sight."

"Hate tofu."

"Me too. Something about the texture."

"Ugh."

"Cheers!"

We clinked glasses and grinned like idiots. I had no idea what I was doing. Zero.

I took off my hat and threw it down next to the puke bucket full of flowers. Matt put two plates of food at the table, and I got up and grabbed two forks. He tutted at me and handed me chopsticks. Laughing.

I loved when he laughed.

I loved that we were doing this.

And I was shit scared of messing things up. Honestly. I wasn't good at friendships. I wasn't good at anything involving other people. Most of all, I was totally crap at looking after my poor, neglected heart.

"You staying then?" He peered at me from under his fringe and took another mouthful of food from the tips of his chopsticks.

"Is that all right?" I asked. My stomach did another little jolt.

"Are you going to wander around naked again before bedtime?"

"Absolutely. I need to practise my lines for tomorrow."

"Naked?"

"I do my best work naked. Have you not watched my show?"

Matt rolled his eyes. "I have some work to do, but feel free to strip off and throw out lines. Any time. *Mi casa, su casa* and all that."

I smiled, suddenly self-conscious. "Sorry about the naked thing. I don't always think."

"Conny, it's fine, really."

Conny?

"I think we should make it a new rule. Being naked. You should be naked too."

Fuck.

FUCK.

I shoved another load of food in my mouth. *Shut up, Con. Shut the fuck up!*

He'd just called me Conny, and it was ridiculous how much I liked that.

Matt snorted, and for a moment I thought he'd choked on his food, but no. He was laughing, hard, tears rolling down his cheeks.

"Nope," he croaked out. "Not happening."

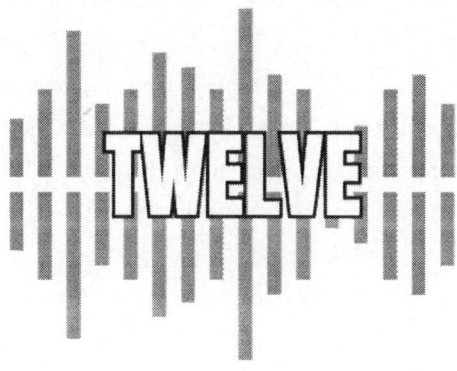

Matt

It should have been driving me crazy, having him here. I liked my own space. He should have been getting on my nerves, but then...

Asadghsagihnaobnasbhafb!

Con Telford had totally inserted himself into my world.

It would never be the same again!

Last night, I'd gone to the gym on my own, as usual, come home and tried to watch TV, which I couldn't because his gym bag was on the floor, his clothes were flung over my sofa, and my once-immaculate apartment smelled weird. Wherever I tried to find the right headspace to relax, he would somehow be there despite not being anywhere near where I was beforehand.

His toothbrush stood next to mine on the shelf by the sink.

My happily single life was over. Ruined forever.

It was hard to get those thoughts straight in my head because this could only go one of two ways. Either he'd get bored and stop turning up, breaking my heart into a million pieces. Or he'd stay here forever and my life would turn into some kind of irreversible, Con-Telford-infused chaos.

He'd told me he was going to a big event in central London and would probably not be back until late, so he'd stay at the hotel, let me have a break from his overbearing presence. His words, not mine.

I didn't find him overbearing. In fact, I spent the evening moping around the flat and missing him like the obviously crazy person I was. It was ridiculous.

I'd managed to do some work, then caught up on my family WhatsApp chat. My sister teased me about having met someone since I was 'unusually quiet'. My brother told her to shut up. My parents were full of questions, which was normal. I never talked about my private life, yet they still asked ALL the questions. Questions I had no answers to.

I didn't want to talk about Con. What we had was too fragile, too...splintered. There was nothing I could say to explain what had happened in my life over the past couple of weeks. Why there was this bloke turning up at my flat every night like he lived there, his dirty underpants meshing with mine in my laundry basket.

I'd put a wash on yesterday morning before I left for work and come home to find all our clothes neatly hung on the drying rack, his socks and mine side by side. He'd made the bed up, fluffed the pillows, even folded my TV blanket into a neat square, just the way I liked it, but it worked for both of us.

Shit.

Were we an *us* now?

I liked my flat to be a certain way, and he made it look different, in a good way, but my head was such a mess I could barely function. I seemed to do an awful lot of silent screaming these days.

I was exhausted by the time I crawled into bed, and I tried not to think about him, but it was hard when he'd left my sleep socks, freshly laundered and folded, under the duvet.

I reached out and touched the pillow. *My* pillow that would forever be his pillow now. See? I was slowly going insane. I even sniffed it, devouring the faint scent of him. He smelled of...butterflies in my stomach.

I needed help. Seriously.

I fell asleep quickly but woke up before my alarm again, and as I reached out in the dark to find my phone, squinting at the light from the screen and stretching...

"Hey."

I nearly leapt out of my skin. Fuck me. Where'd he come from?

"Sorry!" I gasped out, trying not to fall off the bed. "I didn't mean to wake you! When did you get here? I didn't even hear you come in. I could've been robbed and not even noticed! Are you a trained cat burglar as well as a famous actor?"

"I'm not just a pretty face," he said.

Phone still in hand, I shuffled around so I could look at him. He squinted at the brightness of the screen and swatted my hand away.

"You're not just a pretty face," I agreed. "Did you have a good night?"

"Yeah." He pulled the duvet up under his chin, smiling a little when I brushed a strand of hair out of his face. I don't know how or why it happened, but we did it all the time—touched each other's face. He still stroked my cheek, pretending to soothe my now invisible bruise. I brushed his hair out of his eyes. He needed it cut, but he wasn't allowed while filming as Cass Powell.

It drove me mad.

He drove me mad.

"I need to get up for work," I said softly. "You working today?"

"Not until later." He shuffled around under the sheets. I bet he was naked. He always slept naked.

"Want dinner tonight?" That was me hoping.

"I shouldn't be too late. Need to go work out, but perhaps we can grab noodles after the gym or something?"

"Like a date?" I was kidding, but that didn't stop the blush forming on my face. The room was dark but not dark enough. I could see every little freckle on his skin...and his smile.

"Go to work, Matt."

"Have a good day, bed thief," I retaliated. His chuckles shook the bed.

Once I was dressed and had tamed my hair into some kind of half-tidy state, I pottered around the kitchen and poured some of the twatty cereal he'd bought and milk into a bowl. I ate it standing against the kitchen sink. It wasn't bad, but it wasn't good. Like eating damp sawdust. Ugh. I'd have to go shopping at some point because I was once again out of everything.

I smiled, imagining going around the supermarket with Con. He'd told me he'd never been shopping. His runners went for him, and his mum ordered everything online. It was funny, the little things I'd picked up about him. I'd guessed his favourite food would be some ridiculous protein shake. He'd told me it was croissants. I wanted to take him to the little French bakery next to the Tube station for coffee and pastries. Ones with chocolate inside. And jam tarts. I loved jam tarts.

I didn't notice until I turned around to dump the last dregs of clumpy milk in the sink that he was standing right next to me. Not naked, although he was only wearing boxers and hugging his chest. He looked...scared.

"I wanted to talk to you before you left." His face was all scrunched up.

"OK?" Now I was scared too. I didn't like 'talks'. I didn't like how nervous he looked. Most of all, I didn't like that I couldn't function when he was in my space. I lost all sense and sensibility and said things I would later regret.

"Sorry for sneaking in here last night. I did mean to give you some space, but I...I got back to the hotel, and I couldn't settle. I hate it there. It's like I'm being watched and judged when I know I'm not. I can't relax. I can't even leave my dirty laundry out because I worry about the cleaner judging me. It's stupid, but that's what happens when you're alone all the time. The only time I can relax is when I go home to my mum's on the weekends. I can breathe there, like I can get rid of this Con Telford bullshit and just be me. I can breathe here too, with you. You have no idea how nice it is to walk through that door and just hang out with you."

He stopped and gasped, having said all that in one breath.

For a moment I just stood there staring at him. Then, remembering that he was actually a real person, not just an actor on TV, not a figment of my imagination, I reached out and stroked his arm.

"You know I don't mind having you here. I think we're good for each other."

"You're good for me," he said. "I've never met anyone like you. You...You get me."

"I don't understand half of what goes on in your life, but Conny..."

I didn't know what to say, how to explain the millions of thoughts rushing through my head. He was still standing there, hugging his bare chest, while I was here in my suit and tie and still holding a damn spoon.

I put it down, got my two hands on his arms and gave him a little shake.

"I never thought I'd enjoy having someone in my space, but having you here? You're good for me too. I'm always stuck in my own rut, doing my own thing. I don't know where this is going or what we're doing. I don't even know much about you—I've no idea what your favourite colour is or how you got into acting or how you identify—I don't even know how you take your tea. I've never offered you one because we're never awake at the same time in the morning."

"I drink coffee." His voice was barely there, but he smiled, and...God.

There was no point denying it.

I was totally smitten with him. His sweet face. Those lips...

"Coffee. OK."

"I don't have a favourite colour, but I can tell you about how I got into acting later if you like. I must warn you, it's not that interesting."

"Well, I'm interested," I said far too enthusiastically.

"And the other question..." He was squirming internally. I could feel his discomfort.

"I shouldn't have mentioned it. I'm so sorry. It's none of my business what you identify as." I was speaking too fast. Too loud.

"I don't know what I am." He said it so quietly I could barely hear him. "I always thought I knew, but I don't anymore. Everything is so fucked up at the moment, and most of the time I just want everything to stop. I want this goddamn career to stall, just for a few weeks so I can get my head screwed on straight. There's going to be pictures online today, stories in the press, because there's some official line our management expects us to toe, Tara and me. It's good for our brands and fuck knows what else, but Matt, can you promise me something?"

I wasn't sure I wanted to know. My little fantasy bubble was the only thing keeping me sane, but he was staring at me, biting his lips as he figured out what to say.

"What?" I asked.

"Everything you see is fake. Remember that. The only thing that's real is me, right here and now. I can't control shit out there, but when I walk through this door..."

Now he was getting emotional, and I was too. I grabbed his face and held it tight, made him look me in the eyes as I slowly spoke.

"It's OK. Whatever is going on, I'm right here. You have me, OK? Because Conny, I really mean this. I like you. The *real* you. I have no idea who you are beyond these four walls, and I kind of like it that way. OK? So don't worry."

All that meant nothing. I knew that. I didn't know what else to say to the tired, sad man shivering in front of me, so I just rose up on my toes, nudged his nose with mine.

And then I pressed my lips against his and kissed him.

Con

I think my heart stopped for a moment. I know I held my breath.

Then he did it again.

It wasn't a dirty kiss or a friendly one. It was just...so very, very him.

He pulled back slowly, and I stood there like a fool, my nails digging into the skin under my arms.

"Oh God," came out of my mouth.

Matt smile melted away, leaving him suddenly looking distraught.

"Sorry. I'm so sorry. I shouldn't have done that," he muttered and took a step back. Finally regaining my senses and the use of my arms, I stepped with him, crowding him against the kitchen sink.

"No...yes...it's just..." I smiled. Wiped a stupid tear out of my eye. What the fuck was wrong with me? "That was...my first kiss."

"Bullshit," he accused softly. "I've seen your work, remember?"

I stroked his cheek, where the bruise had been, and he let me.

God, I loved his face. He was so bloody handsome. And confused. I replayed what he'd said.

"Oh. No! I mean, that's work. That's acting. Nobody has actually kissed me before...without a script. Just like that, because they wanted to. Well, I assume you wanted to?"

"Of course I did, silly." He was still flustered. "But I should have asked you. Consent is important."

"Yeah." I knew about consent. I'd had to sit through endless eLearning courses. Get signed off that I was aware of project policies. Every new production had its own way of ensuring we were up to date and compliant with every regulation and procedure before they made us sign NDAs and all the other legal stuff that came with the job. Inappropriate behaviour could end your career in an instant. Which made me snigger because last night?

"Matt." I had no idea what was going on in my head. He'd just kissed me and here I was, deep in thought over NDAs?

"Matt, Matt...Matt."

"I know. You don't have to say it. You don't feel like that about me. It's fine. Honestly. It was just a stupid kiss. We're still friends, right?"

"Friends who kiss?"

"Yeah." He looked slightly horrified at that prospect. Weirdly, so was I.

"Matt, I like you, and I have no bloody clue what's going on right now. I wake up every morning and all I think of is you. Then I go to bed in the evening, and I can't sleep if I'm not in your bed with you snoring next to me."

"I don't snore."

"You do snore. Trust me. I know. My hearing is very good."

"Now I hate you."

"No, you don't. You kissed me."

"Without a script."

"Listen." He once again wasn't hearing what I was trying to say. Not surprising. My communication skills were abysmal. But. Fuck, this was important. "I've—"

"I need to go, Conny. I want to stay here and figure all this out, and I want to know what happened last night and why you're so upset, but I have four minutes until I need to be on the Tube."

"Go then!" I said with a smile.

"You and me. We're going to talk later."

"OK."

"Go back to bed."

"I'm going to go to the gym. I might as well since I'm up."

He laughed. "You're an idiot."

"Yeah." I was, and so was he because I still had him penned in against the kitchen sink. "Can I kiss you back?"

God. Morning breath and stale beer repeated on me as I gulped down air. What the hell was I trying to achieve here?

Nothing, apparently, as I grabbed his tie and smashed my mouth on his.

It was a well-rehearsed move. Season two, episode eight. Detective Hamilton, played by some dude whose name eluded me. Grab tie and yank. Nose to nose. Stare at him. Smash mouth on his. Kiss.

Detective Hamilton had pushed Cass Powell away, and I was half expecting Matt to do the same, until he wrapped his arms around me and...fuck.

Fuck. Fuck. Fuck. Matthew Winston could kiss. And I was now...

Weak in the knees. Trembling a little.

"So..." he said, with a smile. "I just missed my train." Then he nudged me out of his way and grabbed his bag off the table. Then he came back and brushed a stray hair out of my face before letting his finger come to a rest against my bottom lip.

"You! Are going to be trouble."

"Why?" I asked weakly.

"Because you have no idea what you do to me, Conny. And I don't know how to behave around you anymore."

I could throw the same statement back to him. I had no clue what I was doing, but he'd walked out the door before I could muster a comeback.

Frustrated and confused, I did what I did best. I went to the gym and kicked the shit out of a punching bag, then I ran until I couldn't breathe. Took a long hot shower, let the water soothe my aching limbs and racing thoughts.

Lucia had sent me a selection of links from today's social media and press, followed by a bunch of cheerful emojis, which I assumed meant she was pleased with my efforts.

I texted Tara. Just a quick, *hello, are you OK?*

I wanted to say more, but last night's shenanigans now felt surreal. I'd been paraded around a party as normal, Lucia one step behind with her phone in her hand.

"This is Zach Kwan. Currently starring in the new Paramount series *Exposure*," she'd stage-whispered as I'd given Zach a hearty man-hug. I'd known him since my first big film job. He'd been my on-screen boyfriend, and he was one of the few people I still kept in touch with. Occasionally. He was as fucked up as I was. We'd happily posed for the required uber-friendly, best-mates-in-the-world shots. He'd kissed my cheek. I'd clung to him like we were closer than we were.

As I'd moved on to the next person, Zach had grabbed my hand and mouthed *call me!* and I wanted to. We should hang out or at least talk, but I doubted I even had his number anymore.

Tara had been Tara—professional and direct—and we'd done our duty for the cameras. Held hands. Smooched. Stared and smile at each other with affection.

My girlfriend wants to kill you and my head hurts. Otherwise, all good, Tara texted back with a screenshot from Instagram. I groaned when I saw what it was.

At the end of last night, the driver had dropped Tara off first. I'd walked her to the building entrance, and we'd high-fived as she'd slipped through the door. We'd obviously been papped, no surprise there, and now the headlines were screaming that I'd rolled out of there in the early hours, doing the walk of shame like a pro. Photoshop was a marvellous thing because I'd been in bed before midnight—Matt's bed—yet the photos looked like they were taken in the early morning light.

I was apparently the 'walk of shame of the week' in some gossip column. No wonder Tara's girlfriend wanted to hire a hitman and put an imaginary bullet in my head.

I was happy I'd got to at least warn Matt before he'd gone to work, because the internet was not a pretty place this morning.

I'd posed with multiple glasses of champagne and quite a few of the sponsored posh beer bottles. I'd probably drunk half a glass in total, taking a cheeky sip between talking to people I needed to talk to and having my picture taken, but some hack had got a shot of Tara and me stumbling out of the event, holding onto each other as if we were pissed as farts, Tara's face a picture of happiness, while I...

Looked like I wanted to eat her.

Usually, I would have laughed.

Today, I felt sick.

Matt had kissed me.

I'd kissed him back.

I had no idea how I was supposed to feel about that. Apart from that I wanted to kiss him again.

What kind of idiot did that make me? Because kissing meant attraction, which meant that eventually, he would want to take his clothes off, and did I want that?

I screamed into the gym towel making a bloke next to me snigger.

Yeah, totally normal behaviour. *Not!*

I went back to the hotel and shoved all my belongings into my two holdalls. I couldn't justify my actions and wasn't thinking clearly, but with one bag in each hand, I left the door to my room to slam shut behind me.

I nodded politely at the receptionist as I passed by.

I could already imagine the tweets about me moving in with Tara.

It was common knowledge where I was staying. I'd had fans wait outside before. I'd had fans outside the gym. Inside the gym even. Thankfully, today, there was nobody around, so I put on my grumpy face and pounded the pavement with my eyes to the ground all the way to Matt's place, using my key to let myself in. I'd held my breath the whole way over, and when I finally sat myself down on the sofa, I was gulping for air.

In. Out.

I closed my eyes for a moment.

In. Out.

Took out my phone.

In. Out.

More messages from Lucia.

One from Tara: *I think we need to break up. There are pics of you kissing that Louis Pereira.*

I've known Louis since season one. Played my dirty hook-up. Killed off in episode seven. I was distraught, I replied. Yes, we'd snogged for the cameras. It meant nothing. Just acting.

Because nobody had actually kissed me before...without a script. *Just because they wanted to.*

I wanted to cry. My chest hurt, my head hurt, and I should probably have followed Matt's advice and gone back to bed.

Instead, I reopened my messages. Another one came in from set telling me I wasn't needed today. They were using Hamish for the shot. Of course they were. Hamish cost them a cool hundred quid a day, while I cost them a small fortune. I didn't usually care. I earned more than enough already, and it gave me a break, but this morning, it pissed me off.

I needed to talk to Aisha and get Zach Kwan's number.

I needed to get Lucia to pipe down on my official Instagram, where I'd supposedly been up at two in the morning commenting on a load of posts and posting drunk selfies.

I agree we need to break up. This is insane, I texted Tara back.

Welcome to my life, she replied. *At least you're a sane, normal person. My last stunt was with someone who was too stupid to hold a normal conversation.*

Did your commitments keep you apart, but you'll always remain great friends or something? I teased back. She replied with a load of vomiting emojis.

I needed Matt. I needed to go home to my mum. I needed out of all of this.

I pulled up Matt's number. Sat there and stared at the phone in my hands.

I had no idea what to write. How to explain. What to say.

I scrolled the net instead, squirming at photos, and shot off an irrational angry text to Lucia, then another one apologising for my brusque tone. It wasn't her fault. She was doing her job, like I was doing mine.

I tried to go to bed, but I couldn't sleep, so I sat around all day on the sofa. Finished a book on my Kindle. Read through next week's script. Checked my messages.

Everything hurt. My head was a mess. My muscles ached. I should have taken it easier at the gym. I needed...I had no idea what I needed. I stared at my bags in disgust. What the hell was I thinking?

The time went slower than ever before, just sitting there, waiting for Matt to come home. I wanted to cry. I didn't.

Then, at last, the key was in the door, and he walked in, casually throwing his bag on the floor.

"Hi," he said cheerfully.

I couldn't even open my mouth. Instead, I got up and closed the distance between us. Wrapped my arms around him and...

I sobbed, big, ugly tears running down my cheeks.

"Oh, Conny," he said softly.

"Sorry," I slobbered out. I didn't know what I was sorry about. Well. Everything. Being me. Being stupid. Having this messed-up job. Having no idea how to be a grown-up. Not understanding shit. All of it, swirled into this festering mess filling my head.

"Nothing to be sorry for," he said, pushing me gently away so he could wipe the tears from my cheeks like I was a child. I felt like one. "I was going to go straight to the gym, but I wanted to see if you were here first, so we could talk. Because this has to stop. Right now. OK?"

Matt

"What needs to stop?" Con snivelled, wiping his face with the back of his hand. At least he was wearing his own clothes, so his T-shirt was stretchy enough for him to pull up and dry his blotchy face. It was a pointless task since the tears kept on coming.

"All this messy panic you're carrying around. I mean. You've been like this since the first time I met you."

"I'm not messy," he protested feebly. "I'm just over-emotional. It goes with the territory."

I didn't believe a word he was saying, but he was here, in my arms, and I was strangely level-headed and on track, so I just held him.

"Conny, you're the most brilliant person I've ever met, yet at the same time the most chaotic. And yeah, perhaps you're a little over-emotional, but that's a good thing, don't you agree?"

"So I don't need to stop the crying?"

I was a bit lost with how to handle him because even though he was a full-on adult human being, there was something incredibly naïve about the way he sometimes worded things. It brought out all my protective traits, in overload.

"What's with the bags? You leaving?" I asked, having spotted the two large holdalls by the door. "Please don't move out."

"No."

"No, I'm not leaving or no, I've just packed my bags for fun?"

"I picked up the rest of my stuff from the hotel. I can't stay there anymore. It's…a long story."

"OK." I had to stop. Breathe. Stroke his hair. Smile at that ridiculous face I'd been dreaming of all day. I wanted so badly to kiss him again, but I didn't dare. The fact was that he was this big lump of a man, and I wasn't, and that I was struggling to stand up when he was hugging me like he was because he…

God help me.

"Conny, we need to stop this thing we have going on where we're basically boyfriends who don't talk to each other. At all. We need to hash out what's going on here and not just jump each other in the kitchen and then go to work like nothing happened…" I had to stop again because he wasn't crying anymore. He was laughing.

"*You're* the one who jumped *me* in the kitchen." There was that twinkle I adored, even though his eyes were still full of tears.

"Uh-huh? I just gave you a supportive, friendly kiss. Then *you* pushed *me* into the kitchen counter and snogged the living daylights out of me."

I was being somewhat economical with the truth there, as I'd run to the Tube station trying to disguise my semi under my cheap work suit, and I wasn't proud of that. It was one thing dreaming about being kissed by Con Telford, another actually being assaulted by him naked apart from boxers and bed hair. He was irresistible in the morning, and had I not had my wits about me, I'd have dropped to my knees and given him a blow job.

I'm glad I hadn't. That would've no doubt had him sobbing. Seeing what one small innocent kiss had done to him, he was nowhere ready for anything like that.

But it hadn't been *just a kiss*. I kind of understood that.

"Come here," I said and towed him over to the sofa. I got my suit jacket off and threw it on the floor, then tugged at him until he sat next to me.

I'd only intended to initiate a friendly chat about where we both stood. Instead, he pretty much plonked himself on top of me and snuggled his face into my shoulder.

I wasn't complaining. Not at all. I hugged him, stroking my hands up and down his back.

"Yesterday looked like an absolute shitshow," I started carefully. Not that I knew anything about Con's line of work, but it was clear the photos told a story that had absolutely no anchor in reality—the set-up, Tara Marie trying to kiss him, both of them looking wasted—mostly because the sheer amount of alcohol involved would've put him in a coma. I may not have been an expert, but the Con I'd kissed at six o'clock this morning had been stone-cold sober.

"It was," he said into my shoulder.

"You don't drink, and you were definitely not drunk this morning. I would have smelled it a mile off. I have a little brother who insisted he didn't drink on nights out when his beer intake was ridiculous. He was seventeen at the time. He learned his lesson, but yeah. I was that big brother. The one who picked him up in the middle of the night and sobered him up enough to drag him through the house so our parents wouldn't know he'd been smashed. So, I know."

"It's business," Con said. "I have a show to promote. A play coming up and a potential big deal in the States where Con Telford needs to be seen as the man of the moment. It's all fake. I'm told what to do, what to say, who to talk to..." He snivelled again. "I mean, I can say no, but it's easier to play along..."

He shuffled up so he was looking at me.

He was terrifying this close up. Because of who he was. How he made me feel. How I just wanted to wrap him up in my bed and kiss him until we both fell asleep.

"It's true what I said this morning. I've never been with anyone. Never been kissed. Never been intimate with anyone for real. I mean, I know how to do it. I know how to make all kinds of things look amazing on camera. I know what expression to wear to look like I'm having the best orgasm of my life. I've just never...done it for real."

"Not even masturbating?"

Wrong question, Matt. He faceplanted my chest and groaned. I nudged him, but he wouldn't look up.

"Yes. But that's different from actually being with someone."

"Would you like to, though?"

"Of course I would. But not with just anyone. I...I'm...let me explain from the start. Because I'm not...*fuck*."

"It's OK. Just talk to me."

Those words seemed to make him relax. Moving off my lap, he sat beside me on the sofa, leaning back, legs stretched out in front of him. He took a deep breath.

"I left school at fifteen and finished my education with a tutor on set. I missed out on all those years when kids experience things. When they figure shit out and experiment and do stupid stuff. I never went to uni or went backpacking or even had a summer holiday. I've never had another job. I don't know anything about how to live a normal life. Going to a supermarket gives me palpitations. I live in a hotel, and I'm shit-scared half the time because people know who I am and recognise me and want things. I mean, it's not like I have stalkers waiting for me every day, but things creep up on you. Like today. I'm on every fucking website, falling drunk out of some event, doing some imaginary walk of shame, when I was here, in your bed, just before midnight, for crying out loud! It's not a big secret that I live in a hotel, and it's not the first time I've panicked and asked Lucia to move me somewhere else."

"Where are you moving? Who is Lucia?"

"My agent. Manager slash publicist slash everything kind of thing. She gets me my gigs, sets up appearances and meetings and auditions and all that, has a whole team dedicated to me being me. Books my tickets. Pays my bills. Organises my clothes. Like that suit over there. It's not mine. It's borrowed from some designer. There's a courier collecting it...from the hotel. Shit."

I hadn't noticed the posh suit hanging on the door, and I recognised the leopard-print shirt from the pictures on social media. I was glad it was going back. I never wanted to see it again. "You have more important things to worry about than some rental suit."

"Designer collaboration." He smirked. "Such bullshit."

"Whatever." I smiled, stroked his cheek. We needed to get into our normal groove. It made things easier.

"What other worries do I have?" he asked, rubbing his nose. His eyes were red and swollen, and he was still tearful. Fuck. I hated seeing him upset.

"Firstly, we need to find space for your stuff somewhere. Secondly, I'm starving."

"You said boyfriends earlier." He spoke slowly like he was tasting the word. "I'm not actually gay. I don't think."

I laughed. Tactless, I know, but it was a ridiculous thing to say.

"I was chatting to some of my students today. We're doing a project on ethics for Pride. Afterschool club. I run it. We were talking about queer actors playing straight roles and straight actors playing queer roles, and your name came up in that conversation."

Oh Matt, shut up. He looked mortified.

"Yeah, I'm the ultimate queer-baiting bastard in the business—despite everyone thinking I'm gay."

"You know it doesn't matter." I was trying so hard here, but Con Telford was *not* straight. No straight man kissed the way he'd kissed me this morning. And if that made me the arsehole?

"It *does* matter when people hurl abuse at you," he said. "When directors are afraid to touch you because you might bring bad vibes. And what the hell does the public know? If you count the number of people I've supposedly dated, shagged, got engaged to and no doubt married in the press... Lucia keeps pushing the uncertain bi narrative, because it works for my brand, and look where that gets me. Crying on the sofa because I can't handle all the bullshit."

"Ehhhr, you're not just crying on any sofa, baby, you're crying on *my* sofa. Big difference."

"But we're not boyfriends. Baby."

God, he was hard work. But yes, I got it.

"I'm not going to push it, but listen. You don't have to be anything, you hear me? But I know one thing. You like me. And God knows I like you. We sleep together. Note. *Sleep*. We adore...well...*I* adore you. I think you kind of like me too. Your bags are in my hallway. You've got your toothbrush in my bathroom, and your bloody flowers are still in my kitchen!"

I paused to catch my breath and look at him. He seemed a little taken back with my little outburst.

"So we are boyfriends?"

"Conny, this whole set up screams boyfriends! Even the bag of coffee in my bag that I bought for you agrees with me."

"And we kissed."

"Yes. We kissed. Not a scripted kiss. Not a work kiss. Kisses should be fun. They should feel good, and I can't think of anything more fun than dragging you into bed and kissing you for hours. Don't worry. I won't, but I want to. You need to remember that when you get all wound up. You're amazing, and you have someone here who's hoping you'll stay. Long enough for me to prove to you that I'm right."

"You're kind of bossy when you're mad."

"I'm not mad."

"Yes, you are. Because I said I'm not gay."

"Well, it's a shitty thing to say to the guy who had to go to work with a hard-on because his non-boyfriend-platonic-roommate decided to snog him."

"I know." He looked bashful again and chewed his lip. "It's a shitty thing to say to anyone. I agree. But I didn't say I wasn't bi. Or that I'm not straight."

"Hallelujah!"

"Shut up."

We grinned at each other.

"Seriously, Con, you don't have to be anything. As long as you promise me that we'll work on this and that there's a chance I get to kiss you again..."

"Matt, I'm...I'm shit scared."

He was, I could tell, but talking was good. I was learning to read him now, figuring out how to help him stay calm. For now, I just listened.

"My life is such a shit show. I don't know how to handle it at the best of times, and now I'm here...forcing myself into your life because you're the only thing I have that's good. Everything else is just bullshit. I'm no bloody Prince Charming, and I can't give you anything in return. I can't even tell you how I feel because I have no idea how to put words on it."

"Well, it's not like I'm going to jump you and demand blow jobs, just because I said the boyfriend word." I stroked his cheek and lightly tugged at the fabric of his shirt, bringing him back where he belonged. In my arms. Against me.

"So, what happens now?" he asked, snuggling under my chin. I kissed the top of his head.

"Friendship. Hugs. Roommates. Who sometimes...kiss. Naked sleeping—"

"Is it all right if I stay for a while?"

"Yes. Definitely."

I was aware I was pushing my own agenda and probably making this even messier than it had been to start with, but for now, everything seemed to be under control. He gently pushed away from me and stood up, then my hand and pulled me up too.

"Would you like me to take you out for food?" He didn't look too keen on that idea.

"I don't think we have anything in the fridge."

"Nope. I would have gone shopping, but I...couldn't."

I had a feeling even getting him to leave the flat would be traumatic today. I got it. God, I did. If that had been me splashed all over the media, I would have been hiding under my bed taking a lifelong vow of solitude.

"We'll get noodles delivered. OK? Go wash your face, and I'll pop the kettle on...or do you want another one of those pink gin things?"

"Go on. I think we deserve one after the day we've had!"

"You get the ice?"

"Did you really have a hard-on going to work this morning?"

God, he was so bloody stupid, and I was even worse because now we were both smiling, and he was just...bloody irresistible. All wrinkled and messy, and his hair was all over the place, and he looked like he needed...a hug.

I'd lied when I'd said things were under control. They weren't. Because I fisted the front of his T-shirt and pulled him forward, and then I assaulted his face with my mouth.

And he let me.

FIFTEEN

Con

It was like I couldn't even breathe anymore. I couldn't function, no blood running through my veins. Death had claimed me.

No. Not really, but I was breathlessly dizzy, and I had to push him away, turning around in juvenile shame.

I was tenting down below, and that was not even the start of it.

"Sorry." His voice came from behind me as I steadied myself against the wall with one hand, adjusting my junk with the other.

"Don't you dare apologise."

"Whatever is going on in your head right now, just tell me. Because nothing here will ever be right if we can't talk to each other."

"I...just need this unfortunate boner to go down," I squeaked out. This never happened on set. Ever. I was the ultimate professional. Everyone knew I was reliable and steady. I delivered. Over and over again.

"Unfortunate boners happen to all of us," he said calmly. "Trust me. I teach teenagers. Girls in short skirts. Boys with vivid imaginations. Queer kids with insane crushes. Sports day is always interesting."

"Matt." I rolled my shoulders and tried to figure out what to do while he patiently waited behind me. I needed to go sit in a dark corner. "I can't even look at you right now."

"Says the man who walks around naked more than he's dressed."

"That's different. I didn't…"

"What?"

"You're…you drive me crazy. In a good way."

"Thank God for that."

"And we weren't boyfriends when I was walking around naked."

"We've been boyfriends since you hit me in the face. Fact."

I turned around, stood up straight again. I was fucked. So bloody fucked. Especially since he was pulling off his tie and loosening his top button. Removing his ID, he let it drop to the floor, followed by his white shirt, grey slacks… He shook out his hair.

"Have we?" I was probably drooling, my juvenile stupidity at an all-time high. Right now, if someone had told me to marry him, I'd have done it. No questions asked.

"Let's change the subject. Food. What do you usually order?"

He was brilliant, always knowing the right thing to say.

"Number forty-two. Extra egg."

"OK…" He smiled. "And what is that?"

"Don't laugh. It's bad enough that the guy who works there ridicules me every time I put an order in."

"It can't be that bad. Mrs Wu has won awards for her cooking. You've seen the place. They're all on display behind the counter. Chef of the Year in 2016 or something."

"Which makes it even worse."

"Do you want me to order something else? Broaden your horizons?"

"Says the guy who only ever orders number seventeen."

"You are absolutely my boyfriend. You even remember my noodle order."

"Of course!" I was staring at his naked chest harder than I should.

"I need a shower," he said, folding his arms and obscuring my view. "Shall I place this order then?"

"I have the app. You go shower." At least I was useful for something.

He disappeared into the bathroom, leaving me alone in his apartment, ordering our food like this was normal when it was anything but. I had an almost uncontrollable urge to follow him, drag him under the water and soap down all his dirty places.

I'd filmed a scene like that once. It was supposed to look like you were pulling off the hand job of the century when instead you were giving your co-actor carpet burn on their thighs and trying not to get the camera soaked with the camera guy's face up your bum. It was messy and painful, but the thought of it wasn't helping the problem in my underpants, and I whined in frustration as I flopped onto the sofa and opened the app on my phone.

"Do you want rice?" I shouted towards the bathroom door.

"With noodles?" He casually walking back out into the room, towel around his waist, wet hair still dripping onto his shoulders. That was quick.

I stared at him. His gorgeous body. I'd seen it so many times now—even his arse and balls when he changed out of his clothes—because he was as comfortable around me as I was around him, but this evening, it made my stupid little heart go all funny.

I'd never fit with anyone before. Ever. Not at school, in friendship groups or on set. I didn't regret the way my life had gone. I couldn't. I knew how bloody privileged I was; the state of my bank account gave me palpitations just looking at it. I was lucky. Goddamn lucky.

But I was also fucked in the head, clearly, because for a moment I forgot why I had my phone in my hand, and I was panting like I'd just stepped off the treadmill. I snapped myself out of it.

"What do you want to drink?"

"Diet Coke."

"It's not good for you," I said and blushed. Fuck me, that was rude, but he laughed. See? We fit.

"I bet Wei will deliver," I continued nervously. "He usually does," I had no idea how he made me feel this way.

"I can't believe you remember his name."

"Of course I remember his name. I'm not a complete arsehole. We should always treat people around us with respect, which includes using names. My mum taught me well."

Matt nodded. "Yeah. Wei's a nice guy. We've kind of become friends since I moved in here. He gives me long lists of books to read, and they're good books."

"I gave him a list of books too, but he said he doesn't read sci-fi. I told him he should get started on that. I'd rather read a book than watch a film. My head's weird that way."

He shrugged. "Maybe it comes with the job. Everything's scripted for you at work, but reading lets you visualise things your own way."

"I guess." I'd never thought of it that way.

"So, food then..." he prompted.

"Yeah." I pressed submit on our order and double-clicked the side button to pay. Easy. And now he was sitting next to me on the sofa.

"You know you said you're scared?" His voice was soft. I loved when he talked to me like this. When he put words to all those things I couldn't even start to understand.

"I'm scared too," he continued. "Remember that. I'm terrified that I'll wake up alone one morning and all your stuff will be gone. I know it's only been a few weeks, but...I've...honestly...I love having you around."

"We fit." Yeah, I could memorise pages' worth of script in an instant, but my skills in speaking from the heart?

"God, we do. You have no idea how nice it is to feel...accepted. Even liked."

"Matt, you have thousands of followers on Instagram. You're, like, really popular."

He smiled, but it wasn't a happy smile.

"I know a lot of people. Most of those are people I've worked with, union officials, or members of the associations I'm part of. I try to keep former students out of there, but a few have slipped through. There's only a handful of real friends, people I talk to. Colleagues. Not that it matters. Social media isn't real."

"That's what I mean. You get me. God, Matt. You have no idea how scared I was that you'd see those pictures and think...that was me."

"I *know* that's not you." Now he smiled. Properly. "It's not like I'm sat here thinking, any minute now Tara Marie will burst through the door and demand her boyfriend back."

That made me chuckle. My stupid arm automatically reached out so I could stroke his face again.

"Tara would definitely burst through the door and demand her boyfriend back. She's quite the joker. But she'd be dragging her girlfriend along with her and come armed with a bag of homemade macaroons. Tara doesn't drink either. We bonded over black coffee and pastries. She bakes. I eat them. We make the perfect couple."

He laughed. What I loved even more than his laughter was that I made him laugh, just being myself. And my stomach was once again full of fire.

There was a drop of water running off his shoulder. I wanted to lick it off.

I loved how real he was, the natural shape of his body, his chest—hairless apart from a few stray hairs around his nipples. I wasn't allowed any hair. Cass Powell groomed. Well, Peter did, yanking every little, microscopic hair out of my battered skin.

My fingers wandered from Matt's face down to his nipple. I gently stroked those little hairs and watched in wonder how what had been a plump area of soft skin tightened into a hard, bumpy patch.

Fuck.

Fuck.

There was no script for this. No intimacy coordinator to advise me on the right way to place my hands on him, inoffensive touches that would look good on camera. In real life, I wanted my mouth on that nipple, and it terrified me. I snatched my arm away and sat back on the sofa hyperventilating.

"You know, you can touch me. Anywhere." He reached out and stroked a finger over my hand. "I have no issue with you trying things out. And if something doesn't work for you, it really doesn't matter."

I gulped air. I had no idea why I was like this.

"Come here." His voice was gentle, but I couldn't move.

"Conny? Just come here."

I wanted to, so much, and he must've known that because in the end he pulled me to him, tugging at my sleeves until my cheek was flat against his chest. The noises coming out of my mouth were ridiculous. I gasped, clung to him, closed my eyes at the sensations of his warm skin against my face, his lips in my hair, my fingers gripping his arm.

"You're always safe with me. I will never do anything you don't want me to do. We're just going to take this as it comes. But hugs, Conny? I really need hugs. Lots of them. You against me, like this? This is the stuff I live for. Connection. Knowing that you're here because you want to be not because we met on Grindr or something. I have no expectations. All I need is you. Here. OK?"

"OK."

I lifted my head and looked at him. Pressed my lips against his. The thrill of being able to do that was...intense. Almost too intense when he smiled and kissed me back, little soft pecks all over my face.

Which, of course, was when the intercom went. And since I was all polite and dressed and all that, I shot up and went to answer, leaving him sat on the sofa.

"Uh...hullo?"

"Ha!" Came from the speaker. "I knew it! You're the only one who orders that crap. Mum almost refused to cook it. You need to thank me because I bribed her."

Matt was laughing his head off.

"Buzz him in," he said, getting up from the sofa. "I'll grab some clothes." There was a wet patch on the sofa cushion from his hair.

I stood there like a lemon, holding the front door open, as Wei the Noodle Man skipped up the stairs.

"This isn't what it looks like," I started, immediately on the defence and for no reason whatsoever.

"Matt's a nice guy. I'm glad you're...friends." He smirked, unzipping the carrier slung over his shoulder.

"Hey, Wei!"

Matt to the rescue. Thank you, God.

I took the bags off Wei and tried to skulk away.

"Con, those books? I read the first one. Great choice! I may need another list off you because my friend had already read everything you recommended. That cool?"

"Absolutely." I grinned.

"Also, Mum needs gossip."

"I know. She keeps telling me. If I don't spill the oolong or whatever, she'll put washing-up liquid in my omelette."

"You need to stop ordering omelette. With extra egg. It's an insult to my mother's skills."

"It's really hard to make a good omelette. Your mum knows this. She does make an extraordinary omelette." I didn't mean that in a bad way.

"Conny, please tell me that isn't what you order!" Matt's jaw hung slack in horror.

"I like an omelette! Simple and tasty. But the portion size is ridiculous. Hence the extra egg."

"We thank you for your feedback," Wei said flatly. "You don't even let Mum put spring onions in it. Seriously. I added four bags of chilli sauce. I mean. Come on!"

"Just because I like plain food, doesn't mean I don't like good food."

"Of course my mum's food is good, even the bland crap you order. At least Matt orders something decent."

"Do you insult all your customers like this?"

Matt was laughing and shaking his head.

"Of course! People would be disappointed if I didn't deliver their food with a good dose of abuse. I'm known for it." He flicked his hair back and zipped up his bag. "Anyway, Mum will be very pleased to know that I found Matt, half dressed, with my favourite famous customer. And that fancy shirt hanging behind you looks awfully familiar..."

"Wei," Matt warned, but there was no need. I was laughing because this? This was the kind of shit I *could* deal with.

"You want it?" I asked. "It's, like, super famous. Been in seen on all the major entertainment sites this morning, attached to some idiot who deserves all the washing-up liquid in his omelette."

"It's Gucci. You can't just give it away."

"Take it. Seriously. Your mum can use it as a tea towel or something."

Bingo. Now Wei was laughing.

I grabbed the damn shirt off the hanger and held it out to him. "Only used once. As seen in...what was it?"

"Walk of Shame of the Week. But will it get me laid?"

"A hundred percent...not. It's a vile shirt. Itchy as anything. But it will make a good rag to wash windows with if that would work for you?"

"I'm going to treasure it. Wear it with pride." Wei shoved the shirt in his jacket pocket. It made me smile. "Dude, you have good taste in books. Just next time, please let me put some spring onions in your dish? A dash of chilli sauce, garlic mushrooms—"

"Bye Wei."

He grinned and waved as I closed the door in his face.

"I hated that shirt," Matt said.

"Not as much as I hated it."

The bag of food hit the floor as I ripped the T-shirt over his head and launched at his mouth.

Because I could. Because he was right there, and the food?

Fuck the food.

Matt

He was all over the place, and I probably should have stopped him. Sat him back on the sofa and talked him down from this frenzy of feelings. That would have been the right thing to do. The sensible option.

I wasn't sensible. Not anymore. Not with his lips against mine and the way he was clawing at my boxers, trying to get his hand where he wanted it, which was... There. OK. He had my arse in a firm grip, and it was crazy how much that turned me on. Cranked me up. Blimey, and there was his tongue in my mouth and...fuck.

I never swore except during sex, when I could be rather bossy and in control, but I had absolutely no control here, and I needed to do something about that. I turned him around and slammed him into the wall behind us, managing to elegantly drop my boxers in the process.

Then I grabbed his face and made him look at me.

I wasn't having any of this. None of it.

OK. I was.

Because his face.

Shit. Fuck. Hell.

I carefully kissed his upper lip, then the lower one. Slowed everything down so I could actually think.

"Are you...OK with this?" I whispered as he once again tried to ravage my mouth.

His boner was back, stabbing my leg through the flimsy fabric of his shorts—the only thing between us. Carefully releasing him with one hand, I pulled down his shorts and let them slip to the floor, then reinstated my grip on his chin and made sure he was looking at me. Really looking at me. His eyes were glassy, and his cheeks were flushed pink.

"I'm not going to do anything you don't want me to do, but you have to show me what you...need."

I tried to keep my voice steady, but it was hard with his hand around my dick. His breath hitched.

Ah. OK. Words were kind of unnecessary then, but I was nervous on his behalf because I'd once been through this too. The dreaded first time. Mine had been OK, as good as it could have got with someone, I thought had been boyfriend material but turned out to be anything but. I didn't want to think about it.

What I *did* want was for this to be good. For him. I didn't care what happened as long as he got what he needed. So I kissed him, hard. Smiled as he moaned and put his hands back on my arse, gripping tightly as he humped into my groin. I'd have marks there tomorrow, and that kind of made me happy.

So much for me taking charge. With one hand now on my hip and the other now gripping my arm, he walked me backwards and threw me onto the bed. So was this how we were doing this? Him in control and me pinned to the mattress as he crawled onto the bed, on all fours, on top of me.

Oh God. His dick. I'd only caught a glimpse of it hard, but fuck me sideways.

Like I said, I only swore during sex. And in my head.

"You're...bloody stunning," I murmured. I hadn't meant to say it out loud.

"Thanks...I guess."

That made me laugh. Fuck. I was so bloody in love with this guy it was ridiculous.

His lips on mine were addictive, and now I was squashed, breathlessly trying to roll him onto his side until we somehow ended up stomach to stomach, chest to chest, his hand sliding over my hip and gently squeezing my arse. If I didn't know he'd never done this before, I'd have begged for him to fuck me. Just one glimpse of that dick of his had ruined me forever. I wanted it. I wanted him. Fuck. I wanted that cock in my mouth, and I wanted him to...

"Conny," I moaned as his hand snaked down between us and once again gripped my cock. My rock-hard cock. No surprise there. My fingers trailed over his chest. His body was insane, all hard firm muscle, curves to die for. And those nipples. I peppered kisses down his pec, letting my tongue play with that perfect skin, and sucked a nipple into my mouth. His breath came out as a soft gasp.

"Anything you need, I will give you. You can do anything you want to me." God knows what I was promising him, but I'd give it to him. All of it.

"Anything?" came from above my head in a voice that was barely there.

I leant back and allowed myself to look at him. His chest blushed bright pink as I dropped my gaze and gently traced my fingers over his erection. He was...the expression well-endowed wasn't descriptive enough. I'd seen him naked; his cock sat prettily over his balls. Erect was a completely different picture and...there it was. A long, drawn-out groan as I gave him a couple of good tugs.

He grabbed one of the pillows and tried to hide underneath it, which, of course, I wouldn't let him.

I threw the pillow on the floor before pressing my mouth against his. "I'm going to make you come. I promise."

"Matt?" he whispered.

"Yeah?"

"I have no idea what I'm doing." There was a small smile forming on his face. I kissed it. I couldn't help myself.

"Nobody knows what they're doing," I said softly, letting myself get comfortable as he moved into my arms, one around his back, one carefully moving back down so I could resume my attempt at giving him a slow, lazy hand job. He was calmer now. Turned on, but calm. "I have no idea what turns you on, what you like. What drives you crazy or what's too much."

"There's no script," he said quietly.

"Most of my hook-ups have been through the apps. You kind of get a clear list of likes and dislikes from people's profiles. Gives you a framework to start with."

"Trust you to talk about frameworks during sex." He laughed.

Good. Now we were getting somewhere.

"Well, I am a teacher, you know." I smirked and kissed his stupid face.

I loved how he tasted. The softness of his lips. The light stubble. He hadn't worked today, so he hadn't shaved. He was just him. Au naturel.

"What do you like? What's on your menu?"

His hands were all over me, stroking down my chest, fingers carefully circling my nipples. I mirrored his actions, admiring the firmness of his muscles as I walked my fingers back down to his cock. He was feeling more comfortable because now he was mimicking my movements too, my dick getting the attention it desperately craved. I was going to say something, but I was struggling to talk. He was good at this. Really good.

"My menu is simple. I like things that feel good," I panted out.

"And does this feel good?"

"I'm... Conny...I'm going to come if you keep that up."

"That's kind of the whole point, isn't it?" he sassed and locked his mouth on mine.

I was kissing Con Telford.

Ugh.

But at the same time, he wasn't Con Telford. Con Telford was some drunken idiot in a leopard-print shirt. An actor on TV.

This was a guy called Conny, who was going into overdrive, trying to hump my hand and lick my face at the same time.

Was I complaining? Nope.

And all my efforts of slowing this down, plans to meticulously devour his body? Went out the window as I rolled on top of him.

Fuck.

Fuck indeed.

I really wanted to grab a condom and roll it on his dick. That would be fun. Cover him in lube until he was shaking with need. Then he could just flip me over and fuck me into oblivion.

No, scrap that. I wanted to suck him dry. Swallow him down as he screamed.

My arse twitched at the thought, but no.

Yes.

Fuuuck.

Somehow, he knew exactly how to touch me, how to gently move the foreskin in that way that made me shiver. I did it back to him, strong, firm movements, twisting my wrist and smoothing my fingers over his tip then back down again as he panted into my mouth. I was no better than him.

We rolled again until he was on top of me, and our hands tangled. He was humping against me, and I was jerking into his grip as the headboard thumped the wall.

This wasn't just sex.

This was desperation. Need. Fucking desire.

My head went into that strange place where I wanted to swallow him whole, get on top of him and be where he was. In the moment. Us.

I rolled him over, straddling his legs, and got our dicks lined up with my hands around them both, as his arms flew up so he could hold himself steady. With his head shoved up into the remaining pillow, banging against the headboard, I jerked us both off in a frenzied manner.

I should have got the lube out.

I should have stopped.

There was no way I could stop.

His whole back arched off the bed, his face twisted in what looked like pain but I knew was that state when your mind went blank.

And he roared.

Fuck. Fuckety-fuckety-fuckety fuck.

My dick next to his would've been enough, but his cum hitting my fingers was more than I could take.

Sex was never like this.

It wasn't like what you saw on TV. Or in films for that matter. In reality, people didn't come like this. Together. It was a joint effort, teasing that elusive orgasm out of your partner. Working for it. Using little words to slowly and carefully tip the other person over the edge.

He'd just nosedived straight off the cliff, and now I was smearing his cum all over my dick and carelessly throwing myself headfirst into a blinding crevasse of an orgasm.

I didn't think a single, coherent thought after that. Not until I found myself on his chest with his arms around me and my head being bounced around by his erratic breathing.

"Matt?"

"Yeah?"

"The fuck was that?"

God, I laughed. This man. He'd be the death of me.

"That, muffin, was one hell of a messy hand job."

"Muffin? What the hell?"

"Muffin. Suits you."

He just laughed.

"Good."

"Good?"

"Yeah. Just checking. No idea what happened. I didn't plan on that."

"These things are rarely planned. It's apparently what happens when we order take-away noodles."

He laughed and kissed the top of my head as I wriggled further into him. I had no idea what that conversation had been about but, anyway.

His body. Insane. My leg over his crotch, my arm slung around his shoulder, my lips somewhere in his neck.

"The noodles will be cold."

"Luckily, I have a microwave."

"Oh. Lucky."

He went quiet again, his breathing slowing down. Little sniffles coming from his nose as I played with the wetness on his stomach.

He'd come all right. So had I, and I had a sneaky suspicion that this was one of those defining moments. Where everything changed. Because this?

This had been...sex. A messy, funny moment. New. Fumbling. Gorgeous. I didn't think I'd ever want to have sex with anyone else, ever again. Because once you found that connection, where you just let yourself go and did what you wanted, and the other person was there with you in the moment, laughing...

I barely knew him, but I felt like I did, and it made me emotional as he tugged at me and wrapped me up in the monster of all hugs, holding me so tight that I thought I would break.

"Thank you," he whispered.

"For what?" I whispered back.

"For letting me do this. With you. For... Matt, I don't know what to say. I'm not...I never thought this was something I wanted. Or needed. But I think I always have. I just never met the right person. You're...you're amazing...with me."

"We fit. You said it yourself."

Those words were not enough. They never would be. But what I wanted to say was hard to say right.

He just kept holding me, his breath warm against my forehead, my fingers tracing the smooth skin on his back.

Chest to chest. Heart to heart.

"My menu is simple," I said. "Not that I'll be using those apps ever again. I don't mess around. I only used them when I felt desperate enough to want someone. Just to get off, and sometimes when I just needed to feel...I don't know. Loved? Sometimes it was really good. Other times, I felt like crap, dirty and used. It's not as simple as people think it is. Sometimes it doesn't work out at all. I met up with one guy who took one look at me and just walked away. Another time, I got my shirt off and the guy just laughed. Said something about killing the moment as soon as I got my kit off."

"Rude," he said and pressed his lips to my head. "It's like auditions. You turn up already with the script perfect in your head, and they take one look at you and dismiss you. Like you're rubbish. You don't even get a chance to prove your worth. Other times, they circle you and touch you. Like you're just a prop."

"You're not a prop." I wanted to say so much more than that. Tell him how beautiful he was. How perfect. That I would love him forever. That if he got up now and left, I would never recover.

"I feel like it. All the time. I'm put in a place—there's usually a taped X on the floor—and I stand there. Do what I am told. Move my body the way they tell me to. Then I go home, and I have no idea how to actually be human. It messes with your head."

"I think you're the most human being I have ever met," I said. I meant it. "Because you know what is work and what is life. And what is real. Not many people do. Some people get a promotion and think they've become God. Others lose all grasp of reality and forget that they were once a terrified teenager with baggage and burdens. Hopes and dreams."

"That's why you're so brilliant, Matt. You see people. Not just the outside, but you see what's on the inside too. You didn't just dismiss me, even though you knew who I was."

"I don't always. I'm not perfect. But why would I have dismissed you?"

"I think you're perfect," he said, shuffling down the bed so he was nose to nose with me. "Most people dismiss me because they think I'm an idiot. A *Love Island* kind of airhead muscle dude that got lucky. The truth is, Con Telford *is* an idiot." His lips leaned in for another of those kisses. A dirty one.

"You're..." Fuck. Now I was getting emotional. Because this guy? He just shrugged off that last sentence and babbled on.

"I need to eat something before I get all shaky. I don't think I had any lunch. I forgot." He pressed another kiss to my mouth. "And we should really go to the gym. But somehow, I think I'd rather just stay here in bed with you."

"Conny." God, I loved saying his name like that. The silky syllables rolled out of my mouth.

"Not Muffin?" He was smiling, soft and relaxed on my bed, his nose pressed to mine.

"Muffin." Fuck. OK. He might be an idiot, but I was one too. I couldn't even breathe when he looked at me the way he was looking at me now. "What d'you need?"

"After we've eaten, can we do more of this? The sex thing?"

Con

It was seven in the morning, and I was splayed out like a piece of meat on the chair, a towel covering my midriff. Totally normal on a day like this, apart from that it was Saturday, and the set was much quieter than during the week. We were filming just the one scene today, and I was all geared up for it. I even had my nude piece of fabric glued on, holding my junk in place, ready for the required nudity in an intimate scene.

I was ready.

My body hair wasn't, though, and Peter was moving across my chest with his tweezers, ensuring I'd be suitably hairless. I was so used to it I didn't even flinch when he found a strand of hair. His hand smoothed over my skin with a wipe after every tug.

"You're very smiley today," he said, giving me a little grin.

"Huh?" I wasn't even paying attention, lying here in my own world, thinking back to last night.

"I think someone might have got laid."

"No! What?"

Shut up, Peter. This wasn't something I wanted to talk about, but he just chuckled and carried on inspecting my skin.

"We need to get Zara back in here."

"She's already done my face," I muttered.

"I'm not bothered about your face."

"Then what?" I smoothed down my stomach. I was clean, plucked to perfection, my privates nicely tucked in under the towel.

"Yes. Well, you're all good to go, but the mark on your neck is slightly problematic."

Shit.

I didn't say that out loud. Instead, I laughed nervously, getting up on my feet and leaning over so I could see myself in the mirror.

"There." Peter pointed it out and held up his hand mirror so I could see the back of my head. And yup. There it was. A small, faint outline of something that absolutely didn't look like a love bite, but I wasn't about to tell anyone that Matt kissing my neck while he played with my dick? Yeah.

"There's a bite mark on your bum as well, Con. Honestly, you knew we'd be doing this today."

I did. And this was my life, in a nutshell. I hadn't even thought, and yes. I was now grinning like a fool, staring at my buttock in the mirror. I remembered it well. He'd gone to make us a cup of herbal tea. I'd been on the bed reading my script. Then he'd bent over and just...nibbled at my bum.

"Can I just ask you one thing?" Peter looked more serious than I was comfortable with. I didn't need a grilling. Not today. "Is he good to you?"

What kind of question was that? Was Matt good to me?

"It's very...new," I said, trying to figure out how to fend off this conversation.

He smiled. "We all have to start somewhere."

"Yeah." I wasn't falling for this.

"I can tell. You keep smiling, like you're remembering things that made you happy. I assume it was this boy of yours?"

"Not a boy. He's actually a senior schoolteacher," I admitted. Fuck. I needed to stop this. Now.

"Oh. Nice. Educated."

"He's also the kindest man I've ever met. Really funny. We fit."

Shut the hell up, Connor! God. Where was all this coming from?

"So your kinks are aligned and there will be a second date?" Peter tried.

"No." I laughed. "No dates. We've pretty much skipped that stage. And there are no kinks involved. I promise you that."

"Well, I don't quite believe you. This boy of yours—"

"Nope," I warned. "You're not getting another word out of me."

He wasn't, and neither was Zara, who was surprisingly unfazed at the state of my bum.

I kept my mouth shut but couldn't stop smiling because Peter was right. Matt made me happy, and it was stupid how much I wanted to throw my hands in the air and declare I'd quit so I could go home, drag him into bed and forget that there was a life outside those four walls.

I liked Matt naked. I liked me naked with Matt, in Matt's flat, and that made my stomach hurt. I'd left this morning taking an overnight bag with me because I was going home to see Mum. Matt had agreed it would be good for me. Give some space to breathe, re-group. I'd be back Sunday night, back in Matt's bed, and things would be OK.

But right now, I wasn't OK. My stomach was all weird, and I couldn't concentrate. Whenever I tried to relax, I was just sitting around with an idiotic smile on my face, and then people would ask questions about why I was especially smiley today.

Fuck.

And here was Toby, thank God. It was a relief to have him back because I didn't think I could handle any more drama today. He gave me a brisk hug as he came into the hair and make-up trailer.

"You all right, mate?" He grinned, and who could blame him when I was naked apart from a glued-on sock covering my bits?

"Yeah, all good," I replied as he ripped off his shirt. We had no shame, the two of us. In a second, he'd be stark naked and wearing a matching sock.

Returning to my trailer, I crammed in another croissant and read four chapters of my book. Brushed my teeth. Stretched my muscles. Sat on my own like a loser. Stared at my phone.

I desperately wanted to ring Matt, but he was probably still asleep. Just hearing his voice would have calmed me down. I didn't know why he made me feel this way. Without him nearby, my body was full of butterflies, and I was antsy.

I pulled up his number and realised I'd never actually texted him. I had his number but couldn't remember having given him mine. I probably hadn't since I was the idiot of the century. We'd chatted over Instagram loads of times, but that was how you interacted with strangers, not people who meant something.

I didn't even know what was going on in my head, as the wardrobe dude turned up with today's ready-and-prepared Cass Powell suit with Velcro instead of buttons and zips for easy removal. Next came Sally, the intimacy coordinator, looking all motherly and concerned, offering me lip salve and gum and asking how I was feeling.

It made me laugh because what the hell was I supposed to feel?

And then I was walking over to the set with Sally nattering on next to me, and I waved to Aisha as she flurried past and then...here was Toby again.

I stared. Of course, I did. Dressed in an open shirt and smart trousers—Cass Powell was about to catch him raiding a crime scene—Toby's chest glistened with sprayed-on fake sweat, as did mine, no doubt, under my Velcro-fastened shirt. Zara bounced around me with a brush in her hand, adding the finishing touches.

I could do these kinds of scenes in my sleep. Honestly. I had no idea why I was nervous.

"You OK?" Toby asked quietly, gently resting his hand on my shoulder.

Now the thing was, we had an intimacy coordinator here for a reason. She was the one who was supposed to notice these things, but Sally was on her phone.

"I don't know," I mumbled. I honestly didn't.

"Don't say you're coming down with something because that bug I caught the other week was bloody nasty. Wouldn't wish it on my worst enemy. Thought I was going to pass out on the Tube going home."

"I had it too."

"Do you need to go over this again or are we good to go?"

Like me, Toby was a pro. We could probably pull this one off in one solid shoot and go home. Job done.

"Nah. All good," I lied. This was not me. I never got like this.

We got into position, and I shrugged my shoulders, tried to get my head into the zone.

"Silence!"

Fuck.

"And Action!"

Toby's lines rolled off his tongue with just the right amount of venom. I snarled mine out in return, hoping I could keep my chill long enough to get through this.

We served insults as per the script, and then Toby went for me, crowded me up against the wall, spitting words into my mouth. Then he kissed me, and I froze up.

I had no idea why.

"Cut! Con, what the hell is wrong with you?"

Not again. I couldn't do this again.

The set was tense as the AD railed me.

"From the top again. Positions!"

We went again. Got a little further this time until Toby kissed down my neck and I fluffed my lines.

I wanted to cry. I wanted to scream.

"Con, do you want to take a minute?" Sally asked, too much in my face.

"Come here, mate." Toby dragged me outside, my half-open shirt flapping as we walked.

He pushed me down onto a chair and pulled up another one, so he was right in front of me, elbows leaning on his knees as he stared at me.

"What's up, mate?"

"I don't know." That was the truth.

"We did this pitch perfect a week ago."

"I know," I whispered. "I don't know what the fuck I'm doing today."

"We all have bad days," he said softly. "But we've worked together a few times now. You're always bang on. Today, you're all over the place. I don't think Sally's helping much, but mate, talk to me."

"I've..." I started. I didn't know how to explain the shit that was swirling around in my head.

"Go on," he encouraged patiently.

"I met someone. Someone really special, and it's all new, and my head is in the gutter, and now I have to pretend have sex with you and it's all bloody wrong."

He smiled. "That makes me really happy, Con, because you're one of those good guys. This business is full of arseholes, I've met a good few of them, but you're a decent bloke. Always on form, always ready for whatever these bastards throw at you. This may seem like an easy scene for us, but trust me, I feel the pressure too."

"It's not the pressure. It's...like...I don't even know!" I was shouting, and I wasn't proud.

"Hey, I get it. I have a wife at home. Two kids. A third on the way. I'm bisexual, out since I was in my teens, but sometimes it's confusing as fuck. Doing these kinds of jobs doesn't make things any easier. I left my wife in bed this morning with a crying toddler so I could pretend-shag you all morning."

"Sorry." I squeezed the words out. "I'm not helping."

"This...person. A man...or shouldn't I ask?"

"Fuck, Toby." I needed to talk about this, not hide. Not be an arsehole. It was just much harder than I'd thought it would be, dealing with all this. "His name is Matt. I always thought I liked girls."

He laughed, but it was a kind laugh.

"Mate." He shook his head, pulled his fingers through his hair.

"I know." And it was bloody stupid, all of this.

"OK," he said. "This is what we're going to do because you're all tense and frustrated, and we need to get that crap out of your system—"

"I just need to go home and get into bed and hide under the covers until I can get my head screwed back on straight." I sighed. "Or not so straight." I knew how stupid I sounded.

"You're as straight as I am, mate, but we wouldn't be as good as we are at this if we weren't fluid about these kinds of things. I always read you as on the spectrum, which perhaps is a crap thing to say right now, but I did. You have zero hang-ups about anything, and it makes filming these scenes with you, such a refreshing thing to do. By the way, what happened with the other guy? The one who was supposed to replace me?"

I smiled despite myself. "Straight guy with an antibacterial wet wipe issue."

"Ah. One of those gay-for-pay types. Met a few over the years. Makes things bloody weird, I can tell you."

"And now I'm the one having issues because I have a boyfriend. I had sex with him, and now I'm frustrated as fuck."

The laughter spilling out of him was freeing, and it made me laugh too.

"Good for you." He slapped me on the knee. "You deserve it, but the frustration is normal. You think everything is chill, and then you meet someone, and there is nothing, and I mean that, *nothing* you can do to stop the total clusterfuck that your life becomes. When you can't eat or sleep and all you think about is being as close to that person as possible. You can't breathe when they're not there, you can't breathe when they are. It's bloody bonkers, but it's true."

"I snuck into his flat and crawled into his bed in the middle of the night because I couldn't bear the thought of not sleeping next to him."

Toby laughed at that. "You can't help who you fall in love with. You just have to roll with it. It's the best feeling in the world, having someone to love you like that. He's a lucky guy. Really lucky."

"Your wife is lucky to have you." I rubbed my nose with the back of my hand. I didn't know what else to do.

"I'm lucky to have her," he said quietly. "Got her pregnant on our first date. Didn't mean to, but the bloody condom broke."

"No!" God.

"Yeah. Not my finest moment. Neither was I the best human being six weeks later when she tracked me down with the pregnancy test in her hand. She wanted to kick me in the balls. I wanted to kick myself in the balls. Then I hugged her, and she cried and I took her home. She moved into my flat, and now we have number three on the way. I apparently have super sperm."

"Crazy." This was helping. I was actually breathing better now. Feeling calmer.

"First time I met Matt, I whacked him in the face by accident, holding an imaginary gun in my hand. I was going through a scene on the treadmill, and he was in the way."

Now he was full-on belly laughing.

"See? We're both pathetic losers. What were we thinking? I mean? You're a Bafta winning actor. I won musical artist of the year. Doesn't mean shit when it all comes down to it. It's the people we love that matter. Remember that when you go all stupid and remember this too. If you love this guy—"

"It's very new."

"Makes no odds. When you know, you know, and every time you mention him, your face lights up like a bloody beacon."

"Yeah." I knew what he was saying.

"You're frustrated because you have to be here with me when all you want to do is go home and get naked with him."

"You're a poor substitute," I joked.

"I'll have you know I was also Mr Surrey in 2019, and you're calling me a poor substitute? I'm offended." He tutted in fake disgust.

"Yeah, and I'm dating Tara Marie." I had no idea where that came from, but he howled.

"Yeah, right." He stood up, dragged me up onto my feet. "Mate, we're going to do this, and do it good. Because you're going to take out all the bullshit and all that frustration on me. Honestly, we're supposed to beat each other up and have hate sex. I need you to beat me up. Use your strength, don't hold back."

"I can't do that." My legs were jumping, and I couldn't stop wringing my hands.

"Yes, you can. We're good at this. We both know how fantastic this scene will be if we get it right. Powell and Rodriguez have been at each other's throats for the entire season. Rodriguez has been taunting him, fucking up his investigation, intimidating his witnesses and soiling his crime scenes with more dead bodies, all while Powell hasn't been able to even get a clear picture of him. He's frustrated—more frustrated than you—and now he's found me, and I'm being a dickhead flirty bastard to him. I don't think a few shoves would cut it in the real world. Go for me. Slam me into that wall. For real."

"Sure way to lose my job," I muttered. He was right, though. The scene was kind of lame the way we were supposed to do it.

"So, I'll go for you, and then you just let it all out. Deep breath. Do it. It'll be good for you, and then we'll just follow on with ripping clothes and getting naked."

"Then we have to fuck afterwards."

"Yeah. But by then you'll be fine, and when we go to break, you're going to ring that boy of yours and have a bit of a pep talk."

I took a deep breath.

"Tobes?"

"Yeah?"

"Thanks for this."

"Sally is kind of useless. Sometimes people just need to level. Thank you for talking to me because now I feel we're chill. We can do this."

"I'm not going to beat you up."

"You're going to give it a bloody good go. I'm not fragile."

"Neither am I."

"We should really have practised it, but I think it'll be better like this. Centre all that frustration in your stomach, then take it out on me. Come on. Let's totally slay this."

He shoved me backwards. Squaring up to me with his chest until I shoved back with mine.

"Bastard," I whipped out.

"I fucking hate you, Powell. Every single one of your witnesses will have a bullet to the brain. The ball is always in my court. Whaddya gonna do?"

"Nothing if you keep putting on that stupid accent," I snarled. He laughed. An evil, horrible laugh.

"I'm up for it. I'm a real dirty bastard, your worst nightmare, and now you finally have me where you need me—"

"Gentlemen, are you two all right?" Sally was finally off her phone.

Toby threw her a dry growl and dragged me back inside.

We took our positions. Waited as my clothes got brushed down.

I shrugged the tension out of my shoulders, stretched my neck. Stared at him as he pretended to chew gum and stuck up two fingers at me.

I would have laughed, but I was back in the zone.

"And Action!"

It felt different this time, my head right where I needed it to be, and Toby was right there with me, egging me on, puffing up his chest more than he'd done in rehearsal, spitting out his lines as I drawled mine back at him. And I did shove him. Hard. Because he was pissing me off. Well, he was pissing Powell off. Rodriguez was all his worst nightmares rolled into one, and I threw him across the room, swung at him. Hurt him, growled out my lines in anger as he fisted my shirt and threw me down onto the desk. Forced his lips onto mine as I kicked him in the balls. Not for real. That bit was in the script, and I landed my knee softly in his thigh as he bent over in pretend pain.

And there it was. That roaring anger. Frustration wasn't even the start of it as I destroyed his shirt, the Velcro in my slacks doing its job as my naked arse was put on display.

Yet there was a tenderness to his kisses as I rolled on top of him, half expecting the *cut!* to come. His hands were rough against my skin, and I welcomed it because this wasn't real. Nothing here mattered.

Yes, I was an actor, and yes, I was a bloody professional at this, but right here, right now, everything seemed to culminate in my head and things just became unbearable. Too much. The tears forming in my eyes were real as he turned me over and held me down, my chest flat against the wooden desk, his lips against my cheek as he whispered the familiar dialogue that I couldn't even take in. His hips shoved against my naked arse, pretending he was inside me. Cass Powell didn't want this. He'd not asked for this. This wasn't right; it wasn't what he wanted. I knew what the scene was supposed to achieve. Cass Powell getting off with his arch enemy. Another triumph for his traitorous dick.

Instead, my Cass Powell was bawling his eyes out as Rodriguez pretend-forced his dick into his arse. Toby was right on top of my back, pushing me down, holding my hands in place as the tabletop cut bruises into my thighs.

Gut-wrenching sobs tore from me.

"And, cut!"

Toby lifted me up. Turned me around and wrapped his arms around me. There were remains of trousers around my feet, and he smelled of make-up and sweat.

"Good job. Really good job," he whispered against my cheek.

"Connor, Toby, fabulous work." That was the director, cutting the deadly silence, which filled with an uncomfortable round of applause.

I was an actor, and this wasn't real, but in a way, it was. I'd finally put something real into that arsehole Cass Powell, who deserved everything Rodriguez had given him. Now all I wanted was to go home and forget that any of this existed.

I skulked off to my trailer with my dressing gown in my arms, then sat there like a fool, waiting for the redness on my face go down.

Picked up my phone and typed words into the text box.

I know I'm supposed to go see Mum, but I don't want to. I feel all kinds of fucked up right now, and I know we should give each other space and all that...

I deleted it and stared at my phone. Grunted in frustration over my inability to know the right thing to do.

I need you.

I couldn't tell you how much my face was burning having sent that. I was childish and needy, and then I laughed out loud.

Who is this?

God. How much of an idiot was I?

Matt, it's me. I'm going crazy here. I just want to come back to yours and lie in your bed and kiss you. I know that's stupid and I need to give you space and all that, and I have no idea what I'm doing still, but I just filmed a difficult scene, and I'm emotional and drained.

Talk about immature word vomiting. My hands shook as I pressed send. He replied straight away. I knew he would.

I'm sat on the sofa watching some cooking show, hugging your hoodie because you're not here and I miss you.

There were the tears again, rolling down my face.

I can't even function when I think of you.

It was true. I couldn't. I couldn't even act like I was normal. And then he replied, and I couldn't stop smiling.

That's why you're my boyfriend.

X

EIGHTEEN

Matt

It was no surprise that he crawled into my bed just after ten that night. I'd half expected it, to be honest. Not that Con had miraculously figured out how to use that phone of his after his surprise emotional outburst this morning, but he'd at least told me he was going to his mum's for dinner. Then, suddenly, here he was, stripping off in the hallway, detouring into the bathroom where the shower went on and off, while I wondered if it was presumptuous to undress or if I should just stay here in my night gear, sleep socks and all.

He threw the wet towel over the bathroom door, letting his feet make sloppy patterns on the floor—something that should have made my teeth clench, but instead I smiled as he rolled naked into bed and made himself comfortable with his damp hair on my chest.

The front of my top was soaking, but I didn't complain. Having him here had again put me in a coma of complete bliss.

"Hello, muffin," I said softly.

"Hello yourself." He smiled. I could feel his cheek muscles contracting against my skin.

"I missed you."

"Yeah. I know the feeling. Mum says hi, she wants to meet you. Said you're welcome to tag along for the weekend, whenever it suits you."

"It's a bit early, perhaps, for meeting the parents."

"Parents...well, you won't meet my sperm donor. But Mum is seriously cool. She'll cook us dinner, ask if you want her to do your laundry, then mock you relentlessly and tell you to do it yourself. I'm kind of nifty with a washing machine. I sort the colours and read the labels and everything."

"Good to know." I giggled, stroking his hair. "So, you told her...about me?"

"Yeah." His hand smoothed down my hip, digging under my waistband until he was cupping my arse.

"You like my arse?" I asked innocently.

"I *love* your arse. And thanks for the bite mark. My make-up artist was scandalised."

"Your bum's rather yummy. Couldn't help myself."

He rubbed his nose against my chest. It was stupid how much I loved that he did little things like that, and how much I loved that I could just grip his arse in return, squeeze all that delicious hard muscle.

"So yeah, I told Mum. She wasn't surprised, you know. About you. She was more concerned about me not having come out to her properly. Told me off for being all sneaky and stupid when I could have just told her. Well, I didn't know."

"Nobody should come out before they're ready."

"No. I know. I had no idea what it would be like, meeting someone who mattered. I mean, you can read all the books you like and watch all the films, but nobody can actually tell you how you're going to feel when you fall in love. It's not all good stuff. It's a lot of weird stuff. Stomach aches. Pining. Bloody anxiety hitting you left, right and centre. I fell asleep on the train back and dreamt that I walked in on you and there was a guy sat in the kitchen. In my chair."

"*Your* chair?"

"Yeah." He laughed nervously. "The one by the window where I sit. Anyway, in the dream, you were all, like, blasé and just went, 'Oh, Conny. This is my next hook-up.'"

"Noooo..." Fuck. I shouldn't have told him about my hook-up...thing.

"And then I woke up and I hated you for about one second until I realised I was sitting on a train and the lady opposite was staring at me."

"She'd probably seen all your naughty bits on TV," I teased.

"Yeah. And. Eh. Sorry for just turning up again."

I didn't know what to say to all of that, so I kissed the top of his head. This was fast. Too fast. High speed on a grand scale, but somehow?

"You never have to apologise. I've lived here for two years, and now all of the sudden, the place feels wrong when you're not in it. I feel wrong."

"I thought about us today. Quite a lot."

"No more hook-ups, OK? I promise. I'm not an arsehole."

"I know you're not. Which is weird because *how* do I know you're not? You could be some huge scam artist—no...wait, a superfan and stalker, and now you're going to tie me to the bed and chop my fingers off or something."

"Wow. You have read far too many novels."

"I was into horror books for a while. Messed with my head. Nightmares and all."

"I promise you, I'm no stalker. I'm a proper normal nerd. I don't do anything naughty or silly or dangerous. Ever."

"Well...you go to the gym?"

"Where I get assaulted by famous actors."

That made him smile and hug me tighter.

"I'd clocked you before, at the gym," I admitted. "I'd recognised you off TV and used to look out for you, watch you do your lines. Sometimes I could kind of make out what was happening, like when you pretended to get into fights. Other times, it looked quite tame, like you were handing out traffic fines or something."

"Detective Powell hasn't handed out a traffic fine in his life."

"Nah. I can't see him doing anything menial like that."

"He's a bit of an arse. I mean, I've always thought they wrote him a little bit too perfect. He always gets the girl, and then he gets the boy too. And the kid. And his colleagues all think he's awesome, and he's shagging his boss on the side and getting away with it. Cass Powell always solves the crime. Yet he's a bloody bastard to everyone around him. Never says a kind word to anyone, and it's been pissing me off for a while. Because if that is the perfect life, what does that make me?"

"Rather observant," I deadpanned. "But I agree. Cass Powell is not a normal bloke. Nobody lives their life like that. I hate to use that word, but...it's a soap opera with guns. Nothing that ever happens to him is realistic."

"I'm kind of...this sounds awful, but...I hope this season will be the last. Just so I can do something else. I've got a play coming up."

"The one that you're naked in?"

"Everyone will be naked in that play. It's a proper gay play in a Queer theatre. Kind of backstreet stuff but with a solid reputation. I went to see one of their plays with Lucia—you know, my agent—and it was really good. Hard hitting and real. Not that I would know, but anyway. Every show is usually sold out, and full nudity is an expectation. Simulated sex. Graphic stuff. I'll have my dick on display. No protective dick socks. No make-up artist to cover all my bodily sins."

"Can I come and see you?"

"You don't have to. You get to see me naked every night anyway."

"Yeah. Not the same. I want to come, to support you. I'd love to, actually."

"Maybe?" He rubbed his nose against my top again, tugged at the fabric until it was shoved up under my chin and then danced his fingers across my chest.

"I scrolled through some of my social media on the train. Pissed me right off. If you ever feel like things are going right, all you need to do is open bloody Twitter, and in seconds, your head feels like it's going to explode."

I may have loved that he was here, but there was a massive warmth spreading through my body. All because he was talking to me. Really talking.

"What pissed you off today then?" I wasn't being flippant about his words. I just didn't want to pry into things that he may not want to tell me. But as I was figuring out, Con had a lot to say.

"The usual. Firstly, half of the people on there think they're my mum. I already have a mother, thank you very much. The other half are pretending to be the fandom-police and educating the world about not sexualising characters on TV. Do they really, honestly think I care? It's a bloody acting gig! Next thing these people are reading dirty fanfiction and getting off to cartoon porn."

"And you read all this?"

"I don't read fanfiction," he said quietly. "I may have looked at some of the cartoon stuff. Kind of funny."

"Christ." I sighed.

"Yeah. And then I get all the vitriol from people who think I'm straight and hate on me because I haven't declared to the world that probably I like a bit of dick as much as the next person. I'm a grown-up. Who the hell comes out with those kinds of things in interviews anyway?"

"Nobody. And as you said, you're an adult. It doesn't matter. All that matters is that you're here. With me."

He looked up, and his smile was infectious. And a little naughty.

"Matt?" He said it slowly with a long 'a'.

"Yes?" He was definitely up to something.

I loved how he looked at me. How his face softened, a small smile forming on his lips.

"Would you mind if I...got you off?"

I choked on my breath, stuttered out a few syllables. He laughed.

"I just want to try. See if I can do the stuff you did to me. If I...hang on."

My top was yanked over my head and hurled across the room as he turned me around and settled in, spooning me as he tugged my pyjama bottoms down, his fingers circling my dick.

"You have such a gorgeous dick. You're just...bloody perfect. I love your body. I love your face. And most of all, you kiss like...I dunno. You. That's what I said to Mum. I told her I'd taken one look at you, and that had been it. That face of yours, and...yeah. That's why I was trying to get you to come out for a meal. Because you were...you were just so...totally..."

He leaned over. Kissed the breath out of me.

"Pretty. Irresistible. And you make me laugh. You only have to be here and I feel so much better. About everything."

"You can always talk to me," I said, shivering as his lips latched onto my neck. He worked his way back up, leaving little soft kisses on my jaw.

"I've never had...someone like this. Never met anyone I wanted to... Someone I wanted to do all these things with."

"What things?" I tried to sound innocent, but my voice was all breathy. It didn't help that he was stroking my dick. Gentle movements, up and down, making my body shiver.

"I can do the front stuff. But I want to do the...back stuff as well."

"Back stuff?" I had to. Even if it was mean. I twisted a little so I could kiss his mouth. "You can do back stuff."

"I don't know how. It's one thing humping someone on set. In reality? I don't want to hurt you."

"You won't. I'll show you if you let me. You need to prep, though. It's not quite as straightforward as just yanking a condom on and doing the deed."

"You like it?"

"When it's with someone you trust, it's amazing. Real. It's not for the faint-hearted, but it makes you feel closer to that other person than anything else in the world."

"Would you...do it to me?"

"Yes. Absolutely. But baby?" I'd never called him that before. Or maybe I had? I'd wanted to, and now, with his mouth on mine while I helplessly humped into his hand, my chest against his, I didn't hold back. His breathing was fast and erratic as I wrapped my hand around his dick.

"Fuck. We need lube."

When we'd done this yesterday, I hadn't dared step out of the moment in case he lost his nerve. He didn't now, just lay there with his mouth open, watching me rummage in the bedside table. I found it and gave it a few pumps into my hand, then did the same with his.

"Now. Both of us. Together."

I didn't have to explain. He lined us up, his abs contracting as he got his hand around our dicks. I added my hand, and then...

Oh God. The sounds coming out of his mouth. I silenced him with sloppy kisses, but I couldn't concentrate and wanted to watch. His hands. His face. Our dicks. His eyes closing as his lips tightened, deep lines forming on his forehead.

Fuck. He was amazing. Our hands now working together, his fingers tangled with mine in hard strokes, up and down, the lube creating that delicious slide as my mind started to tingle.

We were once again doing that messy hand job thing where I was about to fall off the bed and he was pushing pillows onto the floor and the headboard was banging against the wall and I was pretty sure the legs of the bed were about to collapse.

My poor neighbours.

Fuck the neighbours.

I was close. So bloody close.

I wanted him so badly. My body moved closer to his, trying to get under his skin. His cheek pressed against mine, his breath fanned over my face. Everything was turning white and fuzzy around the edges. Just the thought of pushing inside of him, hearing him gasp as he came...

"Harder."

My head was a jumbled mess of chaos. Skin against skin. Words. Noises masquerading as words.

"Faster. Fuck. Faster." My breaths rasped as he once again drove me into madness.

The orgasm still caught me out, making me stiffen up and arch off the bed as I let my seed spill over my stomach with him leaning over me, the wetness from his mouth on my lips, nose tip to nose tip, his forehead against mine.

"Fuck," he whispered.

"Yeah. We just did," I whispered back, trying to get my body back under control. My leg spasmed as my foot got caught in the duvet.

"You're right. You're such a nerd." He kicked out, rescuing my poor foot as the last of the duvet slipped off the bed.

"I know. And you like a bit of dick...just as much as the next person."

"I don't. I only like *your* dick," he murmured into my mouth, then kissed me, long and deep.

"Can I spend the day with you tomorrow?" He sounded out of breath. I know I was and gulped down air. A faint *yes* came out of my mouth as he rolled on top of me and arranged his arms around my body, only letting go so he could retrieve the covers and pillows while I lay there like a muppet, exhausted, filthy, covered in his cum and mine, with a stupid smile on my face.

I love that he asked. That he took nothing for granted here. That he was always aware that he was in my space and grateful to be there.

My space. It would never ever be my space again. With his bags on the floor, his clothes once again flung on my sofa, his flowers wilting in the kitchen, the smell of him on my skin, his head resting on my shoulder as he relaxed into my arms, his hand adjusting the pillow under my neck...

He belonged here as much as I did.

"Can I stay?" he whispered.

"Conny." I kissed his lips. "Muffin. *Baby.*" I clung to him like a needy child. "I love that you're mine."

"So can I?"

"You're so daft. All your stuff has already moved in here. You can't leave me to babysit your laundry. I'm crap at reading laundry labels. I have to buy new shirts all the time because there's always a red sock or something that turns everything pink. I'm with your mum on this one. I obviously needed a well-brought-up boyfriend. You're going to have to get friendly with my washing machine. So you see? Please don't ever leave."

Or was I the daft one? Was I being delusional, thinking this could work. We were so wildly different. He lived in a dreamworld. I lived in a messed-up suburb of London. I had a whole life that he would never fit into.

Yet he did. He fit so effortlessly, and it made me emotional. Even though I'd probably would and turn his expensive designer clothes pink.

I whispered words into his skin. Words I had never told anyone before. It was reckless and crazy and far too soon, but he lapped up those words and said them back. We fit, and if we could just hang on to this feeling, maybe we could figure this out.

He told me I was stupid for even doubting myself. I laughed and kissed him again.

Then I fell asleep with his arms around me, his chest moving against my back.

And I wondered if fairy tales actually came true. Or if we were going to crash and burn.

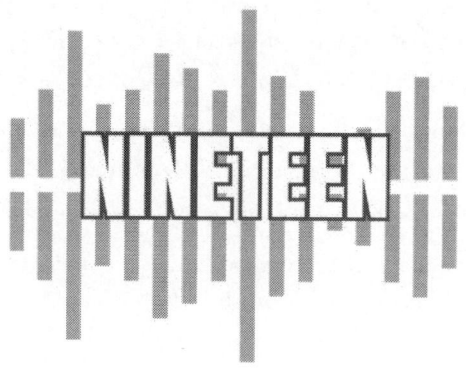

Con

I'd wanted to spend Sunday in bed with Matt, figure out this sex thing. I'd kind of imagined rolling onto set on Monday morning, a virgin no more. But that was clearly a fantasy Cass Powell kind of thing, and Con Telford had no clue. Life didn't work like that.

Instead, Matt and I were in his dad's car, on our way to Matt's parents' house to have dinner.

Fuck my life.

I'd wanted to say no when he'd suggested it. I was nowhere ready for this. Neither was Matt, sitting in the front seat, his leg bouncing nervously as his dad cast weird glances at me in the rear-view mirror.

"So, you're an actor?" he asked politely. I'd shaken his hand when he'd picked us up, but these were the first words he'd spoken.

Matt looked nothing like his dad—well, apart from some kind of murderous streak in his eyes.

"Dad, you've never watched TV in your life, so you wouldn't know Con's work anyway. He's just a normal bloke, OK?"

I wasn't. I was ready to crap myself, to be honest, nodding awkwardly in the back seat.

"So no movies? Just TV?" Matt's dad continued.

"I've done quite a few movies, mostly small parts, you know? Playing the random person in the background. But I've mostly done work for TV, and I've got a run coming up on stage. Theatre work."

I had no idea what I was saying, and this was not an interview.

"Documentaries? Audiobooks?" He clearly had no idea of who I was or my line of work.

"He's won awards, Dad, but that doesn't mean he needs an interrogation. I'm nervous enough as it is."

Yeah, thanks for that, Matt. Now I was squirming.

"He's never brought anyone home before, our Matt. We know he's dated a bit, but you're the first...boyfriend."

Matt banged his head on the side window, groaning.

"I'm honoured." I grinned. Then I met Matt's dad's eyes in the rear-view mirror and wiped my grin off my face. He was kind of terrifying. *This* was terrifying. "I've done some really scary auditions, but I have to say, meeting Matt's family beats them all."

Gulp. What on earth did I say that for?

Matt twisted around in his seat belt and stretched his hand towards me. I reached out and grabbed it. Tried to breathe normally.

"It'll be fine. We're just having a barbecue. My mum's a really good cook. My sister won't be there. Just my little brother, I think. Is Ollie at home, Dad?"

"Who knows? I have no idea what to do with him. He's always out with his mates, going to events and parties and stuff." His dad made eye contact with me. "My youngest is apparently at university, but I have yet to see a single textbook or exam result."

"Sounds like university to me," I replied politely. "Not that I ever went. I should. I want to study something, but I've worked since I was thirteen, and now I have no idea what to do with the rest of my life."

OK. I had to stop this. I wasn't the socialising kind, obviously, meeting new people and straight away talking like I was being interviewed by some high-end magazine. I wanted to sink into the back seat and beg Matt to just stop the car and take me home.

I could socialise when there was a script, like I'd done at the fashion show in Italy a few months back. I'd been dressed up like a doll, told what to do, where to stand, who to talk to—even where to dance so there'd be footage of a bunch of twatty actors pretending to be best mates with a bunch of girls giggling in the background.

I did know two of those actors, vaguely, but the rest were strangers. Even so, we'd hugged and grinned and flopped around pretending to have the most brilliant time when all I'd wanted to do was go home.

Also, I couldn't dance. I had no control over my limbs where music was concerned. Lucia had made me audition for a musical once. Yeah. It went about as well as you'd expect.

"Conny?" Matt was waving his hand in front of my face. I'd drifted off into my own world again. "Dad was asking if you're going to be the next James Bond."

"It's the only film I have ever watched." Matt's dad looked strangely apologetic. "Not much of a cinema buff, I'm afraid."

"I doubt it." I laughed. "I'm not quite in that league."

"You OK?" Matt mouthed at me, once again reaching out his hand, which was why I was so bloody besotted with him. He understood when I got nervous and knew that just holding his hand would make things better.

He kept the conversation with his dad away from me for a bit, giving me another break from having to think. It was bad enough being crammed in the backseat of a small car, but at the same time, it was normal. Comforting.

No expectations.

Who was I kidding? *All* the expectations.

We pulled up along a narrow street, Matt's dad swearing under his breath as he tried to find somewhere to park. At least this bit was familiar, as Mum and I did it all the time. You could be an award-winning actor all you wanted; it still didn't mean you'd magically find parking.

But then we got out, and suddenly I was standing in a hallway, having to air kiss Matt's mother and pretend I wasn't being stared at by a younger version of Matt. And this wasn't just ordinary staring. This was proper, judgy, found-shit-on-his-shoe staring.

"Who the hell are you?" he demanded.

Rude! But I was kind of taking up the entire hallway.

Matt laughed and stroked my arm protectively.

"Ollie, this is Conny. Be nice."

"You look just like that guy off TV. The idiot who's naked in every episode."

Oh. So we were doing honesty here. OK.

"Yep. It's in my contract. *Must not wear clothes.*"

I was giving as good as I got, and Matt's brother just laughed.

"No wonder Matt likes you then. He's totally gay. I'm bi myself, so yeah, I appreciated the nudity in that show, but seriously, dude. You're him? For real?"

"Is that a bad thing?"

"Oliver, let Conny come in and grab a drink. We don't bombard our guests with personal questions in the hallway." That had to be Matt's mum.

Conny. So I was Conny then. Nice.

Evidently, Matt's brother wasn't about to give up on interrogating me, as he pushed me out in the back garden, pointed at a seat and handed me a glass of water.

"So you're Matt's boyfriend, and you're a famous actor."

"Yup." I was desperately looking for Matt, but he seemed to have disappeared, and now I was stuck with his brother, who pulled up a seat next to me.

"Why?"

"Why what?" I wasn't prepared for this. At all.

"My brother is nobody. He's, like, some Year 8 teacher and a total nerd. Why would you even consider dating him?"

"None of your business," came out of my mouth. Because I was an idiot.

"Totally my business. Our sister won't even come over and meet you because she thinks this is ridiculous."

"Y..." Fuck. Brain. Think. "You can't help who you fall in love with."

Ollie grinned. "You've read too many self-help books, mate. Trust me. I have too. It's bad enough growing up with the gayest big brother on earth and a sister...well, you know what big sisters are like. She acts like she knows everything, and then, when you're trying to figure out the most life-changing moments? Turns out she knows shit. Apparently, I'm just the kid who can't make my mind up about anything."

OK. I wasn't following him, but he shuffled his chair closer to mine.

"Matt is Matt. And he deserves better than some idiot who'll shag him and leave him. Then he'll come here and sit and cry in the garden when you break his heart, and I'll have to deal with all his whining. So just fucking...don't."

"OK. Ollie? It *is* Ollie, isn't it?" I was trying here, but I was leaning forward trying to make myself a little more intimidating than I actually was. "Matt is my boyfriend, and

I don't care what anyone else says, he's...mine. I have absolutely no intention of leaving him or breaking his heart. If anyone will leave anyone, it'll be Matt dumping me because I have no idea about anything. Apart from that—"

"Dude. You're dating Tara Marie." His face was a picture. Triumph. Superiority. I laughed.

Funnily enough, he laughed too.

"Hey, I had to say it. I know it's all bullshit. My mate knows her from school, and she's not into men. At all. Nice girl, though. Plus, she's got a girlfriend, so don't even try to pull anything on me." He pointed at his head. "Little brothers know everything. Big sisters think they know it all, but us littluns are the one with all the information. The gossip. All those convenient truths that we can use—"

"To blackmail people with. Dude. Chill. I'm not dating Tara. I'm dating your brother—if I survive long enough. I'm sat here half thinking you'll stab me with those kebab skewers if I even dare to move."

"I would. I'm very protective of my brother. Matt's cool, but he's not good with getting boyfriends, even if he's, like, kind of handsome. Not as handsome as me, though."

"Have you got someone special in your life?" I asked carefully because those skewers looked sharp. Before he could answer, Matt's mum arrived with a platter of salads and stared at Ollie in disgust.

"Water, Oliver? Is that all you offered our guest?"

"Nothing wrong with water, Mum. Anyway, I had to talk to Conny here because—"

"Conny darling, can I offer you some wine? A beer? We have soft drinks. Juice?"

"Mum used to be a flight attendant. Can you tell? Next thing she'll be offering you tiny packets of snacks and showing you the emergency exits. She gave up her career to marry Dad. Wrong move if you ask me. I mean, she was travelling the world, and now she's stuck at home with a bunch of queer kids squatting in her house, doing accountancy work on the side."

"I'm sure accountancy work is very fulfilling." I had no idea who had written this script, but it was becoming more surreal by the minute.

"Accountancy work is what pays your uni fees, young man, so if I were you, I'd be very careful what comes out of your mouth."

I think I liked Matt's mum.

"Ha!" Ollie laughed, leaning closer to me. "I'm getting a student loan next term, so she can't threaten to evict me out of my own home."

"If you're not careful, I'll evict you myself." Matt was back, his hands on my shoulders. It was funny how that suddenly made me relax. "It used to be my room, and now Ollie uses it as his own personal shag pad."

"Boudoir, thank you very much." Ollie tutted. "I'm a language student. French and Spanish."

"Boudoir? Oh dear. I never even got kissed in that room, and from what Mum tells me, there's some serious action happening at the weekends. Dad had to go buy those...what was it?"

"Noise-cancelling headphones," Matt's mum filled in. "Conny, please don't judge us. Matthew and Emily were such good kids, we had no issues at all with them growing up. Then we had Ollie, and I have no idea where we went wrong, because as you can no doubt tell, we have totally lost control."

"Mum, I'm nineteen. It's not like you're supposed to have control."

"Matt, can you please take Ollie away from here, find him a place to live? Somewhere where he can have parties without us needing to install extra insulation in the walls?"

Matt's dad took a seat next to me. I laughed as he handed me another glass of water.

"I'd offer you something stronger, but Matt says you don't drink."

"I do, but I kind of...prefer not to."

"The rock 'n' roll lifestyle." Ollie nodded. "Have you been to rehab then? Done your wild and wacky years partying with the rich and famous?"

I didn't know if I liked him or wanted to slap him. Not that I would, but Matt did. He whacked him over the head and told him to shut up.

"No rehab. Trust me, my life is so boring that they haven't even written the unofficial autobiography on me. It would be, like, two pages. Connor was born and then he just worked."

"Then he met Matt and lived happily ever after, which got boring, so he handed over all his money and fame to one Oliver Winston, who became the most famous actor ever."

OK. It was official. Matt's little brother was slightly unhinged.

"You want to be an actor?" I asked. Unexpectedly, I was enjoying myself.

"God, no. I want to be a rockstar. Play the guitar and dominate the music scene. Only one problem."

"He doesn't play the guitar." Matt smirked. "And he's too lazy to learn."

"Yup. That's me. So, my next plan for world domination is becoming an influencer. I'll just live in my bed, study remotely and have as much sex as possible while raking in sponsorship deals."

"See what I have to put up with?" Matt's mum said. Matt's dad laughed.

"I was exactly the same. At his age, I was backpacking around the world and smoking far too much...of that naughty stuff. And do you know where that got me?"

"No?" I wasn't sure I wanted to know.

"It got me right here. Married to the prettiest flight attendant in the world. And then...yeah. Not sure what happened with the kids, but I'll tell you one thing. I'm so bloody proud of them. Even the youngest, messiest one here. These kids are mine, and I'll love them until the day I die. One day, you'll have kids, and you'll know exactly how I feel."

"Despite us all being a bunch of losers," Ollie said.

"Absolutely."

Matt laughed. "We haven't lived unless we've gone backpacking and done drugs and been robbed at least once."

"Life skills," Matt's dad said, laughing.

"In that case, I'm the biggest loser here." I laughed too.

Oddly, none of them believed me.

I was dragged around the house for a tour after dinner, a younger Matt grinning from the photos on the walls.

"So you never even got kissed in this house?" I teased, hoping he'd let me. It was one thing being away from Matt all day, another being with him and not getting to kiss or touch him.

Dammit, I wanted to drag him into the toilet and see if I could get a sneaky hand job out of him. My dick wasn't playing nice. Matt must've picked up on it, as he stared at me for a minute and then put his hand over my mouth.

"Don't," he whispered. "Don't even think about it."

"What?" I was as bad as Ollie, playing innocent when I was anything but. I'd heard it all now. Ollie had a boyfriend *and* a girlfriend, and they were all chill with that. There had been threesomes too.

Cass Powell had had threesomes. Too many hands and feet and legs, in my opinion, and I hadn't even known which one Cass was supposed to be in love with. I doubted he'd ever been in love with anyone because the looks actor-me dished out didn't match anything I felt with Matt. Threesomes, though. Nope. Complicated angles and stilted dialogue. I'd kneed the female actor in the thigh, and she'd put in a complaint about me being hopeless with the choreography.

Fuck. I was usually better with my moves, but today, it seemed I had none at all because while I had been lost in my thoughts, Matt had dragged me into Ollie's room.

"This used to be my room. It's not anymore, and ugh, it really does stink in here."

"It does," I had to agree and made a mental note to clean my own room before subjecting Matt to my humble teen self and his very poor cleaning habits.

"I never brought any boyfriends home here. It was like a total safe zone. Just me. Friends coming over sometimes, but nothing else. I did wank a lot in that bed, though."

"Matt." I sighed. I could kind of imagine him, all alone here and dreaming of something he never thought he would have. Like me. I used to dream of fame and fortune.

I had the fame, and my bank account was healthy, but I still didn't feel like I'd succeeded. Not in any shape or form.

I'd also wanked. God. More than I wanted to remember.

"Wanna snog me in my room? Just so I can tell Ollie we fucked on his bed."

"You wouldn't! It's his room?"

Matt laughed. "I wouldn't. But I will, one day. Fuck you, I mean. Just so you know."

"Matt," I whispered. I couldn't find any words to respond to that. I wanted to. But then he kissed me and I kind of lost all control. I lifted him up and wrapped my arms around his bum as his legs hooked behind my back.

He was heavier than I'd anticipated. He was a tall bloke, and I wasn't a body builder. The bounce into the back of the door that slammed itself shut was louder than I'd anticipated, but Matt just laughed in my arms.

"You're crazy."

"I know."

Then his lips were on mine, and his clothes smelled of smoke and outdoors, so I dug my face into his neck and just breathed.

I loved his skin against mine. I loved that he let me do this, even as his legs slid back down on the floor, his weight now pushing me harder into the door.

"After dessert, I'm ordering an Uber to take us home. Mum and Dad think you're brilliant, but I however much I love being home, I think you need to go to bed."

"Why? Because I'm tired?" I laughed and decided I really didn't like Ollie. His behaviour had rubbed off on me, and my brain had gone all stupid.

"Yes. You're very tired, muffin, and we have work tomorrow."

He winked. I winked back.

"So we're going home to bed."

"Yup."

"And in bed...?"

"*Before* we even get into bed, I intend to have you naked and desperate."

I'd give him naked and desperate.

I was definitely desperate by the time the Uber pulled up outside Matt's flat. Desperate enough that I probably looked off my face in the picture the driver asked if he could take with me for his daughter. Yeah, right. It was always for someone else. A son. A cousin. The wife loves you, mate.

Matt hadn't said a word the whole way home. Just sat in the back looking out the window, holding my hand.

I got it. Had he looked at me, things would not have ended well. Still, we made it up the stairs and Matt put his key in the door. I followed him, closing the door gently behind me. And then he was ripping at my clothes while I was kicking off my shoes, and his head got stuck in his T-shirt as I got ahead of myself and started kissing his shoulders, and then he bloody bit me on the shoulder because I tried to grab his dick through his shorts.

This was not a film shoot, and thank God for that, as we tumbled clumsily down the hallway, bouncing off the walls with him trying to climb me, and I had his arse in my hands, but my dick was getting none of that lovely friction I'd craved all day.

"Want you to come when you fuck me," he murmured into my ear.

The sound that came out of my mouth was pathetic, a slow whine as he dragged a fingernail up my chest and smoothed his palm over my pec. I shivered and tried to breathe.

"You OK?" he asked softly.

I couldn't even look at him, so I grabbed my dick, held it. Whined again.

"Come on, muffin, let's get you laid."

I loved that he took charge. That I didn't even have to think because he just knew. I trusted him to know what I needed, and I needed all of this. His breath against my skin as he kissed down my chest. The scent of his sheets all around me. His bed that had become more than a home. This was the place where I could relax, where my breaths didn't hurt when they left my lungs. Where life was simple and full of him.

Where his face was now down in my groin, his cheek stroking my dick or the other way around. I didn't know which, but my dick throbbing, sending shudders through my entire body.

"I love you," he said. "It's stupid and too soon, but when I'm with you, those words make more sense than anything else.

"I love you too," I huffed out. It wasn't easy to speak when his mouth was suddenly around my dick and there was all this warmth and fire in my body that I was only just learning to control. To use. To share. I flipped him over as soon as he came up for air and climbed on top of him, trying to get my mouth everywhere at once. On his lips, his face, his chest, sucking on one of those nipples as my hand travelled down over his hips, the other fisting his hair.

I needed it all. All at once. All of him and all of me. All of this, in this strange dance of being us.

He smiled and arched off the bed so I could get closer. "Let's get you slicked up because I'm gonna come if you keep on licking my nipples. They're very sensitive. And I kind of...ahgrhg..."

OK. Good to know. I moved up, flicking my tongue across his neck then back down to the other nipple, which hardened as soon as I got my mouth on it. Little things like that—who would have known? I whined again and had to hang on to my dick as Matt reached over and grabbed the lube.

"Condom?" I asked.

"Need one?" He wasn't mocking me, but I still felt stupid.

"Well, I've been on PreP for years, and I've always used condoms with hook-ups. I got tested after the last time I got laid, but if it makes you feel better, we can use a condom." He was already leaning over towards the bedside table, and my hand was already tugging at him to come back.

To me.

I wanted this, and he did too. I wasn't going to question things that didn't need questioning. The whole thing was so surreal that all I could do was smile and wrap my arms around him, hold him against me as we just breathed.

"I don't want this to end," I said. I had no idea where it came from.

"What to end? I just want to have sex with you, but stamina is a thing, muffin."

"I love that you call me that. Muffin. It's such a silly name, but it makes me...I don't know...happy? I want to do this forever. Be with you. Have you lie with me on this bed. I want this to last, and it's making me all panicky that I don't know how to do that. How to...make you fall in love with me and want to be with me when I'm just this big clueless oaf who has no idea how to even start making you happy."

"You already make me happy," he said quietly. "You make me happy by just saying that. And there's no need to panic with me. I'm right here. Always right here. You'd have to do something pretty stupid to make me give up on you."

"How stupid?" I got out before my brain went into melt down. It was hard to think with his expert hands smearing lube all over my dick. I groaned at the sensation of his fingertips firmly moving up and down.

"You've never done this?" He already knew the answer, which was as well. I didn't have the oxygen to reply, small gasps coming out of my mouth as he squirted more lube into his hand and then straddled me, so he was sitting on my stomach. Well. Not sitting as such. My stomach was full of food and my head was full of static, and his dick was just there, proud and erect, smooth skin in a bed of dark curls. So I stroked it, taking it fully in my grip. He rewarded me with a squirt of lube at the tip, one I made full use of. Like a pro.

I was no pro. But I was happy we hadn't done this the first time around. Or the second. Now, though?

"One day, I will ask you do to this for me. But right now... Conny, I want you inside me...ahhhh..."

His hand was behind his back, and he was humping into my grip. My neck stretched as my dick caught his arse. More lube. I had no idea what he was doing, apart from that my dick was now getting the full treatment from his hand and he was making cute little huffing noises. I wanted to watch, yet all I could do was feel. Groan. Want. Need.

His hand pulled up, squeezing my foreskin together over the tip of my cock, lube bloody everywhere, then he was right there, and...and...

There were no more words left in my head to describe what we were doing. But I suppose that was sex—when words didn't matter anymore and all that was left was feelings. A massive sense of pressure around my dick. A smooth warmth. More pressure. Those sounds he was making, pushing down onto my length. I was watching now in complete awe, my mouth wide open as I felt myself disappear inside of him. My hands grasped at his hips as he groaned.

"Fuck, you're big. Everyone wants a big cock, and then when you get the perfect cock, you kind of go...damn...ugh...oh, fuck."

I loved that he always talked to me, made me smile when I couldn't even function.

"You OK?" I asked as his head hung between his shoulders. I smoothed dark curls away from his face.

"Yeah. Just need a minute...to adjust...I mean...ugh...fuck...fuck you and your huge cock."

"My cock is very normal." My cock was anything but normal. It was happily pulsing inside of him, and the urge to just flip him over was overwhelming. Yet if I did that, I'd have no idea what to do, so I waited patiently while he did whatever he was doing.

Then he moved, and fuck and hell and the devil and shit and all that. I think all those words came tumbling out of my mouth as he rose up and sat back down. I fisted the sheets, pretty sure my dick was screaming with joy, as he fell forward and kissed me.

So this was sex. Fuck-sex. With his mouth clamped on mine, my hands flew to his arse. Somehow, somehow my legs were arched up and my heels were digging into the bed, and my dick was...was doing things I had no idea how to do. My hips sang in exhaustion, and his arse was just...

We were having sex. Real sex. Him on top of me, my dick inside of him, and I couldn't...

"I can't..." I slobbered out as he suddenly made a noise that was so obvious even I could read it. There was wet stuff on my stomach, and he was all tensed up and I was...well, I was rather proud even thinking the word, but I was still fucking him. Me. Inside of him. And he was beautiful. *This* was beautiful. This was my idea of...

He'd said he loved it because it made him feel close.

Close was nowhere near enough. I grabbed his sides and pulled him to me, held him as hard as I could as my hips made their last thrusts, in and out, as I moaned into his hair. He was right here with me, clawing at my arms as I started to lose my mind.

Everything went black. Totally black. I was in that state where I was barely conscious, caught between pleasure and pain as I shook my way through an orgasm. A real one. A sex-induced one.

My body spasmed into something I couldn't control. More like a death knell. I didn't know what was up. Nothing was down. The sky was black, and he was right there as my breath hitched with every attempt at getting oxygen back into my lungs.

"M...att...I..."

He shook his head.

"I get it. I get what you were saying," he whispered into my chest. "I don't know how to make this last either, but I never...bloody ever...want to not have you in my life. I need you. Conny. Promise me we'll at least try to do this."

"I think we just did," I whispered back. "I want to be this close to you. Always." I wasn't sure I was making sense, but somehow, I didn't think it mattered.

My softening dick was sliding, and I almost yelped in disappointment, grabbing his arse and trying to stay inside of him. Just a little longer.

I never wanted this to end. Ever. I only wanted this. Him. Here. Where the sun was still shining, and our bed was a mess, and our clothes were all over the floor and the flowers in the bucket on the table had started to wilt.

Because if this was what my life was going to be like?

I'd take it. All of it.

Matt

I never thought we would, but we did. And it was bloody horrible.

I came home from work to find that the bed was as I'd left it. Messy duvet half on the floor and pillows in all the wrong places. The sheets were empty and cold.

I could live with that.

But his bag was no longer on the floor and all his clothes were gone.

If that wasn't cruel enough, that twatty suit was still hanging over the bathroom door and the scent of him was everywhere. The flowers in the bucket now smelled sour as I walked around in a complete panic.

I hadn't heard from him all day. Nothing unusual there. Con wasn't a communicator, and I hadn't wanted to push, but he could have said something. Anything. Left a note.

I gave up on the silent screaming I'd had going on since I'd got in and instead roared into the fridge, where the idiotic pink gin sat smugly in its fancy bottle. I wanted to tip it all away, smash that stupid bottle to shards in the sink.

I didn't. Because I had no idea what to do. The shock of it all was debilitating. Paralysing.

He could have gone to the gym.

But then he wouldn't have taken all his clothes. There were no dirty underpants in the laundry basket, no shoes by the door.

It hurt my head more than I wanted to admit.

I'd known this was coming. I just hadn't expected it so soon.

I couldn't even think back to yesterday without cringing. Fuck. It had been too much, obviously. Meeting the family. Then I'd forced him to have sex. Or had I? I couldn't make sense of the muddled memories in my head.

I ripped the suit off the door and kicked it violently into the bathroom. I had no idea why, but...

FUCK!

OK. I needed to ring him. Get answers. I shouted into thin air, undressing as I ranted, dumping my suit jacket in a heap on the bed. My tie landed in the flowers. I couldn't be bothered to rescue it. I stepped out of my trousers and fury took over.

Grabbing the bucket, I thundered down the stairs in my underpants. I took great pleasure in dumping the stupid greenery in the bin, letting the lid close with a satisfying slam.

Then I shivered in unease, standing there with just my shirt covering my bare legs, my socks no protection from the gravel beneath my feet.

I was losing it. That was clear.

My head was spinning with insane thoughts. What if he'd had an accident? No. He hadn't. He wouldn't have taken all his clothes to a random car crash. I made no sense. This made no sense. Why the hell wasn't he here? What on earth was going on in his head to make him...bloody leave me?

He wasn't coming back. That suit was probably loose change for someone like Con Telford. And me? I'd been an expendable little experiment. Someone to have a bit of a laugh with.

WHAT THE HELL DO I DO NOW?

I didn't know. Normally, I'd have gone to the gym. Made some food. Instead, I slumped on the sofa and tried to breathe.

Fuck.

I hadn't expected this. I didn't want this. Con Telford was an arsehole, and I was a bloody fool.

I never swore, but I couldn't stop the filth spilling from my mouth, sentences that made me want to put myself straight in detention.

Outside, the sky was blue, the evening sun was shining, birds were singing somewhere far away, and yet the air around me was strangling me. The whole flat felt pitch-black.

Nothing made sense.

I made a desperate dash for the washing machine, only to find that empty as well. I slammed it shut and kicked at the metal in despair.

Then my phone rang, and I picked it up in a panic.

"Conny?"

"Hold your horses." Nope. Ollie.

"Ollie, I can't talk." My mouth was dry as I tried to form words.

"Why?" Typical Ollie. Couldn't take a hint. Ever.

"I just need...no. No, Ollie. Whatever you want, it's a no."

I couldn't deal with my brother. Not today.

"I just tried calling Conny," he said.

My heart jolted in some kind of fear.

"What?"

"Yeah. Swiped his number from your phone because that is one seriously cool number to have. He mentioned football, so I was going to ask him to come play next weekend. Like, you know, Sunday lunch football combo kind of thing."

I said nothing.

"Matt?"

My stomach hurt. I hurt. Every bloody breath came out wrong.

"He left."

There. I'd said it. Another twist of the imaginary knife in my chest.

"Bullshit," Ollie said. "What makes you think that?"

I wasn't going to cry. I wasn't going to cry. I was stronger than this.

"He took his clothes, and he's not here anymore."

"Matt, he has a home. He must have gone home. He's allowed to go home."

Yeah. I was an idiot. He didn't need to remind me.

I swallowed.

"Conny is a nice guy," Ollie went on. "So, there's something you're not telling me here."

Trust him to talk me down. He was nineteen. It should've been me teaching him all about life, supporting and gently guiding him through his heartbreaks and infatuations. Yet here he was, and I could almost hear him rolling his eyes. Well, watch him actually. We were in the twenty-first century, after all. I accepted his video call request, even though I didn't really want to.

"OK. Talk, Matt, because you're being stupid here."

"I'm not." My chest was doing strange things, and I didn't even know where to start.

"Did you let him fuck you?"

"Ollie!"

"What? That's what you always told me. Don't let them fuck you because then all the fun is over. String them along. Make them work for it."

"I never said that!" I protested.

"Well, maybe not, but we both know how this works. So he fucked you and then fucked off. Doesn't sound like Conny at all."

"You don't even know him!" I wasn't sure why I was defending him. I was angry, beyond ashamed, and my little brother just laughed.

"I'll ring you back," he said. He hung up.

I frantically jabbed at the phone and brought up Con's number—only because I didn't want Ollie to get to him first because what if he hadn't left? What if I was just...

It went straight to voicemail.

I wasn't having that.

My fingers shook as I tried again.

Nothing.

I jumped out of my skin when my phone rang. Ollie again.

"What?" I snapped.

"You're such an idiot."

Sometimes I loved my little brother. Sometimes I wanted to strangle him.

"OK. I googled that show. The production set is at Shepperton, but they mostly film on location. The main set is about twenty minutes from you, but they also use several other sites."

"And?" I wasn't following, and my hands were shaking to the point that I could barely hold the phone, despite him laughing at me.

"Follow *White Noise* production on Insta. Someone posts daily set updates. You would think your boyfriend would tell you these things. They had to dash to Norfolk today to reshoot something, and the weather is closing in up there, so. Yeah. Your boyfriend is in Norfolk for the week. With all his clothes. And you have egg on your face because he's probably on some kind of NDA ban and can't use his phone. Not even to text you. Or something."

"Ollie," I whined.

"Conny is a nice bloke. And bonus points for the shagging. Kudos. He's, like, mega famous."

"I hate you."

"No, you don't," Ollie replied smugly but with a smile. "You need to ring your Conny and get him to come over for lunch on Sunday. I've kind of told everyone he'll come. I'm the one who'll have egg on my face if he doesn't."

I flailed, tried to breathe. In and out. It wasn't relief flowing through me, it was need. Desperate, stupid need just to hear his voice.

I slammed the phone down on Ollie and rang Con. Voicemail again. I hoped Ollie was right about the NDA ban.

I attempted some work. Ironed my shirt. Tried to remember what I'd done with my time pre-Con. I had no idea.

I put on the TV and loaded up *White Noise*. Season five.

It hurt listening to him because it wasn't him. I barely recognised the man on the screen because my Conny didn't speak like that. The intonation was wrong. The words were different. Even his breathing seemed to come from someone else, and there was definitely something wrong with me because suddenly I hurled the remote control across the room, screaming at the frozen picture on my TV of some woman gasping as Detective Cass Powell cupped her breasts.

Everything was wrong.

I had a shower. Tried not to cry. Wondered how I'd ever got myself into this mess. In this state, I doubted I'd be able to stand in front of my form group in the morning.

I was scared. Terrified. I didn't want to believe anything my head was telling me. In desperation, I looked up the *White Noise* Insta account, and there he was, looking pissed off and tired. If I'd been in his shoes...

Fuck.

I went to bed and lay there, pathetically awake, watching the headlights of passing cars flit across the ceiling.

I hadn't cried. Yet.

My phone was silent, mocking me with that screen void of notifications. I hated that I was like this. Needy and possessive. Overbearing. I looked up that photo again, his face stern, his stubble noticeable. I wished he was here with me.

He wasn't, though.

I almost fell off the bed when my phone lit up.

Incoming call. Unknown number.

"Hello?" I answered in a shaky voice.

"Matt?"

"Yeah."

We were both silent for a moment. My heart was racing.

"Sorry. I was going to ring you, but today turned out to be an absolute shitshow."

"OK?" God. What was I supposed to say?

"Are you OK?"

Was I OK? No. I was not, but I nodded into the receiver. Pointlessly. His voice was coming from a blank screen.

"I'd completely forgotten to check my phone, and then my driver was outside the hotel this morning, and I had to pack in a hurry, and then I spent the entire car trip up here memorising a brand-new script. I didn't want to disturb you when you were working, and by the time you weren't, I couldn't find my phone. I think it's locked in the hair and make-up trailer, and I'm in a hotel by the beach and it's raining like crazy, and I miss you."

Now I wanted to cry. All the awful feelings from today came crashing down like a hailstorm. I clung to the phone and tried to speak, but I couldn't.

"Whose phone is this then?" I hacked out, trying to wipe my eyes with the duvet.

"My driver, Dave. Lucky for me, I'd memorised your number. I'll text you when I get mine back. We're filming some stupid scene with me standing on top of a cliff at like fuck-this o'clock in the morning and then something else. I just want to come home. I mean, I knew this was coming up, but it was supposed to be weeks away. Then everything got changed around. I never used to mind, but now I have you..."

"Yeah?"

I waited silently as he breathed.

"I don't like being so far away from you."

"I know," I said, my chest warming. I hadn't realised how much I'd needed those words to come from him. Well, anything really. Just having his voice in my ear had soothed a million worries. "We're adults," I said matter-of-factly, like I hadn't been through a total meltdown today. "Sometimes work will take us away. I have a conference in autumn. Two days in a hotel."

"I suppose I can...deal with that."

"And you'll be doing this theatre thing."

"I have a driver. I'll be coming back to you every night. I'll probably drive you mad waking you up in the early hours, but I'm looking forward to not having to get up at the arse-crack of dawn like I am now."

"When are you back?" I hated not knowing.

"Two weeks." The way he almost whispered, it could have been two years. "I asked Aisha if she could bring you up here on Friday so I could at least see you, but we're shooting all weekend too. It would be awful for you, stuck in my trailer for days in the rain. Good weather for the show, though. I'm going to be caked in mud looking for bodies all week. Fun times."

"You're crazy. Your life is crazy."

"Even crazier when I have you," he said softly.

"My deranged brother has left a load of messages on your phone. Something about football."

"Oh." He giggled and snorted. I loved that sound. For a moment, it was like he was right here beside me.

"I'll have to text him too then."

"He said you're dead famous and that all his mates will be super jealous that he knows you. Swiped your number from my phone."

"The little shit."

Yeah. I laughed too. Funny how everything was suddenly brighter now.

Two weeks. I could survive two weeks, couldn't I?

"Conny?"

"Yeah?"

"We can do this. Can't we?"

"Of course we can. I'm not giving up on you."

"So...we just have to have phone sex now?"

He laughed. Coughed. Tried to compose himself. It didn't sound like he was having much success.

"Matt, we're not having phone sex on Dave's phone, but bear with me. If I get signal on top of that cliff tomorrow morning, I might treat you to...well. I don't know."

"Don't fall off that cliff!" I growled.

"I promise." He was smiling. I could hear it.

"I love you," he said, and I smiled and said it back, then sank into my pillows, tucking the duvet under my chin the way he always did, and stared out the window. The sky outside was dark, but my room was full of light.

Con

I hated how I felt, and the worst thing was I didn't know how to fix it.

Well, I did, but that would involve running away from set and becoming that ridiculous diva person I had promised myself I would never become. I was a responsible human being, and I would not force Dave the driver to take me to London on a whim. I also knew how much trouble I'd be in if I did, even though the car was right outside my hotel room, so in theory, I didn't even need Dave. Except I didn't have a driving licence. Something that had never bothered me before but did now. I was a grown-up, and I was...I didn't even know what I was, apart from an idiot.

Matt had been upset with me; it didn't take a genius to figure out why. It wasn't the same talking to him over the phone, so I had kind of...not called him, which was a dick move, and I would've been pissed off with me too if I'd been him.

Now it was Sunday. We'd been here a week, and I still didn't know what the hell we were doing. I'd had my phone back for days and was sitting on the bed in the room, the week ahead already turning into all my worst nightmares since the light was perfect. I'd barely had any sleep, and now they wanted to drive Caroline and me out to some bog again so they could film us crawling in mud in the dark.

Our director had lost the plot, and I wasn't the only one complaining. Aisha was too. And she was supposed to knock.

"Normal people knock," I snarled at her as she flung the door open and walked into my room. I was not in the mood.

"Yeah, they do, but we're not normal people. Caroline is threatening to contact the union. I'm dangerously tired, and I don't care if you're Kit...whatever his name is...the one with the hair, muscles, brooding face..."

"Connor?" I suggested.

"No...no, the other one."

"Which other one?" My mind was just fog.

She flopped down next to me on the bed. "This is your thirty-five-minute warning. They want us in the car and rolling. The light's fading."

"I can barely move." Truth. I was cold and aching, despite the long shower I'd had. The day had been too long. My body had had enough. *I'd* had enough, and I'd already typed *I love you* to send to Matt but hadn't pressed send. I was just so tired.

"Don't lose your phone again. It's not in my job description to run around asking everyone if they've seen a phone in a nondescript cover with a nondescript background photo. Your phone is, like, the blandest thing I've ever seen." She waved her own phone in my face, the cover full of stickers with too many things hanging off it.

"Suppose that's me. Nondescript." I sighed. I had no idea why we were talking about phones. None whatsoever.

"You're not. You're Con. But you are kind of bland. At least, you used to be. You've been much more fun lately. Need any more shopping?"

I had to smile.

"I kind of need relationship advice."

"Oh, no." She stared at me. "You're asking the wrong person. I'm married to my radio, and my last boyfriend dumped me when I got up in the middle of sex to answer my phone. I love this job, really, but it sucks balls. Big time."

"I upset...the boyfriend." I didn't know how else to phrase it.

"OK." She picked up her phone, which was making some incredibly annoying noises, and then put it down again. "We're wanted, but I didn't see that text...yet. What did you do?"

"I think I may be really bad at being in a relationship, but I don't know what I'm bad at, but I think I should be, like, telling him things that I don't."

"Like what?"

Oh, fuck. I should never have started this.

"Things like, 'Hey, I've just gone away for two weeks.' I'm not stupid, Aisha. I know I should have told him, but I'm just... Crap. And now I am avoiding texting him because I don't want to disappoint him further by being a clingy idiot."

"Ah. Yes. OK. So, we need to step up the flowers and send him large gifts. Is that what you're suggesting?"

"I don't know. Should I?"

"Sometimes I wonder who the talent is here." She shook her head. "No. Fucking hell."

She sighed and picked up her phone again, stabbed some words into it and slammed it down on the desk next to the bed.

"I very much doubt gifts and extravagant gestures will do the trick. If this boyfriend is a nice normal person, then maybe flowers and gin wasn't his thing."

"Yeah. That stuff was stupid."

"Agreed, but also sweet. Romantic. We all need a bit of fluff in our lives. But I think the two of you are past that. Am I right?"

"It's been...a few weeks."

"Yup."

God. It was like pulling teeth. I just needed her help, preferably before being caked in mud and thrown into a bog with a camera up my back.

"Can I suggest something?" she said.

"Anything." I sighed. "Please."

"Use your phone. Text the guy, morning and night. Tell him things, even the trivial stuff, and always tell him you miss him. Dudes love that shit."

"Do they?"

She laughed. "And no more gifts. I know what you need. You need him, and he probably needs you, so let me check the rota and see if I can get him up here for you. Just one night. I may be able to swing that. Does he work?"

"School teacher."

"Okaaaay." She smiled. Yeah, driving Matt up here for the night sounded like heaven, but it would be impossible, and I would be exhausted, and people would talk, and did I care?

"Aisha, I really appreciate this." I did. I wasn't just saying it. I was in way over my head here, and there was truly...I just...fuck.

"Don't worry about it. Problem-solving is my entire résumé, which is why I'm still here doing this crap while my flat hasn't been cleaned for a year and my one and only pot plant has died a cruel, horrible death. My friends don't even bother texting anymore, and my hotel room in this dive doesn't even have a window."

"At least you have a room. Dave's sleeping in one of the trailers."

"Yeah. The set coordinator fucked up the head count."

"I think we all fucked up," I mumbled. "I hate this. Am I the only one who's getting pissed off with this whole shoot?"

She stared at me because I was never this candid. I never said anything. I was the one who turned up and did whatever I was told.

"It's mega fucked up. But we all smile and nod because we have three weeks to go. Seriously, Con. Just do it. But I'll tell you now, if they think they're going to ask me back for the next season, they can think again. I've worked on every single season for this arsehole show and never once been offered promotion. Aisha's great, give her a runner's job. Again. Tell Aisha, she'll fix it. Again. Then I get the blame when whoever else fucks up. I can do better for myself. I don't have to settle for what they offer because it's safe."

"You're really good at what you do. Everyone says so." It sounded so lame, but I felt guilty because I'd never considered it from her point of view. I had Dave, who picked me up whenever I needed to go somewhere. I never questioned it. I had Aisha, who made sure I got everything I needed. Everyone else around me worked like a well-oiled machine making everything happen. All I had to do was turn up and deliver.

And I would deliver again, right now, as Aisha pushed me out the door with her phone glued to her ear, as usual. Her radio crackled in the darkness as I got in the car with Dave and set off down the road.

"You all right?" I asked him.

"Bog tired, kid."

"This is a clusterfuck, isn't it?"

He didn't reply out loud, but he nodded.

I slept all day the next day, and the only thing that got me up was another text from Ollie to get my arse into gear and ring him.

So I did because I needed to do something that wasn't this. It was Monday. Well, that's what my phone told me. I'd lost track, wallowing in loneliness and frustration because my boyfriend wasn't where I was.

Spoilt and entitled wasn't the start of who I'd become, and it made my head hurt.

"Finally!" Ollie said as the call connected.

"Hey," I said weakly.

"OK, dude? Matt says you're away working, so I'll give you that, but seriously?"

"What?" I sounded defensive. I hadn't meant to.

"Rules, mate. Rules."

"What rules?" I wasn't just dumb. I was full-blown stupid.

"If you're dating my brother, then there are rules. You don't diss him and you don't ignore him, and you ring him every morning and every night and you bloody tell him that you love him. I'm getting pissed off with Matt being a nervous wreck because you seem to have lost the ability to use your phone."

"I lost it." It was a poor excuse.

"Bullshit."

I took a breath. And another one.

"I warned you what would happen if I had to spend the whole weekend in the garden with Matt whining."

He had. I remembered.

"If you're messing him around, I will hunt you down and hurt you."

Ollie was terrifying. Even his voice sent shivers up my spine.

"I'm not," I whispered.

"I will hurt you, and it will...hurt."

Not so terrifying then.

"Ollie, mate." I was trying not to laugh, even though it wasn't really funny.

"He's upset!" Ollie shrieked down the phone.

"I know, and I don't know what to do about it!" I shrieked back.

"You're such a dumbass."

"Asshat," I retaliated. "I saw your comment on Insta."

There'd been several, actually, from someone called Oliver Winston on my official Instagram account.

"I thought you celebs didn't look at your social media."

"Well, this *dumbass* does. And I do know how to use my phone. I'm just bloody new to all this relationship stuff, and I'm a chicken because I don't know how to not be bloody clingy and overbearing and all that."

"All that." he laughed. "Mate, you're a mess."

"A mess?" My voice was pathetic. I was pathetic. "I miss him. And I've rung him twice, actually."

His laughter was not kind.

"I have rung him twice! The rest of the time, I've been on set and there's no signal where we are, and my runner is really annoyed with me because I keep asking if she has signal, and even my driver keeps putting his phone away as soon as I'm near. The whole set is in meltdown, and the director is off his head. We're all being worked to the bone, and I just want to go home and be with Matt."

"Yeah. Being with Matt is not your job. You have to work. I get that. But ringing him twice in a week is not good enough. You're with him, and you need to put some effort in."

"I don't want to ring him in the middle of the night." That was a feeble excuse. I could tell just saying the words out loud. The truth was I had almost called him in the middle of the night. Every fucking night.

"If you were my boyfriend, I'd be delighted to have you ring me in the middle of the night."

"Also..." God. How much of an idiot was I? "Matt mentioned phone sex. I don't even know what that means."

Yeah. Good work, Conny. I was way in over my head here, and Ollie wasn't even trying to contain his laughter.

"I'm going to hang up on you now. Unwittingly hilarious as you are, you need to ring Matt. Right now. And you need to tell him all this crap because these are things *he* needs to hear, not me. I'm not going to sit here and teach you how to have phone sex. Mate. Seriously. Have some boundaries."

I almost threw that back in his face. Instead, I said, "OK." Quietly. And then I stared at my phone because Ollie had actually hung up on me.

My phone rang again, but I ignored it and sat up in bed, looking around the room. I smelled really bad, and I was starving. I was also due on set in an hour. My voicemail kicked in. Then my phone rang again. With a sigh, I answered it.

"Lucia." I tried to sound composed.

"I need you in London next Saturday. Event, with Tara."

"Absolutely not." I never said no, but...no. I was too bloody tired.

"Connor, stop it."

"No. Tara and I are over. Work commitments or whatever crap you want to throw at me—no. Just stop. I'm doing Pride on the Saturday. I'll be on the *White Noise* float. I've never done it before, but even Caroline is doing it this year. I want in on that. No bloody events."

"You know how this works, darling." Lucia was doing her pleading voice. I knew her far too well.

"I do, and I've had enough." I was not backing down.

"You sure you want to pull the contract?" She wasn't as stern as I'd expected her to be. "It's been very successful for both your brands."

The whine that came out of my mouth was ridiculous, but so was all this.

"I'm out, and I have a boyfriend. It's not like it's some big secret. I don't care anymore. I just want this circus to stop for a bit. I need some time off. I need to just bloody breathe."

"I know this shoot has been difficult for you, and there's been a lot of chatter in the background with regards to the future of *White Noise*. I'm sure you've heard."

"Heard what?" I asked, but I had heard. Caroline wanted out, and I didn't blame her. The crew was pissed off. Even Hamish had started to grumble and was being difficult to reach, while I was holed up in bed, letting the stress get to me.

"They're planning season seven," she said quietly. "With a new cast."

"Yeah, no surprise there." My heart hurt. Just a little. It was a shock hearing it from Lucia because if she'd already had word, then it was probably true.

"Which is why I need to do Pride," I insisted. It had nothing to do with this. And everything to do with being sick and tired of not being real. Of being an actor. Of being so freaking scripted. I wanted to be out there and be honest and just live. With Matt. I had a whole crew who did the bloody Pride parade. The grip team. The second camera man. The girl who worked as our best boy. The scriptwriters. A bunch of extras. The bloody fake nurse who had stood on the top of the float last year, waving a flag. I remembered seeing it on Twitter and wishing I'd been there. We were well known for our Pride appearances...well, apart from me. I'd never done it. I couldn't even defend my absence. I suppose I'd never felt part of it. But I did now.

"Why Pride? You've just never mentioned it before." Lucia sounded genuinely confused.

"I know," I agreed. I wasn't sure why I'd brought it up. Another whim? No. This was no bloody whim.

"I'm bisexual, Lucia. Always have been. And I'm in love with a gorgeous guy called Matt, and he's the only thing I have in this pathetic existence of mine that's real. So, stick me on that Pride float and I'll come to London. Also, no more Tara. She's a lovely girl, but please just make it stop."

"Done," she said.

I hung up on her, like the diva I was.

I barely took a breath, already dialling out.

Matt picked up on the first ring.

"Hello, stranger," he said, but he was smiling. I could hear it in his voice.

"Hey, boyfriend," I said back cheerily. Then I hated myself for it. "I love you. I'm sorry I'm rubbish at being your boyfriend, but I do mean it."

"You're just stressed and working too much. I know."

He was being too kind, and I was just huffing and puffing as I tried to figure out what to say. It sounded like he was in a car, and even that insignificant detail made me nervous. I wanted to be where he was. Not here wallowing in desperation and stupidity.

"We'll figure this out, Conny," he said softly.

Which was when Aisha barged through the door, and I bloody screamed in frustration.

"Why does nobody ever bloody knock!" I shouted as Matt laughed in my ear. I was glad it wasn't a video call because...well...

"I *would* knock if you locked the door!"

"I had!" Hadn't I? Fuck this hotel. Bloody crap old building falling apart. The window didn't open. The carpet stank, and the bed was giving me a backache.

"You need to ride down to set with me in the minibus," Aisha said flatly. "And you need to get up—and put some clothes on."

"Who's that?" Matt asked, still laughing.

"My slave," I said with added sarcasm.

"I hate you," Aisha muttered as her radio went off, then her phone. I just wanted to cry. Run away and never come back.

"Where are you?" I asked Matt in desperation. "Wait. Can I just get dressed and ring you back?"

"Yeah, OK."

This was my life. Two minutes. I'd only had two minutes with him and now I was jumping around trying to get a pair of clean pair of underpants on. Aisha tutted in disgust and walked out the door.

Yeah. Inappropriate, but she'd started it.

It got worse. Much worse. By the time I was dumped back at my excuse of a hotel, I was shivering, covered head to toe in cold mud, my shirt and trousers clinging wetly to my limbs under an oversized dry robe. I could barely walk, having had to climb rocks for the past couple of hours. Caroline's hands were a mess, and we'd both walked off set after the medic had shut us down on health and safety grounds. It had been dangerous and stupid and surely illegal, and even the AD had started to question the whole set-up. There was some kind of mutiny brewing within the camera crew, and the prop guy had been in tears, as they kept demanding that he move the fake body we were supposed to find. On a fake clifftop! Why we were filming this crap on location was beyond me when we could have safely done it in a studio with a greenscreen and warm clothes and bloody showers.

And when I tried to get into my room, the key wouldn't work, which made me bang the door in a fit of rage. I'd had enough. Totally enough. Until the door opened and there was...

Matt.

I gasped in surprise and flailed my arms through the air as he looked at me uncertainly, and then...

Then I burst into tears.

I cried. Like a bloody baby. Again. And Matt dragged me in and took the dry robe off, asking me why I was wearing a duvet. Was it some kind of new costume prop?

I couldn't even laugh because my chest was still convulsing with sobs. Fuck. I had no idea what I was doing, but I'd survived almost a week without him, and it hadn't been good. Not good at all.

But he was here now, hugging me and shushing me and somehow taking my clothes off and...and...and he'd even figured out how to use the old electrical shower on the wall in the bathroom.

"My nan used to have one of these. I can't believe this hotel. When was it built? In the 1800s or something? It's only got one socket! No wonder you haven't rung me. I bet your phone's been constantly out of battery."

I wanted to tell him that wasn't true, but I couldn't speak anymore. I'd been working and sleeping, and I hadn't seen a gym for days. My body hurt everywhere, and now he was here, I couldn't even think of anything but sleep. With him. God, please.

He got me into the shower, got himself undressed and joined me, holding me up as I leant against him, my face in his neck as he tried to get the soap under my arms.

"You stink." He smiled into my skin.

"I know," I whispered. At least I was calming down.

"I'm right here," he whispered back. I wasn't sure why we were whispering, but I needed it. I needed the calm. His hands stroking down my back. His voice in my ear.

"I love you. Whatever is going on, that's all that matters. Your...Aisha, is that her name? She's so lovely. She rang me and asked if there was any way I could take a day off because you were losing the plot and needed a cuddle. Her exact words. You needed a cuddle, and how can anyone resist that? Anyway, the head's given me a couple of days' compassionate leave, although if I worked anywhere other than a school, I could probably have taken a month off, the amount of overtime we all do.

"Then there was a guy in a big black car outside the flats—I thought I'd been kidnapped when he whisked me off to this nightmare of a place. No wonder you're all going crazy here. Your Dave is a funny guy. Didn't say a word for the first hour, but I asked for a loo break, and he bought me a sandwich. I didn't even ask. Then he stopped again for coffee, and he told me he's signed so many NDAs in his career that he doesn't dare open his mouth in case he says something that would jeopardise his driving gig."

"Yeah. That's Dave," I said, the words merging into a yelp—Matt yelped too—as the water turned cold.

"Bed?" he suggested.

I looked at him. Truly looked at him.

"You came all this way for me." It wasn't a question.

And he just nodded. "Yeah. Of course."

"I..." No wonder I'd struggled to text him. I could barely speak when he looked at me. His face. The sharp angles of his jaw. Those thick, thoughtful eyebrows and those eyes. Too deep. I kissed him. There was nothing else I could do. Well, other than stand there shivering.

"Bed," he said again. "And food. Want anything to eat?"

"Did anyone feed you?" I had no idea what was happening here, but he pushed me over to the bed, then got in beside me and pulled the duvet over us, snuggling close.

"Whatever you need, I am always here for you. You just have to ask. I've eaten—the receptionist was very accommodating. I almost ordered you an omelette. With extra egg. But then I was worried it would go cold before you got back."

He made me laugh, and it was just so comforting I almost burst into tears again. I had no idea what was wrong with me. All these emotions were...ugh.

"I...want to be better at looking after you," I snuffled out.

"You look after me fine. I'm kind of figuring out how you work. We don't have to be joined at the hip. As long as you're you and I'm me and we're together, we'll just do fine. And anyway, I got a chauffeur-driven mini-break to a...fine hotel in Norfolk."

"Fine hotel." I snorted. "The windows leak, the bed is hard as rocks, and the breakfast buffet consists of frozen toast. Not a croissant in sight."

"You're so bloody spoilt."

"I am," I agreed. "Especially since you're here. How on earth did you get here?" I was just musing, but he still kissed me. Stroked down my cheek. Did everything I needed him to.

"I think Ollie's right," he said carefully, like he was contemplating his words. "I've never been in a relationship before, and neither have you, so maybe we need to set some rules, so we know where we stand."

"No bloody threesomes."

He laughed. "Absolutely not. Ignore anything Ollie says."

"And no hook-ups," I added as he got up on his elbow and arranged himself so he could look at me. The soft light from the bedside table made him look almost unreal. I'd been so full of anxiety and doubt this week that somehow, I'd forgotten how stunning he was. How perfect he looked, even here in this horrible place. A place that was less horrible now he was here.

"No hook-ups," he agreed in that soft voice of his.

"Aisha said no more presents. That you don't need things, just me. I think that's the same for me too. I don't need anything else as long as I get to be with you."

I had no idea what I was saying. Well, I did.

"You have me." He stroked my cheek again, his fingertips travelling over my lips.

"I'm doing the Pride parade in London. I've told my agent to scrap the rest. I'm going to be on the *White Noise* float waving a bloody rainbow flag, and I don't care about anything else. I'm tired, Matt. I'm so bloody tired of being other people. I want to start being me. Doing things I want to do. I need to get off the merry-go-round and do things that make me happy."

"That sounds like a good plan," he said, quietly watching me with his eyebrows all raised.

"Yes. It is. I'm going to stand on that float with a shirt saying something like—"

"Matt's boyfriend?" He laughed. "No. Don't do that. That would be really cheesy."

"I was thinking maybe something a little more subtle, but I can totally order a 'Matt's boyfriend' T-shirt. Anything to make you happy."

I loved seeing him laugh. I loved feeling his skin against mine.

I sighed happily as he snuggled closer.

"Are you coming back home? To me?"

Now I was the one who grabbed his chin. I lifted his face so I could look at him.

"I'll be home in a week. And then...I'll move in properly. Would that be OK?"

"Can you leave your bag? And put your toothbrush back in my bathroom?"

"Did you miss my toothbrush?" I had to smile at the way he blushed. This was totally insane, but I realised that this was me. Us. And being us was absolutely fine.

"Of course I did! You left me with your twatty Gucci suit. It's awful and smells of some stupid aftershave. I went into Mrs Wu's the other day, and Wei was wearing your shirt. He looks good in it!"

"Good." I smiled. "When I get back, I want noodles. In bed. With you."

"Definitely. And I *will* make you order something that's not egg."

"Oh, no!"

He was mocking me, so I kissed him.

"We'll do all these things," I said. "I'll take you to meet Mum, and we'll go do football with Ollie, and we'll have lots of sex. We could start now."

How old was I? Sixteen?

"You're too tired for sex. Sleep, baby. We'll have sex in the morning. Aisha told me we have until one o'clock, and then Dave will take me home and you have to go back and get caked in mud or something."

"Yeah." I didn't want to think about that.

I wrapped him up in a hug and kissed his forehead. The urge to crawl on top of him was overwhelming, but he was right. I needed sleep. He sighed happily in my arms, and I wondered how something this small could make me so happy.

"I need to make sure Aisha gets a promotion. And Dave needs a raise," I muttered into his hair.

"She's good at her job. So is Dave," he rumbled against my chest.

And then there was only sleep. For the first time in a week, I slept solidly.

I woke up feeling calm, aware of him beside me, moving in his sleep. I snuffled into his neck, my hand tracing the outline of his body. I was finally taking control of my life. I was grasping at straws, admittedly, but those straws felt good. There was so much left to figure out, but I felt proud of myself.

My phone lit up on the bedside table, and I picked it up, smiling as I read the message.

Tara Marie: That's it. We're breaking up. My girlfriend just proposed.

I texted back in a flurry of fingers. *Awesome. Congrats. That's it. You're dumped.*

Tara Marie: Brilliant. Thanks. How's the boyfriend?

I kissed his sleeping head. *All good. Asleep in my arms.*

He was. My life was taking shape. I was in control. Whatever happened next, things would be fine. Absolutely fine.

I texted Lucia and demanded the password to my Instagram. She swiftly sent it back. Shaking, I posted something before I lost my nerve. It was the right thing to do, and it made me happy. I was allowed to be happy. I smiled as I threw my phone on the floor and wrapped my arms around the only thing that mattered.

Actor Connor Telford: *Hi. I'm Con. Out. Proud. Happy Pride.*

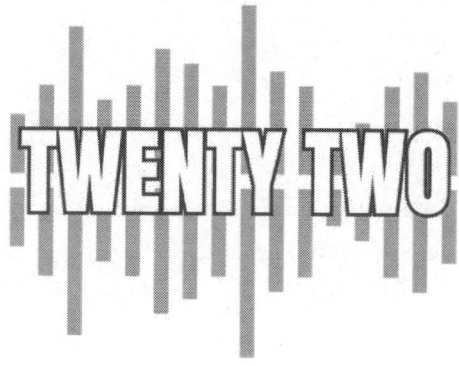

Matt

Things were considerably easier in the week that followed. Con talked more. Well, he communicated more, through disjointed text messages that mostly dropped on my phone during the night, but I was slowly getting to know him. The real him. It was quite scary to realise how similar we were. How our thoughts sometimes crossed like tiny arrows as we'd gone on with our lives. Sometimes I would just remember he existed, and a smile would appear on my face. Other times, I'd look at my phone and there would be a message. It might only be an emoji, or it could be an epic paragraph of words. You never knew with Con, and I'd started to appreciate his randomness. When he did message, it was because he had this overwhelming need to, and I felt that way too.

I shot down the stairs at work and slid into the teachers' lounge area, doing a little happy dance as I grabbed my things. It was Friday, the end of another week, and Con was on his way back...whenever. Timings were always vague with his job.

I was glad he had great people around him. Some not-so-great people too, but Aisha had started to text me updates, which gave me a warm feeling inside, knowing she cared about Con and wanted him to be happy. Hence, I'd just had a message from her saying, *In car*, followed by a heart emoji from Con a few seconds later.

Funny how little things like that brightened my world. Silly things really. We were not kids, but I loved the innocence of what we shared and sent him a heart emoji back as I got on the Tube, then smiled like I'd won the lottery all the way home.

In a way I had. My boyfriend was...wonderful.

The flat was clean and tidy, the bed made with fresh sheets. Yes, I had expectations. We hadn't actually had sex up in Norfolk because. Sleep. We'd woken up just after midday, my head groggy and Con looking more windswept than the night before. But at least he'd slept, and we'd found someone to bring us coffee. I'd not had the heart to say I wanted tea, but Con had remembered later and spent the rest of the week apologising for not looking after me properly.

Aisha had also texted to ask how I took my tea, so she'd know for next time—something about adding me to her little black book of irrelevant yet useful information. I was starting to really like her and had in return asked her if there was any chance, she could put some totally twatty flowers in Con's room with a card from me. I'd even offered to pay, but she'd insisted that there was enough room in her budget to sort twatty flowers. Even in rural Norfolk.

I had no twatty flowers in the flat, though, because we didn't need them. No yellow bucket on the table. I'd moved the gin to a cupboard and filled the fridge with normal foods—milk, yoghurts, cheese and eggs, of course. I'd even bought bake-at-home croissants for the freezer and some nice cereal. Yeah. I was *that* boyfriend.

I changed as soon as I got in and went down to the gym as usual, set up a treadmill and ran with music pumping through my veins. It felt good, really good, like I'd finally managed to run off the last couple of weeks of stress. I grabbed the towel off the handlebar and dabbed my face and neck as I slowed the speed down to a brisk walking pace, letting my heartbeat slowly settle. And I smiled. That's all I seemed to do these days. Everything seemed lighter. Easier.

Or it did until someone threw a towel at me. I looked behind me, ready to serve whoever had thrown it full-on evils, and there was my Con in his gym gear, just standing there laughing at me while I jabbed every button on the treadmill display, trying to get the damn machine to stop.

"Just push the big red emergency stop," he said, pointing out the obvious.

"Yeah," I huffed, jumping off it before it had come to a complete stop because he was here. I practically ran into his arms, laughing at his huff as I almost tipped him over.

"Whoa!"

I planted my lips on his, and there was nothing, absolutely nothing that could have stopped me.

"You back?" I asked, still breathless.

"Yup." He smiled. I loved his smile. "Sorry about the towel. I didn't want to risk getting smacked in the face. You know? Accidents happen."

"Yes, it's a dangerous place, the gym. Especially when people sneak up on you." I still had my arms around his neck.

"I love you," he whispered, and I whispered it back because that was who we were, and I didn't care if people were staring.

They weren't, for the record. This was a very busy gym, and people couldn't care less about two idiots hugging in a corner.

"You're wearing the same shirt you wore that day," he said. "I remember. Bright red."

He was stupid. So bloody stupid.

"I'm glad you hit me in the face," I said.

"So am I."

Then we laughed because there was nothing serious or adult about us. At all. We were just two giggling fools, and I didn't know how to stop smiling.

I smiled a lot these days.

"Wanna give me an hour to work out? Need to do some weights and legs, desperately. I haven't seen a gym in two weeks, and my body is screaming for a run."

"You had a whole beach to run on in Norfolk," I teased, and he put his hand over my mouth.

"Don't mention Norfolk. I never wanna see that place again. Did I tell you Dave went for a walk on that beach and managed to get stung by a bloody jellyfish? He could barely walk! Yet he drove me all the way back here, didn't say a word. I've now officially named him Silent Dave. He's putting in a report about me harassing him with stupid nicknames."

"Really?"

"No. Not really. He got seen by the medic and had a cooling plaster strapped to his leg. He was OK. But yeah. I don't think anyone on set ever wants to see Norfolk again. Not even Silent Dave."

"Will you even watch it when it comes out? I mean, the scenes you just shot?"

"To be honest..." He wrapped his arms around my waist. It was amazing how comforting that was, having him hold me, the scent of him all around me. "I couldn't tell you what we just filmed. The plot is above our heads. Nothing in that dialogue made sense, but I need to watch it because I have no idea what's about to happen."

"Seriously?"

"Seriously. The plot is a well-kept secret, and we've all signed our life away. Even I have no idea what's going on."

"Apart from that it's almost done."

"And thank fuck for that."

"Well, I think you should go lift some weights and run so we can get out of here. Get food. Get home."

"Sounds like a plan." He kissed me again.

I went and found the rowing machines and pretended I knew what I was doing, when in reality I was just sat staring at a certain Con Telford lifting weights in the room next door.

An hour and a half later, he was in my arms in our bed—yes, *our* bed—and everything was back the way it needed to be. His bag by the door, his clothes were haplessly thrown around the room, and he'd made a big song and dance about putting his toothbrush back next to mine by the sink. Where it belonged.

He belonged right here too, which I kept reminding him off. His dirty laundry in the laundry basket. His shoes next to mine by the door.

We were both freshly showered, clean and naked—he'd ripped the towel off me the second I'd come out of the bathroom—and he was flat on his back while I sat next to him, casually playing with his nipples, stroking down his chest and admiring his nicely swollen dick.

Exactly where I wanted him.

"I bought lube," I said. We'd used up the two small bottles I'd owned, so I'd bought some of the expensive stuff—in the big bottle.

"Yeah...about that." He suddenly looked all shy.

"We don't have to do anything," I backtracked. I knew better than to push it after how things had ended up the last time.

I took a deep breath as his hand stroked my cheek, then travelled down to grip my bum.

"I was kind of doing some research."

"OK."

"And I think I know the basics of how to do it. So..."

"So?"

Don't push, Matt. Don't. Even though all I wanted to do was to flip him over and stick my dick where it was desperate to go and then I would fuck him and come all over his butt cheeks, and every single one of my dirty fantasies would have come true. Right there. Well. Almost.

"Do you think you want to...fuck me?" he asked uncertainly.

"Do you even have to ask that question?"

This was not the time to be sarcastic. So, I lay down next to him and kissed him.

"Yes. Yes, please."

"I mean, I trust you. But I would be lying if I said I wasn't a little...apprehensive."

"You absolutely do not need to be apprehensive. I will look after you."

He still seemed a bit scared. To be honest, so was I.

"I'll go slow. Be really careful with you, and I promise you, you'll get one of the most amazing orgasms at the end of this. Then..."

"Then what?"

God help me. He looked terrified.

"I'm not going to hurt you, Conny." I sat up again and dragged him up too. We were better like this, when there weren't so many expectations and we kind of switched off the foreplay for a bit.

"You don't have to agree to anything. If it's all too much, I'll be more than happy to give you a blow job. End of. Not even that. We can just lie here. I'm more than—"

"Shut up, Matt."

He didn't say it in a mean way because he was laughing at me and then he was kissing me and rolling on top of me, and I pushed him over and rolled on top of him, and honestly, we were both kids and shouldn't be allowed anywhere near lube.

"Just do it. No condom. I hate condoms. They smell bad and have that horrible slime all over them, and you said you were tested and all that? I get tested on set before every intimate scene. It's standard practice. We're all good...aren't we?"

"We are." I stared at him. Stroked my fingers over his skin.

We were good. Totally good. Everything in my life was as long as he was here with me.

"You're not going away again. Is that right?"

"Not for a few months," he confirmed. "Well, I'm doing Pride tomorrow, and—"

"So am I. We'll be on different floats and in different zones, but we'll both be there. And then afterwards..."

"We'll be together. Maybe go for a drink? Do normal things that people do when they have a day up in London."

"I want to go for a drink. And have food. I'd really like to do all that."

"OK. Let's do it."

"The drinks or the penetrative sex bit?"

He laughed at that.

"God, you're such a nerd. Which is why I love you so, so much."

"And you're an idiot. Which is why I love you right back."

I loved that we were like this. Just us with no stress and so much laughter. And then less laughter as I got the lube out and smeared it all over my fingers.

"I'm going to touch you...and make you feel all good. Is that OK?"

He went a little pale but spread his legs.

"How do you want me?"

"Just like this. On your side. Knees up."

"Feels weird."

"Yeah, but it's comfortable for you, and easy. And I promise I'll take it really slow."

He didn't reply to that because I let my fingers reassure him, easing them right between the gorgeous globes of his arse and lightly moving them up and down over that little opening that...

Con Telford was waxed. Smooth. Not a hair anywhere. Which I kind of hadn't expected, though I'm not sure why, and I almost said something but didn't. I carried on playing, pushing gently and pressing kisses on his hip as he panted.

"All good?" I asked.

"Awesome."

He made me laugh, but his breath hitched as my thumb put pressure on his hole. I eased off, only to push again.

He was looser than I'd thought he would be, relaxing as my thumb made itself a little home in his opening.

"More," he said.

Who was I to argue?

I was kind of good at this because I knew exactly what I needed, and I really enjoyed being fucked when someone took their time with foreplay. So that was what I did for

Con. I kissed his hip, his stomach, and slowly moved my thumb, focusing on his reaction to what I was doing. His arm came up to play with my hair, and I pushed a little deeper inside of him.

"Good?" I asked.

He nodded. Vigorously.

I replaced my thumb with two fingers, gently moving around, shushing him and urging him on.

"You're doing so well."

"Matt?"

I stopped.

"Don't stop. More!"

"So impatient," I scolded. He just laughed.

"Get your dick in there. The fingers are all good, but I really want you in there. Properly."

"Spoilt as well. My fingers are offended."

"Your fingers are much appreciated, but my dick needs company."

"Really?" I laughed. Grabbed his rock-hard dick. "Get yourself off, baby. Wank away."

"Wank away? I thought you were classy, Matt."

"I'm super classy," I smarmed, grabbing the lube and coating myself. God. I was horny, my dick well and truly ready for action as a moan slipped from my mouth. I mean! He was in my bed with hands on his arse, holding himself open.

"You want me on all fours or like this?"

"Like this. Knees all the way up."

I liked this position. Liked how I had control. I could touch him everywhere, and I did. Smoothed my hands over his thighs. His back. His hips. Leaned down so I could kiss his elbow.

I pushed my dick against his opening.

He moaned, and I whined, grabbing my dick so I wouldn't accidentally come.

I almost had. Because this right here?

"Do it," he whispered. "I need to feel you."

"OK," I whispered back. This whispering was insane, but in a way, I was grateful for the calm. My head functioned better when we were quiet.

I pushed, gently moving my body and holding onto his hips. A sound came out of his mouth, not quite a word, followed by puffs of air as the tip of my dick slowly, slowly edged inside of him. Just the tip.

I had to pant too because it was...

So bloody special.

I'd remember this for the rest of my life. The sounds he was making, his ragged breaths.

"Good?"

"Yeah."

I pushed a little further. Added more lube to my finger and smoothed it over where his skin had stretched around my dick. Tried to breathe as I pushed further in.

His top leg was shaking. I pressed on it with my palm. Gentle strokes. Up and down. I knew how this felt, and I wanted so badly for him to get past it until it started to feel good.

"Relax. Let it take over."

"It's...intense," he panted out.

"Yeah. I know." And I knew what I had to do. I pushed all the way in, one final slide. He roared.

It wasn't pain. Just that feeling of being impossibly full. We were joined together, and our bodies were—it sounded ridiculous, but it was all I could think of. We were one. Him and me. The Con-and-Matt of humanity. Together.

He breathed. I breathed with him. Bent over his body at some impossible angle as he grabbed my hand and held on tight.

"I love you," came out of his mouth. I closed my eyes, let myself feel.

I knew he was ready when his opening started to relax, and I began to move gently as his mouth made sounds. Good sounds.

We didn't need words now anyway. My head went into that space where I was just floating, my hips doing their own thing, his hand grasped tightly in mine and my other hand holding me up so I could keep the angle right. Him half bent over the bed, me across his back keeping up a steady rhythm of thrusts. I wouldn't last. I couldn't.

Then I lost his hand as he slipped out of my grip and started jerking himself off at an alarming speed, and I followed his lead, slamming into him, my dick singing and my mouth wide open as the static built.

I loved it. Loved him. Loved the feeling of being so incredibly lucky to have this. Right here. Right now.

The room faded away, and my mind went dark, small, twinkling stars flying across my eyelids as somewhere in the distance I heard someone shout. Roar. Sounds that made no sense but were right here in this madness.

Madness. That was what this was.

Howling, I spilled my cum inside of him, and it made me feel invincible, like I was the king of the universe, and I held all the secrets of life and the world right here in my hands.

I didn't, of course. It was just the orgasm talking, but then I opened my eyes, and he was laughing.

"Fuck, that was intense," he said. Grabbing my hand, he pulled me down as I slid out and tumbled over him, landing in an uncoordinated heap in his arms.

He tugged at me, rearranged me where he wanted me. Kissed the tip of my nose.

His breathing still wasn't right, and neither was mine. I panted, swallowed, tried to get myself into some kind of conscious state.

"You OK?" I had to ask because he was still laughing a touch hysterically.

"I just came. Like proper mind-blowing-shoot-your-brains-out-your-ears came."

"OK?" I laughed. He was ridiculous.

"I loved it. Really loved it. Intense stuff. Truly intense. Made me re-evaluate all those sex scenes I've filmed. Cass Powell is obviously faking it. In every scene. Thank God I'm not filming any more smut this season because those orgasms were a crime against queer men. I may have to post on Instagram and apologise."

"No!" I shouted, laughing almost too much to speak. "Don't. Honestly. Not a good idea."

"I think it is. *I hereby apologise for my very bad acting.*" He sounded so pompous, and he was waving his arms around. "*My fake-orgasm acting will forever be a blight on my record. I hereby hand back all my awards.*"

I put my hand over his mouth and hid my face in his shoulder. His body was still twitching with giggles.

He was so stupid, but so was I. High on love. On sex. On orgasms.

"Can we do that again?" he asked, his face suddenly right up in mine, honesty all over it. But he was an actor, and I didn't trust a thing coming out of his mouth right now.

"I love you," I said.

He smiled. "I love you too."

It was funny how life was so simple when you were happy.

He handed me the lube. "Give me half an hour to recover, and then I want your dick back up there. Doggy style. I want to try all the positions, and then I want to fuck you too. Can we do that?"

Yeah. We could. Because Con Telford was right next to me, in my bed, breathing my air.

"You hungry?" he asked.

"Starving," I admitted.

"Sex or food?"

"Both?"

Neither of us moved. But to be honest, it didn't really matter. Not right now.

TWENTY-THREE

Con

I was never nervous. Well, almost never, but sitting in some kind of tent erected down a central London side street, feeling out of place wasn't even the start of it. The city was showing herself in her best light, the sun bright in the sky and the temperature already too hot and muggy. And I didn't even have my Kindle to keep me company.

I was sweating, trying to fan my face with my hand. Well, only because I was early and apparently the first one here, which sucked when the volunteers were huddled in a corner staring at me.

At least Dave had dropped me off in the right place and thank God for him knowing where to go because I hadn't even thought that far. I was used to being met by handlers and being ushered around like a dog on a leash, yet here I was, on a rickety chair, not a complimentary water bottle in sight.

I stuck out like a sore thumb.

Matt had gone off with his teacher friends in their minivan hours ago, and now I wished I'd reined myself in and stayed at home.

Someone else arrived, whom I vaguely recognised from set, wearing a rainbow-coloured *White Noise* T-shirt—our uniform for the day, and yes, once again Dave had come to the rescue, handing me mine in the car and making me dump the stupid posh one I'd been wearing on the back seat. Lucia had had a small panic about some designer wanting to dress me, but I'd known about the matching T-shirts and told her that was what I was wearing. Fuck everything else.

It still felt strange standing up for myself, saying no to things I'd previously accepted with a smile. The cheap rainbow-coloured *White Noise* T-shirt was fine. The size was good, clinging nicely to my curves, but the girl in the matching one was talking to someone else, while I was sitting here like a big blob of nerves.

I had no idea what I'd been thinking. This wasn't my cause. Or maybe it was. It didn't feel right. It had, earlier in the week, when I'd insisted that I needed to be here. Now, I had no agenda, no script to go off, and I was starting to realise something I'd never thought of before. Being an actor was easy. Playing someone else? A piece of cake. Playing Connor Telford? It was the hardest thing I'd ever done.

I wasn't gay. I wasn't straight. I was nothing I could put a label on, and the press would have a field day. Maybe they already had. I hadn't dared to check social media since my last post, preferring to stay in my bubble of ignorant bliss, and now I was going to throw myself out on some kind of rickety ride around central London, shouting loudly about my queerness.

The tent was filling with more people, who stared at me while I pretended to look at my phone.

Silence.

Well, good. Non-silence usually meant drama, and I couldn't have coped with that right now.

Another new arrival.

Dave.

Oh, thank fuck for that.

"Hey."

He was wearing a matching rainbow shirt. I stood up, a little bewildered.

"Are you...joining us?" I asked. He rarely spoke, so I didn't expect an answer.

"I'll be walking next to the float. Support crew."

"Nice." I must've still looked confused because he smiled at me. Dave rarely smiled.

"Dude. I don't talk about things, but it doesn't mean I don't have a life. And I enjoy my job, so sometimes keeping those words on the inside isn't a bad thing."

"Silent Dave." I was a dick.

He rolled his eyes. "I could say the same about you, Silent Con."

Now I was smiling too. "Just two silent dudes running around in a big fancy car."

"Just two silent *queer* dudes running around in a big fancy car. Sometimes silences are comfortable. And to be honest, you're a good guy to work with. Easy. No stupid demands. Regular pitstops. No drunk hook-ups in tow. It's appreciated."

OK. If I had been confused before, now I felt totally blindsided.

Dave threw his hands in the air. "Look. My husband works on set too. It's chill. We just keep it real. Private. And that's the way things should be. Doesn't mean anything is different. But I'm really pleased you're here. It's needed, OK? You being here will mean the world to people, so just roll with it. Have fun. And don't worry too much. The world doesn't change just because some bloke rides around on the back of a lorry, but sometimes it can be just what someone else needs."

"Yeah." Too many words from Dave was weird, and my own words were in short supply as my brain seemed to have imploded. I swallowed and blinked to refocus.

"You're a cool guy, Dave."

"Ditto," he said. "If you need me, I'll be walking on the left of the float."

Then he walked off. Typical Silent Dave.

"Connor!" As if my brain wasn't already fried, here was Caroline looking far too serious for my liking as she dragged me towards a corner, slipping us out the back of the tent. I hadn't realised how hot it was inside, and the cool shade against a concrete wall was heavenly.

"Need a word," she said, sounding concerned.

"OK?" I had no idea what was happening right now, but I had a bad feeling in my stomach, as she got her vape out of her pocket and took a deep drag.

"You need to get off those things," I scolded her.

"At least I'm off the cigs." She blew out air. "Not that I haven't wanted to get back on them. I almost bought a pack yesterday, having a panic in the car."

"You OK?" I asked. She looked a little unhinged, and that wasn't Caroline. She was usually much more put together than this. She was wearing an un-ironed shirt tied around her waist and her hair was up in a messy top knot, yet her *White Noise* T-shirt was immaculate and tucked neatly into her jeans.

"Not really. But listen, Con..."

"I'm listening," I grabbed her arms, holding her as she took a deep breath.

"I don't know if you know, but I've had some interesting conversations. Did you know that the entire set is still up in Norfolk? Everyone is still there, but they sent us home."

"Really?" That made no sense.

"They have Hamish, Justin, Natalie and Paya up there, the whole stunt team alongside our body doubles. You know Paya and I talk all the time?"

"OK?" I needed coffee and a sit-down. My heart was doing strange things and my thoughts were making no sense, but Caroline was looking at me, waiting for the coin to drop.

Goosebumps formed on my arms when it. Oh...shit.

"First, they sacked Sally. Rightly so because that last scene you filmed? People were worried. It wasn't right."

"It was fine. I was just over-emotional."

"You were a bloody wreck, Connor. Even I was worried. Production was having emergency meetings."

"And nobody talked to me?"

"You know what they're like. Bloody dickwads, the lot of them. I knew you were all right. I can always tell when you're off, but people were worried. Then you posted that thing on your Insta, and now Production think you've lost your marbles. Sally was rubbish, but it doesn't matter now—"

"She wasn't rubbish." Well, maybe she had been. What did I know? I just rolled with it and pretended everything was OK even if it wasn't.

"But that's not the worst of it. It's been a thing all season. The whole storyline with finding the final prize—you know? The bodies we've been looking for?"

Now I was shivering because, yes. There was something taking shape in my head, and it made me feel a little faint. Suddenly it all made sense, and at the same time as this was a bloody genius plot twist, it was also so bloody obvious. I didn't know why I hadn't clocked it earlier. How I'd been such a fool?

"We've been looking for our own bodies. We're the ones, the final prize, aren't we? Rodriguez's final game? Fuck. FUCK! We don't make it, do we?"

"No." She looked a little shocked herself, sucking on that vape like it was oxygen. "This is the end. Which is fine. I've been wanting to pull the plug anyway, but this has been my life for so bloody long, and they didn't even have the decency to give us some notice. Talk us through the fact that we're being sacked!"

"Not sacked," I stuttered out. "We're just not getting renewed. There will be new people to take the lead in the next season. Lucia already told me, but nobody has actually said anything officially."

"They never do on this shitty production. The communication is awful. Everything is secret and under wraps—I barely know what I'm doing from one day to the next. You know I did that film last year? Totally different vibe on that set, I couldn't believe it."

"I know." I had done other jobs too. "We're so used to being here, always in the dark like bloody mushrooms, that we've become blind to how this awful stupid production works."

"It's not a good place, Con. Not anymore. We're treated like shit, and the crew are starting to grumble. I know at least ten people who aren't coming back next season."

"At least they pay us."

"Yeah, but the new people are cheaper. Production's being sneaky about all sorts of things, and it's not just that they're getting rid of us. They're getting rid of a lot of good people. I should be relieved. I should be happy I don't have to resign, but I expected more."

She was devastated. I was a bit myself, to be honest, and all I could do was stand there and squeeze her arms in comfort.

"I'll miss you," I said quietly. "You've been in my life for years."

She smiled, settling my heart rate to a steadier one.

"Please keep in touch," I begged, and she shook her head.

"Con, you couldn't get rid of me if you tried. I can finally do an internship and finish my degree. An internship! I'll need support. I'll need to call you and scream all my frustration down the phone at you so you can laugh at me and call me an idiot. You've always been my sounding board, and my brother and my partner in crime. That's not going to change. And you have a boyfriend! Thank God you've finally come out. I was starting to worry that you'd implode and go crazy. You needed this. And do you know what?"

"What?" I asked, trying to hide that my eyes were watering.

"You're my favourite person in the world. You always have been. I never know who to trust or who I could talk to or what to even say to people. Yet you were always there making the world a better place. That's who you are. You're my Connor. We'll be fine."

She wiped her eyes. I gave up pretending and wiped mine too. "You need to come for dinner. I want to meet this man of yours."

"He's on the Teachers Association's float...somewhere. I don't even know where." I was talking rubbish and rocking on my heels. Caroline laughed at me. "Yes, to the dinner," I said, trying to make sense of myself. "Are you still with that—"

"God no! That dickhead was shagging everyone else apart from me. And now we need to go ride that float and pretend we're all happy and everything is fine and that the people we've been slaving away for, for the past what...six years? That those people aren't about to royally fuck us over in every orifice imaginable. No offence intended."

"None taken." I smiled. "I don't know how to feel. It's a bit of a..."

"Shock?" she filled in, giving me a nervous smile and blowing vape in my face.

"Yeah, but not really. I've wanted it to end for a while. I just didn't expect them to kill us off."

"Yeah. Me neither. I was hoping we'd finally see the light and get married even if Cass Powell is gayer than this entire parade and Stella is a repressed asexual mess. Honestly, I don't know why I've played her like that, but she's starting to make all the sense to me now, and it's made me re-evaluate everything lately."

"OMG, you didn't actually start to think? Caroline! You know that's not allowed! We're actors! We don't think! Seriously, babe!"

"I know. No wonder they're killing us off."

"And we're not even allowed to play the dead us. I've always wanted to do a death scene." I hadn't, but she was laughing, and we needed that now. And I laughed too as Caroline did her worst impression of dying in disgrace.

"That's why I'm here," she said, her voice low. "This show has done so much good for people, but the production team is a bunch of arseholes. It's all about money, and nobody actually cares about what we do. Like this. We do Pride every year, but it's all about how much sponsorship and how many collabs we can snag, not about giving something back to the community who have, let's be honest, put us here. So, I'm thinking..."

"Yes?"

"This show changed my life. *You* changed my life. It let me explore so much of myself, and for that, I am grateful. But if we have to go, then let's go. Let's bloody go out on that float and make today awesome. And then, if you're up for it..."

"Yeah?"

"Let's mull on this. Do something together. If we can do a podcast or even just a good interview with some big press, talk about the things we were never allowed to talk about. Discuss being who we are. That there are never labels that fit all of us. I'm not straight. I always thought I was but fuck you. You've made me bloody brave with that post of yours. I saw that, and I wanted to find you and slap you right in that pretty face of yours. Because you're braver than me, and I hated you for...yeah, a minute or two."

"I'm not brave," I admitted. "I don't even know why I'm here."

"But you *are* here." She took another drag of her vape. "That's all you need to be. You know that, right? You're here because you're a great guy. You're here for that man of yours. Because you feel and you breathe, and you're human. Whenever you wobble, just remember that. You're also here to hold my hand. I need that today. Can you do that?"

I leant over and gently kissed her. Because I needed it too—that connection we'd always had. She was part of me and would always be, and I was part of her, and in that moment, my heart ached. There were things in my life that needed to remain stable, whatever happened, and Caroline was that for me. A friend. That person who would hold my hand, just as I would hold hers.

She leaned in and lowered her voice. "There's a rumour in the fandom that you and I have fallen out and aren't speaking. Fuelled by Production, of course. Drama always makes for great numbers."

"Seriously?" I laughed. "So now I need to hold your hand all day and cast longing glances across the float?"

"Too right! We also need to remember to completely diss each other and make our rift obvious. Make sure there are lots of pictures of us looking pissed off. Yes, reach out to touch me, and I'll shrug you off. With a death glare."

Like that was going to happen for real after everything we'd been through together. She threw her arms around me, and I reciprocated, feeling my heart return to where it should be. Steady and slow.

"I love you, Connor. Remember that. Whatever happens next, we'll be fine. OK?"

"You will be fine. You're amazing. I'm so bloody happy you're here with me today. Let's go out with a bang. A big one."

"Will that man of yours hate me if I snog you on the float? Just to get the fans all riled up?"

"Love it." I grinned. "I'll pre-warn him. You do know I'm the best snogger, right?"

"Of course! I taught you everything you know!"

I laughed, filled with bubbles now instead of fear.

I stood on that float and the adrenaline was insane. The people all around me were just like me. Where I'd wobbled and felt like a fraud, I was now dancing around and singing at the top of my voice—even Silent Dave couldn't stop smiling, walking along next to the float while I was being thrown about. We were all, strangely, family, and it made me want to cry knowing this was the end. However much anger was brewing on the inside—I would probably be fuming by tomorrow, and there would be times when I looked back on this day with bitter tears—I was grateful. Hopeful.

I fished out my phone, snapped a selfie with Caroline hanging over my shoulder and sent it to Matt with a heart emoji. *Whatever you see online today, remember that it's not real.*

He replied straight away with a photo of him surrounded by smiling people whom I assumed were his friends. Colleagues. People who loved him. It wasn't jealousy, it was happiness in my chest, knowing that he was loved too. That he had good people around him. I hope he knew how much I loved him.

I was grateful. I was loved. I didn't doubt it for a second. Those kinds of thoughts should have made me wobble. Matt and me. We'd only been a thing for weeks, but I knew. I knew I'd never felt like this before. There had never been anyone who had made me feel the way he did.

Safe. Home. Love.

I smiled into the sunshine, listening to the crowds around me cheer, then we passed a group of people with *White Noise* flags, screaming at us as Caroline wrapped her arms around me.

I laughed, and she grinned at me, and we kissed. Just the way it should be. We could make our own ending. Whatever happened in that show, we could make today matter. So we did.

That kiss wouldn't change the world, but I smiled and waved, and Caroline jumped up and down, and then I did something stupid. Well, not stupid. I grabbed a marker pen from a fan on the ground, signed their arm with a smile and then...

Then I held out my arm and wrote I LOVE MATT in big, thick letters, and I waved to the world.

The sun was shining, and the music was playing, and I knew, whatever happened next? Things would be fine.

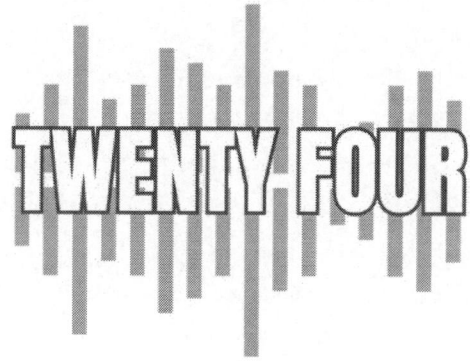

Matt

"You should ask him to come. Come on, Matty! Don't split on us now!"

My colleague Otis was all flushed, the two beers he'd downed already making him slur. Not that I blamed him. We were all hot and bothered, and the cool air inside the Korean restaurant where we'd found ourselves was heaven on my skin. I was soaked in sweat and probably stank a bit. We all did, and the poor server was trying to get all ten of us seated around a small table. The couple next to us got up and left. I didn't blame them. We were a rowdy bunch, and the table was only meant for about four.

It was London on Pride weekend, and the city was packed. I usually didn't mind it, but for the first time ever, I didn't want to be here.

I wanted to be where Con was, and it was doing my head in. I'd quite happily survived two weeks without him, yet it had been just a few hours and I was having a breakdown.

"You're away with the fairies again, Matthew." Sadie was always blunt. "I don't know what's up with you, but the last couple of weeks you've been all off. You meet a bloke and suddenly you've completely gone gaga."

"I've not gone gaga," I protested, and she just laughed.

I would have laughed too, apart from that my entire work team was nodding in agreement.

"We need to meet him. Why isn't he here?"

"Yeah! Where is he?"

"He's busy!" I tried, but they were having none of that.

"You said he's here. At Pride. On his company float."

"Then you refused to tell us who he worked for."

"Is he ugly or something?"

"Ooh, I smell drama!"

"He's probably a straight, married dude and Matt is his bit on the side!"

Otis needed to stop drinking because now he was being downright rude.

I decided to give them something, hoping it would shut them up. "He works for *White Noise*. You know? The TV show?"

"God, that Cass Powell is the hottest thing I've ever seen!"

Grunts of agreement came from several people as someone loaded up a dirty picture of a half-naked Con and passed it around.

"He's a nice bloke and just like us. We're all with our work colleagues. He's probably out with his mates."

I was digging myself into a hole.

"So, there's a *White Noise* float? They should join us! They might even bring Cass Powell," someone shouted at the end of the table.

"Ugh. I'd die. Can't stand him."

No, Sadie wouldn't die. She would hug him and say something deeply inappropriate, and Con would walk out in embarrassment. I needed to direct the attention away from myself. My colleagues were brilliant human beings, and normally I would have laughed along, but there was no way I was subjecting Con to this.

I got up and excused myself to a corner and tried Con's number. I didn't expect him to answer, but surprise, surprise, he did.

"Where are you?" he asked, clearly sat in a car. I could hear the engine running in the background.

"Say hello to Dave!" I said, hoping he would offer to pick me up and I would have a valid excuse to slide out the door.

"We're stuck in traffic somewhere in Soho. Where are you? Can we come to where you are? Dave will know how to find you."

Very Con. As always, Dave knew everything. I'd learnt that bit.

"We're in a Korean dive called Kimchi. Chinatown?"

There was silence, then Con's voice blending with someone else's.

"We'll be there in a minute."

Then he hung up. I was going to have to have words about his phone etiquette. He was obviously not alone in the car and any excess words would have been inappropriate, but what had that all meant anyway?

I went back to the table and sat nervously scrolling my phone, hoping he would at least give me a clue. Was I going outside? Was he coming in? *Please don't come in!* A fresh beer appeared in front of me; I really shouldn't drink any more, but—

"So, is the boyfriend coming?"

"Please don't," I hissed at Sadie.

"Hey, I'm being polite. It's always nice to meet a partner."

"Says the woman who won't even show me a photo of her girlfriend."

"Some things are private!" she huffed.

"Exactly!"

Sadie went red and fiddled with her phone and I let out a little smile. I could be pushy too, but I was getting nervous.

And rightly so because here was Con, walking down the stairs with...Inspector Stella Rubin.

"Hey!" I stood up, not knowing what to do, as the table had fallen silent, and Con looked as shell-shocked as I felt.

"Oh," he said.

I wasn't sure what he'd expected, but not this. Definitely not this. I went into overdrive, giving Stella Rubin an awkward hug. We hadn't met before, but she clearly knew who I was, and me calling her Stella made her grimace. Her name wasn't Stella. I knew that, but I couldn't make my head function.

"Caroline," Con whispered in my ear as I did the most awkward round-table introduction to my colleagues, who were all gulping like goldfish.

"I hate you." Sadie burst out, staring angrily at Con, who was looking a little bemused.

"I do apologise," he stuttered, then he laughed. "Hello, Sadie," he said.

Now it was my turn to do the fish impression.

"You know each other?" I squealed out as Sadie got to her feet.

"That was rude. Sorry," she said.

"No offence," Con said politely. "Is Tara here too?"

"On location. Fucking five-day shoot. Bloody awful, especially this weekend. She was supposed to be here."

"Wait!" I said. I wasn't sure how I was still talking, and if I'd been hot before, I was positively melting now. "Your girlfriend is Tara Marie?!"

"Yep. And Connor here is her fake bloody boyfriend. It's...I can't even describe it. It doesn't sit well with me."

"She always says you're the most jealous person in the world." Con smiled, sitting himself next to Sadie like he was staying when we definitely were not. I was not going to sit here and...

"Is this seat taken?"

Caroline. I sighed. I was sitting in a Korean restaurant next to Inspector Stella Rubin. My life had just gone off the rails. Again. Weird.

"You know these people?" Otis drunk-whispered across the table.

"Caroline, this is Otis," I said, deciding to get it over with. "Head of chemistry and physics. He's a bit drunk, so ignore everything he says."

Forewarned was forearmed, but Otis actually shook Caroline's hand and then Con's hand and mumbled something about loving his work, and Con...

The rainbow-coloured T-shirts he and Caroline were wearing were not subtle. If they were attempting to fly under the radar, it wasn't happening here. Sure enough, within minutes, someone at the next table got up and asked for a photo.

"You. We need to talk," Sadie hissed across the table.

"OK?" There were terrified butterflies trying to flee my stomach.

"Why didn't you tell me you're seeing Con Telford?"

"Why didn't tell me that you know Con Telford?"

We both glanced at Con, who had returned to his seat post-photo and was staring at me with a cute, weirded-out look on his face.

"How mad is that?" he said, reaching out and taking my hand. "You work with Sadie."

God, I wanted to kiss him so badly it hurt, but if we weren't careful, this was all going to end in tears.

"Who's Sadie?" Caroline asked. I'd almost forgotten she was there.

"ME!" Sadie grinned.

"She hates me," Con filled in. "I'm fake dating her girlfriend, and according to Twitter, we're getting married."

"You dumped her!" Sadie pointed out. "I saw the texts! No taking it back, dude. You're split up and staying so."

"Our work commitments were obviously keeping us apart," Con said flatly, like this was a normal conversation. Caroline pretended to slap him over the head, then turned to me and took my hand.

"I need to tell you all about Connor here. All his bad habits. Did you know he's been known to pick his nose?"

Yeah, I didn't need to know that, but whatever. More beers arrived. Sadie threatened to cut Con's manhood into risotto if he ever came near her girlfriend again. I tuned out for a while, and when I tuned back in, they were planning some kind of garden party. My head spun a little.

I needed to stop drinking, but at the same time... Was I really supposed to smile this much?

It turned out Caroline was delightful, and we quickly got talking about education and university studies, and I almost—*almost*—forgot who she was.

Just like I was almost enjoying myself.

I wasn't really a social butterfly. Work meetings with set agendas were much more my jam, but sat here letting the beer soothe my nerves, especially with Con sitting across the table from me, it was actually...OK. He and Sadie were engrossed in conversation, yet he kept reaching over and touching my fingers, shooting small longing glances my way. It made me all jittery in the calmest possible way.

He drove me crazy.

"You!" Chloe, head of Year 10 and also slightly terrifying, plonked down beside me. "What the hell, Matt? You're dating Connor Telford?" She shook her head. "How the hell does that happen in real life? I'm having some kind of weird *Notting Hill* moment here."

Caroline leaned in. "Girl, I work with him. Every day. I keep thinking someone's having a laugh."

Which, of course, made Chloe blush vividly. She grabbed my bottle of beer and took a gulp, then put it down in a flurry of nervous apologies.

"And you're like my superhero," she said, suddenly starstruck. "I use a scene from *White Noise* in my fact-checking lecture. *Always re-evaluate the evidence. Use multiple sources. And trust nothing but your instinct. If you can't trust yourself, who can you trust?*"

"I wish I could take credit for at least some of those lines, but I just turn up and play out a script. Sometimes even with conviction."

"Convincing enough for me. I teach drama and philosophy."

"Now I'm scared." Caroline laughed. "Never actually studied any of it."

"And it makes you all the better for it." Chloe looked at me pointedly. I took the hint and got up, so they weren't talking around me. Caroline jerked her head towards Con, directing me to sit with him.

"To be honest, I don't think Inspector Rubin fully understands her own logic. She lost a witness. Twice. Because she didn't fact-check. She's a little irresponsible at times."

"You're allowed to be a little irresponsible in a scripted drama. In real life, we have to be bang on or we find ourselves in front of a tribunal over calling something trivial the wrong word."

"And you deal with children." Caroline made a face that made me laugh.

"We're inner-city senior schoolteachers," I said. "Nothing fazes us. Not even children."

"We can definitely deal with everything," Chloe agreed. "Apart from having Korean food with famous people. What the fuck, Matt?"

"Yes, Matt? What the fuck? One minute, Connor's your token boring actor with no life, the next, he's losing the plot and causing trouble all over the shop!"

"I don't cause any trouble," Con protested in fake shock. "I'm very easy to work with."

"Lies." Caroline sat up straight. "I know for a fact that you've turned half of the cast queer."

"Have not!" He pouted, although he was laughing.

"He did. Even us girls."

Connor did his best disgusted face.

"I mean, look at me!" Caroline said. "I kiss him on the daily, and God. Never again."

The table howled.

She was funny and clearly a good actor, as she now had everyone in stitches recalling some story about an extra who'd had trouble letting go of Con's manhood. Through his costume. And something about a security guard getting the sack after stealing Stella Rubin's bra.

It wasn't even an excuse, but I had to go pee, so I scooted away to the gents', where I could finally breathe. I washed my hands and stood there for a while, holding onto the sink and studying my reflection in the mirror, hoping my insides could rearrange themselves back into full human order.

I still looked like me, but I didn't feel like me. I felt like someone else. Someone smiling back at me in the mirror.

It had been a long day. A full-on day.

I switched out of my thoughts as Con slid through the door and carefully wrapped his arms around me from behind, resting his chin on my shoulder. He planted a soft kiss on my neck.

"Sorry to just barge in, but I just needed to see you. Caroline is having the best time out there, and I'm just so...so bloody proud."

"So you should be. You are a wonderful, gorgeous human being who I am really, really proud to call my boyfriend."

He laughed. "You and your boyfriend stuff."

"I saw you on Twitter. That kiss is going viral."

"There's nothing behind it. We're just, you know. Friends. And we're messing a bit with everything and everyone, because apparently Caroline and I have fallen out, spectacularly, and are now threatening the whole production. It's all our fault according to some new article in the *Daily Mail*."

"Oh, is it? and...are you now?" I mocked.

"Yeah. And then we're getting married." He smiled.

I just grinned into the mirror, grasping his hands in mine.

"So, what happens next?"

"Well, since I don't actually believe a thing I read online, I thought that maybe you and I could go back out there and have some food. By the way, I ordered for you. With Sadie's help. I can't believe you know Sadie, of all people."

"I still don't get it," I had to admit. I had no idea what had just gone down out there.

"It's been an ongoing thing since Tara's and my management decided to stage our relationship for our brands. Sadie hates it because they wanted to get married. And now they can."

"OK. Sadie's marrying a supermodel. She's fresh out of teaching college. Like...twenty-one or something."

"Probably not." He laughed. "But anyway. Back to the Korean food. They don't do omelette."

"Oh, no!" I teased. God, he was ridiculous.

"Yeah, so your friend Otis has ordered me something full of chilli and stuff, so..."

"We can share."

"Can you...help me order something I might be able to eat? I have no idea what anything on that menu is."

"Muffin." I turned around and cupped his chin, kissed the tip of his nose because away from all the madness out there was this incredibly gorgeous man. All it took was one sentence and I was falling head over heels in love with him again.

"I was thinking, earlier," he said, hooking his arms around my neck. "I've been so scared of this theatre gig, thinking I couldn't do it."

"You *can* do it," I said sternly, hoping I wasn't saying the wrong thing.

"I think I can." He smiled. "Because my life is about to totally change—again. I have so much to tell you, and I think that play will be the least of my worries. I was standing on that float today, and I was bloody terrified. Because I had to be...me. Just me. Nobody else. I couldn't even pretend to be Cass Powell because it wasn't his day. I didn't have a clue who I was supposed to be. So, I...decided to be your boyfriend. That was the only thing that kept me sane."

"I saw," I whispered. I'd seen his arm, still covered in smudged ink. I could still make out the letters spelling out MATT. Con wasn't subtle, and the fact that he was here with his graffitied arm and all his words and his thoughts and that I was the one who got to hear them?

"This is the hardest part I've ever played," he said quietly. "Trying to be a real person. Figuring out who I am. Being able to interact with people in, like...real situations. And I can do it. I never thought I could, but I can. It's hard, but it's going to be fine. Lots of things are about to change, Matt."

"I know," I murmured, letting my lips finally meet his. I needed that connection with him. "All that matters is that I know that this is real. What you and I have is real. Everything else?"

"Is just..." He smiled. And he kissed me. And I kissed him back. "Everything else is just white noise in the background."

It made sense, and in that moment, I could feel it too.

"I also really need to pee." He smiled, and I let go of him. Slapped his shoulder. Pushed him away from me and manhandled him into a cubicle, laughing when he shut the door in my face.

He was too much. Too real. Too...mine.

"Matt?" he called from behind the door.

"Yeah?"

"When we've eaten?"

I knew what was coming.

"Yes, baby, we can."

"Good." I heard him giggling as he flushed the toilet. "Because I asked Dave to pick us up in an hour and take us home. I need a shower, and I need to lie in bed with you and just put myself back together again."

"And have sex?" I smiled innocently.

He walked back out and held up his hands. Then he leaned in and kissed me, and my chest burst with all the feelings that I had no idea how to put words to.

Con - One year later.

I turned my head and buried my face in Matt's shoulder because I still, a year later, couldn't watch the scene that was currently being blasted out on the screen with Caroline's voice shouting lines of pure hatred as my face twisted in pain.

We'd both been so over it, over *everything*, filming those last scenes. And, of course, the test audience had hated the ambiguous ending with Cass's and Stella's bodies lying on a deserted mountain top, played by body doubles so our faces weren't even clear. We'd wrapped and unwrapped and reshot, and yes, we'd still died a horrible death, and that look of betrayal on my face, well Cass Powell's face, as he'd drawn his last raspy blood-soaked breath?

That scene was about to earn me another award. I kind of knew I had it in the bag since I'd been slipped a thank-you speech with pointers and all the names I needed to mention. I'd memorised it already, so the speech would be no problem.

I was still slightly bitter over the way *White Noise* had gone down, but I was also thrilled that Aisha was spilling all the gossip from the season-seven set, since I'd had stern words with her about applying for the set manager job and not accepting anything less. She'd nabbed that job, and my heart skipped a joyful beat every time our little group chat pinged with more news of drama, breakdowns and a new lead actor who was as straight as they came and had a clause in his contract of no full-frontal nudity and no explicit scenes with members of any gender.

Why they'd thought they could make a *White Noise* season without the sex was beyond everyone involved, not least Caroline and me, who seemed to know our fanbase better than the goddamn scriptwriters and producers.

It would be a shitshow. A lazy script, a haphazardly put together cast and a team on minimum pay who'd already caused production delays by working to scheme and union rules. I didn't blame them. If I'd worked to the rules, we'd still be shooting season one, and looking back now, I should perhaps have fought more. Stood up for myself.

Not that it mattered. I was gripping Matt's hand so tight that he probably had no blood left in his fingers, but I needed him here. Desperately.

"And the winner of Best Actor in a Television drama is..."

Cue the obligatory dramatic pause and smarmy smile as some *Love Island* winner wearing an impossibly small dress tried to open an envelope with her too-long nails.

I knew the drill. If it hadn't already been obvious that I'd bagged this award, the two-camera crew in my face waiting for that golden moment of tear-jerking TV would have given the game way.

We'd done this twice already. Caroline and I had been up there to accept Best Scene in a Television Drama and Best Script for a Television Drama. Not that we'd had anything to do with the script, but the writing team had been up there too in the background. No one cared about them; they wanted us at the front, the two of us looking suitably awkward as we politely accepted awards that were then handed to the scriptwriters, who handed them to handlers as soon as the cameras went to adverts.

"Connor Telford for *White Noise*."

Here we went again. Not that I wasn't proud. There were actors here who had done much better work than I had, but still. I smiled. Stood up and put my hands around Matt's face. Kissed him, mouthing *I love you* as the camera zoomed in on me. The viewers at home would have some narrator going over my bio and pointing out that my partner was in the crowd supporting me tonight and that Caroline and the entire *White Noise* team were cheering loudly behind me as I buttoned up my suit jacket and confidently strode up towards the stage.

More air kisses. More awkward smiles. Blinding stage lights in my eyes as I pretended to be shocked and honoured and to not know what to say.

"I would like to thank the production team of *White Noise*, who have endlessly supported me during the past years. Without the fantastic teamwork behind me I wouldn't be standing here. I am incredibly honoured," I waffled on, names and bullshit dripping from my lips as I smiled.

"Most of all, I want to thank Caroline Kováč, who has been my constant companion throughout this amazing adventure. And my partner Matt, who I love more than anything else in the world. Thank you!"

I smiled some more, waved the award around like I meant it and got my picture taken with the *Love Island* woman and her nails as well as some other people who apparently mattered. Then I was ushered around the back for more bullshit and pictures as the award got swirled away, not to be seen again until it would appear on Lucia's office shelf and eventually get packed up and stored in my mum's loft. These things were all trivial ego boosts for show and didn't really matter. Not in my world. Lucia was proud as punch, though, as I gave her a brief hug and returned to my seat between Caroline and Matt.

"Good job." Caroline giggled. "You looked like a stiff."

"Can't help it in this suit. It's too small and—"

"I like too small," Matt murmured. "Makes your arms look massive. Good job you're playing some kind of cartoon superhero next." He wasn't helping and took none of this too seriously. Thank God. He was always there. Mocking me and loving me and holding me at night. Everything I needed in the world.

"It's a children's movie. Based on a very famous children's book," I insisted. Yes. Inappropriate after playing Cass Powell, and I knew it, but Lucia was working hard at broadening the roles I took, and after I'd comfortably survived the *LA Boys* run and then ended up doing a BBC period drama where I once again had been mostly naked, she'd rightly decided that it was time for me to change direction and be more family orientated.

My next job was playing a superhero...who wore very few clothes. I'd tried to point that out to her, but she'd just tutted and threatened to book me another round of auditions in LA.

I refused to go to LA. I'd had so much of my life directed at me and I was finally taking control. I was going to stay here. With Matt. Doing what *I* wanted.

"You did good. We did good." Caroline protectively patted my arm as the camera crew once again swung by us.

We were still a team—and still seen as the stars of *White Noise* since nobody knew what the next season would bring. Well, the viewers were stupid if they thought we'd be back, since Inspector Stella Rubin had been the one to stab me in the chest in a scene of the ultimate betrayal. Ultimate prize, my arse. Then Toby had been back, which had been the only highlight of that pathetic reshoot in Norfolk, and he'd looked as smarmy as ever shooting Stella to kingdom come in a twist that had shocked the nation.

Even I had been stunned into silence when I'd watched the finished season. The scriptwriting team deserved that gong because the storyline had once again tied together to become an awe-inspiring, award-winning show full of twists and turns. Still, I couldn't watch part of it. Too many feelings being triggered in my chest that I didn't want to remember. Too much love for the man who grabbed my hand.

"You did good."

"I know."

We were at another ad break. The stills photography team zoomed in, and Matt was told to move out of the shot so they could get a shot of Caroline and me looking all...cosy.

Which I wasn't having. Neither was Caroline, who always had my back. Wrapping her arms around my neck, she pulled at Matt's tie to produce something that would probably make headline news in the morning. I knew how filthy it looked, her planting a kiss on my cheek while tugging at Matt's tie and me looking at Matt like I wanted to eat him.

For the record, I did. And would. Later. I had Dave on standby and was planning on being in bed by midnight—we still lived in our little place on Cardiac Road—and anyway, Matt had assembly to run in the morning and Caroline and I were...working. It didn't feel much like work.

"Fuck, they're annoying. Remind me to talk about this tomorrow."

"Absolutely. We'll blow the lid off award shows and probably never be invited to one again."

"Good thing Lucia is censoring our shit then. I think Matt and I should switch seats, just to confuse them even more. And Matt? We need to snog at the afterparty. Scandal is the first of my many names, OK?"

My Matt just sighed, taking Caroline for exactly what she was. Caroline and I still took the mickey out of us but now also ribbed each other as a podcast on Spotify. Our weekly episodes of *Beyond the Noise* had started as an afternoon of ideas and too much wine in Tara and Sadie's garden and ended up being a slick production that was now being pitched as a major documentary, which they wanted me to narrate. There was also talk of a book, which filled me with dread because that hadn't been part of why we'd started this in the first place. But apparently, our view of growing up in the limelight and being hounded by a life lived in the shadow of social media had married well with our discussions on sexuality and gender identity. We also knew enough interesting people to support us, and the episode where Tara and I had discussed that now famous photoshoot had shot us straight up the charts.

I'd told Lucia she shouldn't have worried about those pictures, and she'd just huffed at me calling me her problem child. I was nobody's problem child. Well, maybe I was, as my mum and Matt's mum and my auntie Trish waved at us from the guest seats I snagged for them in the balcony above, along with Mrs Wu and Wei. Yes. Friends. I had them now. I had good friends. I...gulp...socialised with normal human beings, and that realisation always made me smile. I was still me, and I could do...most things.

Life had changed, in so many ways.

"Mum just went to the loo and washed her hands next to Olivia Coleman," Matt whispered. "She just texted and...she's like totally flustered."

"I'll get her do a meet-and-greet later. I'll ask Lucia to arrange it." I picked up my own phone to send off instructions to do just that. Lucia managed everyone and knew full well that when I asked for something, it wasn't because I was an idiot with delusions of grandeur. I just sometimes needed things done. Nice things. For nice people.

Like making sure Aisha got the job. Like giving Dave a raise and keeping him on my books. Like...like...

"I need the loo," Matt whispered, standing up to move out of our row of seats. We were still on a break, and I could really do with just stretching my legs, so I followed him. One of the security dudes nervously let us know that we needed to be back in our seats in seven minutes.

"Seven minutes," I whispered to Matt, grabbing his hand as we walked along to the loos.

"Plenty of time." He grinned. He knew exactly what I was up to. What he was up to. And neither of us needed the toilet.

I pushed him into the first cubicle, turning around to lock the door as Matt got his trousers undone and I wasted no time pulling them down over his hips. And his underwear. Whoops! His arse landed heavily on the toilet seat as I got down on my knees.

We didn't need seven minutes. We needed...well...two, max, looking at the state of Matt's dick.

I was good at this. Really good. And I didn't even need an intimacy coordinator or a script these days as I licked around the head of his swollen cock and gently sucked at the tip.

Was Matt enjoying it? I'd say so, the way his hands were clamped against the walls and his leg kicked out to the side as I swallowed him down and then slowly rose up, licking trails along the way. My hand played with his balls, his legs spreading a little further as I unbuttoned myself and teased my dick out.

"Fuck this." Matt groaned. "Let me up so I can turn around and then just bloody fuck me, baby."

"Not enough time," I gasped as he did exactly that. Dragged me up with him and presented me with that delicious arse of his.

"Plenty of time. Here. Lube."

That was my Matt. Always prepared. His pockets always contained a blister pack of paracetamol, my favourite chewing gum, a pen and small, handy packets of lube.

His fingers were already playing with his opening, softening him up as I coated myself in smooth silk.

"Four minutes to go," he panted. "Go hard and fast."

There were other people coming and going into the loos, but I didn't honestly care. There was music playing loudly over the speakers and noise from the main hall blending with the moans coming out of Matt's mouth as I lined up my dick and pushed.

Hard.

He'd asked for it, and I would never say no to this. A hard, fast fuck in a small space where I could let go of the world and just be me.

I was a dirty fucker, and this was my jam. My dick buried so deep inside of him that I practically saw stars, his hand flying back to join mine on his hip, our fingers tangling as another deep moan escaped his mouth.

"Come on, don't hold back," he teased.

I'd been scared to hurt him at the beginning, but we'd practised. A lot. Making these moments count, where he was in unfamiliar situations and I needed grounding and we both knew that perhaps sex wasn't always the right solution, but for us, like this, when the world became too big, and we just needed the space around us to shrink, it was perfect.

"Gonna come," he huffed out, his hand back pumping his dick, the other holding him up over the toilet seat as I shifted my feet to get a better angle. Then I pulled out. Slammed back in. Pounded him at speed as his moans grew into a constant roar.

I came. I knew I would, but it still blinded me. Completely. My mouth hung slack, and I was quite sure I was drooling down my chin. I managed to compose myself enough to wipe it off with the back of my hand and tug at Matt's jacket as he clumsily stood himself up, his hand full of cum and his breath all ragged.

"You're a terror," he mumbled as I buried my face in his back.

"Just needed you," came out of my mouth.

I did. I always did. He calmed me. Soothed me. Put me back together again when I forgot who I was. Deep down, I'd always known, but it was still a shock every time I realised that he was mine. That he loved me back. That I was...special. I'd never felt special, but to Matt, I was. I was just as important to him as he was to me. Knowing that, and that it was true, always made me well up.

I wasn't going to cry. I was NOT going to cry in the men's room at the British National Television Awards.

"One minute, muffin," he said softly, kissing my lips.

He was pulling my trousers up, fastening my belt as I fiddled with the zip. My legs were still shaking, and he was laughing as he let himself out of the cubicle and went to wash his hands.

"There's spunk on my belt," I complained as I moved to the sink next to him.

"Just button up your jacket. Nobody will know," he deadpanned as I burst into laughter.

"We gotta go."

"Mr Telford?" Oh. Ugh. Security. "Mr Telford, we really need you back in your seat."

Yeah. Time to face the world again. Become Mr Telford, whoever he was today.

Me. Maybe he was me.

I smiled and grabbed Matt's hand, and we walked back to our seats with confident smiles on our faces. Caroline stared at us in disgust.

"You reek of sex," she whispered.

Matt blushed. "Nonsense, Caroline," he huffed, looking scandalised. "As if we would!"

"We would," I whispered. Then I grinned.

Because this was my life. And I was going to live it.

T hank you to my amazing team of humans who make my stories the best they can be. You know who you are. Debbie McGowan for the brilliant edits and for being so incredibly patient with my messy, messy men. Sarah Coppin at Manor Editing Services for picking up on all my little mistakes. KC Carmine for sorting out my formatting.

Special thank-you to the lovely Rourke for again helping me create the perfect cover.

If you enjoyed this book, please rate it and, if you have time, write a short review. I am always grateful for your words and your support.

Thank you for reading.

Sophia x

Sophia Soames should be old enough to know better but has barely grown up. She has been known to fangirl over TV shows, has fallen in and out of love with more pop stars than she dares to remember, and has a ridiculously high-flying (un-)glamourous real-life job.

Her long-suffering husband just laughs at her antics. Their children are feral. The dogs are too.

She lives in a creaky old house in rural London, although her heart is still in her native Scandinavia.

Discovering that the stories in her head make sense when written down has been part of the most hilarious midlife crisis ever, and she hopes it may long continue.

Find me on social media @sophiasoames Linktr.ee/sophiasoames

Newsletter signup here: https://landing.mailerlite.com/webforms/landing/d7o8a9

Also by Sophia Soames

717 Miles

717 Miles Christmas

The Scandinavian Comfort Series

Little Harbour

Open Water

Baking Battles

In this Bed of Snowflakes We Lie

The Naked Cleaner

The Chistleworth Series

Custard and Kisses

Ship of Fools

This Thing with Charlie

The London Love Series

BREATHE

EXHALE

TASTE

The Rourke stories

Force Majeure

Dirty Sexy Stupid Love

White Noise

With Magdalena di Sotru

Life is Good and Other Lies

Life is Right Here

Printed in Great Britain
by Amazon

7c2b13ee-8c7b-4c02-9fe1-21b1bb1ce10aR02